THE LIGHT AT EVENING

Kevin McManus

The Book Social, 51 Gower Street, London, WC1E 6HJ
info@legendtimesgroup.co.uk | www.thebooksocial.co.uk

 British Library Cataloguing in Publication Data available.

Print ISBN 978-1-91829-1-780
Ebook ISBN 978-1-91829-1-797
Set in Times.
Cover design by Rose Cooper

'*The Light at Evening* is a brilliant exploration of love and care at mid-life. In scenes that are incredibly moving, we follow ordinary characters who must navigate the tightrope between illness and grief. With a poet's attention to detail, McManus creates a visceral experience of Irish country life, reminiscent of the worlds built by John McGahern. Beautifully written and tenderly wrought. A real pleasure to read.'

Carmel McMahon, author of *In Ordinary Time*

'I was captivated by this sensitive, thoughtful and lyrically written story about a man's reflections – and his life journey – in middle age. It is very much in the tradition of John McGahern, evoking the meaningful everyday in small town Ireland, while the banter and kindness of Irish life is set against nature's shifting seasons and existential fears. I came to really care about Ciarán's and Joan's feelings and relationships, and his elegiac remembrance of things past. Kevin McManus has a special literary talent and I found this novel absorbing.'

Mary Kenny

'Kevin McManus's *The Light at Evening* perfectly captures ordinary people living through hard days with grace, humour, care and, crucially, decency. Beautiful in everything it says and leaves unsaid. There are no small lives. A bittersweet delight.'

Gráinne Murphy, author of *Greener*

'*The Light at Evening* is a delicate exploration of how we face the challenges life doles out as we grow older, including a loved one's illness. A poignant read full of empathy and a keen awareness of those small rituals that make up a life – visiting a local lake, sharing a cup of tea, writing a poem – it will make you reassess the things you value in the everyday.'

Nathalie Abi-Ezzi, author of *All the Lives She Lived*

'*The Light at Evening* is a quiet, intimate and thoroughly moving novel, its chapters measured as carefully as finite days. Kevin McManus captures the extraordinary beauty within ordinary lives in a small Irish town with precision, compassion and utmost authenticity.'

Tim Hannigan, author of *A Pathless Land*

Kevin McManus is a novelist, poet and history teacher from Ireland's North West. He is the author of numerous novels as well as several collections of poetry and books exploring history, folklore and local tradition. His writing has been recognised with the Leonard Trophy, while his poem 'Lost Souls' was adapted into an award-winning short film.

This book is dedicated to my father,
Kevin McManus Snr

1939–2024

*He is gone, but not from the places that made him;
I will not see his like again, yet I carry him still, in all
that remains.*

THE LIGHT AT EVENING

Chapter One

Goodbye to a Quiet Man

Even the warmth of the hallway couldn't keep out the cold that came home with him from the grave.

Ciarán closed the front door of his mother's house gently, as though afraid the click of the latch might shatter something. For a moment he simply stood there, letting the familiar narrow hallway hold him. The air smelled faintly of polish, damp wool, boiled cabbage and the ghost of last night's turf fire – the comforting, stale scents of a house that had changed only in the ways it had been forced to.

Outside, dusk gathered at the windows. Early December, yet the light was already retreating, the days drawing tight like a closing hand.

He took off his coat, heavy and wet at the cuffs, and hung it on its peg. His eye went, as it always did, to the peg beside it, where his father's cap used to hang – bare now, the pale oval on the wood still marking where the cap had shaded it from sun and years. A small absence, but sharp.

From the sitting room he could hear the low, electric murmur of the television, the careful hush of someone who had turned the sound down but hadn't the heart to turn it off.

'Tea?' he called, his voice softer than he intended.

There was a pause, the brief shuffle of a sleeve against upholstery.

'There's a bit of ham left from earlier,' his mother answered. 'And the brown bread. It'd do for you.'

She hadn't said yes, but she hadn't said no either.

He went to the kitchen. The walk from the cemetery replayed itself in him as he filled the kettle. He could've taken the car with the others, but something in him had refused. Walking had felt important – each step a small penance, a way of grounding his body in the same damp earth his father had been lowered into that afternoon.

The cemetery had been all slick grass and cold stone. His father's grave, raw and too new between older, settled headstones, looked temporary, as though it might be tidied away by morning. The priest had said his few practised words; the holy water had struck the lid like rain. Ciarán had watched the handfuls of soil drop, each dull thud both too loud and not loud enough.

He had waited for the tears to come – that hot, private flood he had imagined, the dramatic collapse of something inside him. But there had been only a tightness in his chest and a strange stillness, like a lake frozen just beneath the surface.

From there, down through town: the same chipped walls and faded shopfronts, the same black-and-white posters for music nights that had already come and gone. A few fairy lights blinked weakly from the butcher's window. The Christmas market had been postponed 'due to the weather', though Ciarán doubted the weather was the real reason. People had grown tired of pretending to be festive.

The hotel after had been worse – the awkward inevitability of turkey and ham under silver lids, roast potatoes glossy with oil, the low drone of polite condolences over the hum of a coffee machine. Men he only half knew had clapped him on the back and said the lines all men said at funerals: *He was a good man, a quiet man. He'll be missed*. Someone at the bar insisted on buying him a Jameson. Someone else held forth about a digger his father had repaired in record time back in '89, like a legend from an old saga.

He'd smiled, nodded, said *Thanks for coming*, and laughed in the right places. He could remember their faces now, but not the sequence of what was said, only the sense that he'd been an actor in a play he'd rehearsed but never wanted to perform. All the while his father lay cooling in the ground on the hill above town.

The kettle clicked off.

He shook the thought away and poured, the steam soft against his face. Two mugs, the chipped floral one for his mother, the plain brown for himself. He added a little extra milk to hers, the way she liked, and set slices of ham on a plate with two slabs of brown bread, the knife marks in the crust running like contour lines.

Balancing the tray, he went back to the sitting room. His mother sat in the corner armchair where she had always sat, the tartan blanket over her knees, her cardigan buttoned askew. The television glowed in the far corner – the evening news, the presenter's mouth moving silently, subtitles running on ahead.

She looked smaller somehow, more folded in on herself, the way clothes shrink a little each time they're washed.

He set the tray down carefully on the coffee table, careful not to disturb the small glass of sherry sitting there, still full.

'Thanks, love,' she said, looking up at him properly now. Her eyes were red-rimmed but dry.

He passed her the mug. She wrapped both hands around it, not drinking, just holding.

'He'd have hated today,' she said suddenly.

Ciarán eased himself into the armchair opposite. 'He didn't like fuss.'

'Never did.' Her voice grew tight around the words. 'Even when he was young, in London – wouldn't wear a tie to weddings. Said it choked him.'

She let out a little breath that might have been a laugh, but her mouth trembled.

'He liked the quiet,' she went on, almost to herself. 'Sitting out the back with the paper. Tuning the car radio when it wasn't even broken. D'you remember that? Always fiddling with things.'

'I remember,' he said.

She stared past him, into some middle distance only she could see. On the television screen behind him, a graphic about inflation shifted to one about weather warnings. A scrolling ticker announced delays at Dublin Airport. None of it seemed to belong to the room they were sitting in.

'He didn't look like himself,' she said. 'In the coffin. Too ... tidy. He'd hate that tie.'

'You chose it,' Ciarán said gently.

'I know.' She bit the inside of her cheek. 'I wanted him to look respectable.'

'He was respectable,' Ciarán said. 'He just didn't like looking like it.'

That pulled a real laugh from her. Short, but real. The sound made something ache in him.

'I can't sleep here alone,' she said after a while, her voice dropping.

'You won't have to,' he said. 'I'll stay.'

She nodded, as if she had expected no less.

Upstairs, the guest room was cold in the way that feels built into the bricks; an old cold that pre-dated central heating and wouldn't be argued with. The single bed, with its candlewick bedspread and curved brass headboard, looked unchanged since he'd been a boy sleeping there on sultry summer nights with the window wide open, listening to the late silage tractors on the road.

He turned on the little electric heater, its element glowing orange at once, and fetched an extra blanket from the airing cupboard. As he spread it, he caught sight of himself in the mirror on the wardrobe door.

For a moment he didn't recognise the fifty-eight-year-old man looking back at him.

The light was unforgiving, slicing in from the landing window and catching every line. His cheeks were hollower than he remembered, the grey in his hair more salt than pepper now. His eyes looked … used. That was the word that came to him. Not old. Used.

He thought briefly of how his father had looked on the last day: face relaxed in a way it never had been in life, hands folded not for work but for display. The undertaker had smoothed his hair in the opposite direction to how he'd always worn it. Ciarán hadn't corrected him.

Regret nudged at him, a slow, insistent thing, like dull wire under the skin. He'd meant to spend more time at the yard while it was still open, meant to ask more questions about engines, about hydraulics, about the way a man builds something from scratch and then watches the world move past it. He'd meant to say *Thank you* more often. He'd meant to say *I know you tried*.

He hadn't.

He'd been too busy with books and records and late nights in pubs in Dublin, writing poems no one published and playing basslines to half-interested crowds who clapped more for the covers than the originals.

His father had never said he was disappointed.

He hadn't had to.

Later, when the house had gone quiet, he lay in the narrow bed staring at the ceiling. The plaster above him was faintly cracked, hairline fractures running out from the light fitting like tributaries.

Wind pressed gently at the window. Somewhere far off, a dog barked once, then again, then stopped. An owl called from the stand of trees beyond the back field.

He tried to picture his father's face clearly and kept slipping back into earlier images – hands black with grease and streaked with green paint from a tractor, a cigarette cupped in one palm against the wind, his laugh a short burst that often ended in a cough. The way he'd stand with one hip against the kitchen counter, listening to the weather forecast on the radio as if the man in Dublin was reporting on his own fields in real time.

It struck Ciarán then, with a sudden sharpness, that there would be no new images now. No more additions to the internal catalogue. Everything from here on would be rearrangements of existing scenes.

The thought made his throat burn.

He rolled onto his side, pulled the blanket up, and listened to the sounds of the old house breathing around him – pipes settling, fridge humming faintly through the floor, his mother moving once in her sleep and then lying still.

When sleep came, it came not as an escape but as a kind of truce.

He woke early, as he always did in this house. Light seeped weakly around the curtains – that grey, undecided light particular to December mornings when even the sky seems unsure.

In the kitchen, he filled the kettle and set it to boil. The lino under his bare feet was cold. He got out the porridge pot and the oats, measuring by hand the way his mother did. A pinch of salt between his fingers, the swirl of a wooden spoon. The small rituals of care.

The back garden, seen through the misted window, looked exactly as it had twenty, thirty years ago: the same washing line sagging between two concrete posts, the same veg patch now half surrendered back to grass, the same oil tank squatting by the wall like an old animal. Only the shed roof had caved in further.

His mother came in as he was spooning the porridge into bowls, her dressing gown tied tighter than usual, the tartan blanket now over her shoulders.

'You're up early,' she said.

'Habit,' he replied. 'You sleep at all?'

'Some.' She sat slowly, lowering herself into the chair with both hands on the table. 'I kept hearing him,' she added, almost as an afterthought. 'In the yard. In the hall. Moving about.'

He set the bowl in front of her. 'Dreams,' he said gently.

She shook her head once, sharp. 'No. Not dreams. Just … echoes.'

They ate in near-silence, the spoon scraping softly against china. She took her porridge with salt, as she always had. He added a bit of sugar to his own once her back was turned – a childish habit he hadn't quite shaken.

'I'll be back tomorrow,' he said when he'd washed up and dried the dishes. 'You'll have company again then.'

She didn't look up from her tea. 'Will you stay for a few hours?'

'I will,' he said. 'As long as you want.'

She nodded, satisfied, as if a tick had been placed in some unseen ledger.

At the door, he kissed her on the cheek. Her skin felt papery, the bones underneath sharp.

'Ring me if you need anything,' he said.

She gave him a look that said she'd been managing without him for years, but she squeezed his hand before letting it go.

Outside, the frost bit at his cheeks. The car was crusted white, windows filmed over. He scraped the windscreen with an old CD case, his breath pluming the air in pale clouds. The scrape-scrape rhythm was oddly soothing.

The town, as he drove through, was beginning to stir. A tractor rumbling somewhere down a side road. A child in a uniform too big for him being shepherded along by a woman in a padded coat. A man hauling crates from the back of a van into McEntee's. The ordinary machinery of other people's lives, going on.

The road home rose out of the town and dipped again between fields, a thin grey ribbon bordered by hedges browned with cold. The sky was a washed-out blue now, the early fog burning off in slow strips. In the low fields he could see standing water, a thin layer of ice on top catching the weak light.

As he drove, his thoughts drifted, as they always did, to Joan.

She'd been tired at the funeral, too tired to stay for the hotel meal. She'd stood at the graveside, pale under her wool hat, and said nothing, her presence a kind of quiet anchor. After the burial she'd kissed his mother, pressed his hand, and gone home with her sister Maeve, with promises to have the kettle on when he came back.

He pictured her now in the kitchen at home, the light over

the table catching the hollows under her eyes, the thinness of her wrists. The word *oncology* slid into his mind uninvited – a word that had come to shape their days, their appointments, their small rushed meals before hospital runs.

He tightened his grip on the steering wheel and eased the car around a bend. In the field to his left, a flock of starlings rose suddenly from a hedge, wheeled, and settled again further on, as if the air itself were restless.

The house he shared with Joan sat on the edge of town, on a hill that gave a narrow view of the lake if you stood in just the right spot in the garden. It was a semi-detached, pebbledash, built in the late seventies – the sort of place he'd once sworn he would never live in, back when he'd had notions about cities and garret rooms and all-night cafés.

He pulled into the gravel drive and cut the engine. For a moment he stayed where he was, hands on the steering wheel, the silence of the stopped car loud in his ears. He could see the edge of the kitchen table through the net curtain, the familiar shape of the mug tree on the counter. The mundanity of it soothed and hurt in equal measure.

Inside, the house was warm, but not stifling. The heating clunked in the pipes like an old man clearing his throat. Somewhere upstairs, he heard the faint rush of water. He hung his coat on the banister and went to put on the kettle. Muscle memory did the work: kettle, cups, teabags, milk. The small comfort of routine.

He was pouring when Joan appeared in the doorway, wrapped in a towel, her wet hair slicked back, dark against the pallor of her face. The chemo had taken most of it months earlier; what remained now was soft and thin, like the hair of a much younger girl.

'Good timing,' she said, her voice light, but he could hear

the tiredness in it. 'I was starting to think you'd moved back in with your mother.'

He smiled. 'Just the night,' he said. 'She didn't want to be on her own.'

Joan crossed to the table and sat with the carefulness of someone placing a piece of glass. He set the mug in front of her, the one with the blue ring around the rim she'd bought in a craft shop in Galway years ago.

'She's all right?' Joan asked.

'As all right as she can be,' he said. 'She hears him in the house. Or thinks she does.'

Joan cupped her hands around the mug, the steam travelling up over her face.

'She's not the only one who hears things that aren't there,' she said quietly.

He sat opposite her. 'You?'

'Not voices,' she said. 'Just … the way the house used to sound. When I was still working. Before …' She let the sentence trail off, the unsaid words sitting between them like a fourth presence.

They drank in silence for a while.

On the coffee table in the sitting room lay a battered copy of Heaney's *The Spirit Level*, its cover bent back, a library of pencil ticks in the margins. Between the pages were old bus tickets, a dried leaf, a receipt from a café in Sligo where they'd once sat and shared a scone on a bright day that had seemed ordinary at the time but now, in memory, shone.

He reached for the book.

'Will I read?' he asked.

'If you like,' she said, leaning back into the cushions, her eyes already half closed.

He thumbed through the pages, the weight of the book familiar in his hand. He settled on 'The Cure at Troy', the lines so well-worn in his mind he could have said them without the text. His voice was softer by the time he reached the last line. Joan's eyes were closed now, but he could tell she was listening; her fingers twitched slightly on the mug handle in time with the rhythms.

'Read the one about the well,' she murmured.

He turned to 'The Wellhead' and read that too, the imagery of water and echo, of voices rising from depth, cutting closer than he'd expected after the day he'd had.

When he finished, he closed the book gently and set it down.

'I miss music,' Joan said, not opening her eyes. 'Real music. Live. You used to play in the kitchen. Remember? When we were in the flat in Ranelagh, you'd drag out that stupid amp and wake the neighbours.'

He smiled. 'I was making art.'

'You were making noise,' she corrected, though there was warmth in it. 'Good noise.'

'I haven't touched the bass in years,' he said.

'You should,' she replied. 'Even just for me. Before I forget how you sounded.'

The sentence hung in the room. Neither of them moved to touch it.

Later, he helped her dress for the hospital. She sat on the edge of the bed, breathing a little heavier than she would have once, pulling on a soft cotton top and the wool cardigan he'd given her for their anniversary – dark green, cable knit, the wooden buttons slightly loose from use. Her arms had thinned, skin pale and freckled, the sharp line of her collarbone startling against the fabric.

He fetched her scarf from the wardrobe – the navy one with the tiny embroidered stars – and draped it around her neck. She let him, tilting her chin for a moment so he could tuck the ends in.

'You'll come in this time?' she asked as he picked up the car keys. Her voice was casual, but her eyes were fixed on his, searching.

'I'll come in,' he said.

The oncology unit had its own smell – a blend of antiseptic, plastic and something faintly metallic that made him think of coins and blood. The chairs were arranged in a long U around the nurse's station, each with its drip stand, its little table, its careful anonymity.

'Ah, Joan,' said the nurse with the red glasses, her accent somewhere between Mayo and pure hospital. 'We've your chair ready.'

Ciarán helped Joan out of her coat and into the recliner. A nurse inserted the line into her arm with the practised efficiency of someone who did this every day. Around them, other patients sat in their own quiet islands – some reading, some staring at the TV bolted high on the wall, some with their eyes closed, mouths parted in the slack of deep tiredness.

'I'll be back in a while,' he whispered, touching Joan's shoulder.

She nodded, already half turned inward, submitting to the familiar routine.

Downstairs, in the café, he bought a coffee he didn't want and a scone he would later barely taste. He sat by the window and watched the hospital world move – porters pushing beds, doctors striding past with clipped steps, visitors clutching plastic bags with new pyjamas. Two teenagers in school uniforms sat at the next table, laughing too loudly about something on a phone. Life, impatient and indifferent, flowed past the double doors.

His notebook was in his jacket pocket. He took it out,

flicked through pages of half-poems, fragments of images – frost on a window, oil on water in the shed yard, his father's hands steadying a tractor tyre. He turned to a blank page, pen hovering.

Nothing came.

It wasn't that there was nothing to say. There was too much. Grief for his father, fear for Joan, the prickling awareness of his own body's betrayals – that dull ache in his lower back, the toilet trips that were becoming more frequent. He thought of the doctor's gentle suggestion of 'further tests' and had the sudden childish urge to throw the notebook in the bin.

Instead, he closed it and watched the rain begin to bead on the glass.

By the time they got home, Joan was grey with exhaustion, her movements small and economical, like someone conserving battery. He settled her on the couch, tucking the blanket around her legs, placing a hot-water bottle at her feet.

'I'm sorry,' he said, the TV murmuring to itself in the corner, the room lit by the soft glow of the false fire in the insert stove.

She opened her eyes, the pupils huge against the pale blue. 'For what?'

'I'm trying,' he said, the words thick. 'I don't know if it's enough.'

She lifted her hand slightly, and he leaned in so she could rest it on his cheek.

'I know you're trying,' she whispered. 'You don't have to be everything.'

He thought of his mother sitting alone with the television on for company, his father's grave still fresh in the earth, the machinery yard standing idle. Thought of the school expecting him back in January, exams looming, lesson plans blank on his laptop. Thought of the age-spotted hands of the men who'd shaken his at the funeral, saying *You're the man of the house now* like a blessing and a sentence.

He squeezed Joan's hand.

'I feel like I'm nowhere,' he said. 'Half with Mam, half with you. Nowhere fully.'

'You're here now,' she said, with that quiet practical kindness she'd always had. 'That's all that matters.'

They sat like that for a while, the fire's electric glow flickering on the glass, casting their shadows against the wall – his larger, hers drawn in, the two shapes touching at the shoulders.

Later, when he climbed into bed beside her, she stirred.

'You okay?' she asked.

'Fine,' he lied. 'Just thinking.'

'Don't go too far,' she murmured, already drifting.

He lay on his back, staring into the dimness, listening to her breath even out. The ache in his back pulsed, a muted drum. Outside, the wind picked up. Somewhere down the road, the church bell tolled nine, then ten, the sound softened by distance.

He thought of the hallway at his mother's, the peg where his father's cap no longer hung. Thought of how the light had fallen through that narrow, frosted window in the late afternoon, thin and pearled, making even the old coat rack look briefly holy.

He closed his eyes and willed himself to sleep, knowing that in the morning he would drive back down into town, back to his mother's house, back to the rooms where his father's absence sat like an extra piece of furniture.

Between those two houses, between the living and the newly dead, his days were beginning to stretch – thin, taut, but still holding.

Chapter Two

The Invisible Man

On Saturday evening, the town gathered itself into its usual shapes. Light began to pool in windows, breath rose from chimneys in pale smudges, and the main street filled with slow-moving cars and men in dark coats, drifting in from outlying roads like crows homing in on the same field.

Ciarán sat at his mother's kitchen table, his coat already on, the keys heavy in his pocket.

She was rinsing a plate at the sink, sleeves pushed up, the movements automatic. The six o'clock news murmured through from the sitting room, the anchor's voice rising and falling while images of crises in other countries flashed, ignored.

'You're going out?' she asked, without turning.

'Just for a pint,' he said. 'I won't be late.'

She nodded. 'You should go. You need to see people. Not just me and that poor wife of yours.'

He smiled faintly. 'You're people too.'

'Different kind,' she said. 'The kind that drags you down with talk of the dead and the doctors.'

He didn't argue. Instead he stood and put the plate in the rack beside her, brushing her arm lightly as he passed. It felt too thin beneath the sleeve.

'Do you want me to pick up anything?' he asked.

She shook her head. 'I've the press full. Go on. Don't sit in corners all your life.'

He kissed her cheek. It was cool, smelling of soap.

On his way down the hall he glanced, as he always did, at the peg by the door. His father's cap was still absent, but the pale mark beneath it was already beginning to fade, the way a picture leaves a ghost after it's taken down for only so long. He wondered how long before that too disappeared completely.

The pub sat where it had always sat, halfway down Main Street, shoulder to shoulder with the butcher's and the bookmaker's. Its front was painted a tired red now, the gold lettering above the door flaking but still legible: *Dolan's*. Once it had been Kelly's, and before that, legend said, something else entirely, but for Ciarán it had always been Dolan's, as fixed and inevitable as the church and the GAA pitch.

He paused just inside the door, blinking as his eyes adjusted to the amber dimness. The warmth wrapped around him, heavy with the smell of old beer, turf smoke, and the faint sweetness of spilled stout soaked into wood. Voices overlapped, a low burr of conversation threaded through with sharper notes of laughter, the scrape of chairs, the clack of pool balls from the back.

It was busy enough to feel like company, but not so crowded that he'd have to fight for space.

'Ciarán,' said Joe from behind the bar, as if noting something mildly surprising but welcome, like the reappearance of a regular migratory bird. 'Haven't seen you in an age. Sorry about your father. He was a grand man.'

'Thanks, Joe,' Ciarán said.

'The usual?'

He nodded.

Joe pulled the pint with the slow care of someone who considered it a minor sacrament. Ciarán watched the stout rise, the brown shifting to black, the creamy head swelling toward the lip.

He took his glass and moved to the corner by the window, the place he'd always favoured. The stool creaked under him as if remembering. Outside, the street was a blurred reflection on the glass, the headlights of passing cars smearing white lines across his view.

From his corner he could see almost everyone. There were the usual knots: the retired farmers by the fire, caps on the table, talking in half-sentences; a group of lads around the pool table, all hoodies and tracksuits, laughing too loudly; two women at a small round table near the door, coats still on, lingering over gin and tonics as if unsure whether they were staying or going. The TV above the bar showed a football match with the sound off. No one seemed to be watching.

Near the darts board, he spotted Declan Walsh – a few years younger than Ciarán, his hair receding but his belly prospering. Declan was mid-story, hands drawing shapes in the air to illustrate some misfortune with a trailer and a stubborn bullock. The men around him roared, each laugh a little too big, as if performing enjoyment for one another.

Declan caught sight of him and raised his glass.

'Jesus, Devlin, look who it is!' he called. 'I thought you'd taken holy orders. Or moved to Spain with the rest of the retired teachers.'

'Not retired yet,' Ciarán called back. 'Just hiding.'

'You're welcome to join us,' Declan said, gesturing expansively. 'We're solving all the world's problems here.'

'I'll let you get on with it,' Ciarán replied, lifting his pint.

They both smiled, and Declan turned back to his audience, already moving into the next piece of the story.

Ciarán took a long sip. The Guinness sat on his tongue, cold and bitter and soft all at once, the familiar weight settling into him. It eased something in his chest, or at least pushed it aside for the length of that swallow. He looked down at the foam left on the glass, the pattern it made – rings of slow consumption. He set the glass down carefully on the cardboard coaster, the little circle of pretend reverence under the real thing.

It occurred to him that he'd had some version of this drink in some version of this corner for over thirty years. Post-match when he was young, flush with the temporary invincibility of a win. After school on Fridays once he'd started teaching, still full of chalk dust and adolescent drama. Later, with Joan sometimes, when they'd walk down together in the summer and sit out the back in the beer garden, sharing a bowl of chips, her face turned toward whatever light remained.

Now he sat alone, watching the town revolve around him, and felt … unnecessary. Present, but not required. Two men he knew from school days – Kieran Brennan and Liam Ward – settled at a nearby table with their pints and nodded as they passed.

'How's things, Ciarán?' Kieran asked. 'We were sorry to hear about Sean. He did a gearbox on a Ferguson for us back in the nineties. Never a whimper out of it since.'

'Thanks,' Ciarán said. 'He'd like to be remembered for that.'

They laughed softly, the appropriate amount.

'And Joan?' Liam asked, a little more carefully. 'How is she keeping?'

'Up and down,' Ciarán said. 'Still doing the treatments. Some days are better than others.'

'You're not having an easy time of it,' Kieran said. 'Mam

was saying you're back and over to your own mother as well. You'll wear yourself out.'

'I'm grand,' Ciarán said, the automatic lie. 'Keeps me busy.'

They nodded, but he could see in their eyes that they didn't quite believe him, or believed him only in the way people believe in the weather forecast: as a polite possibility rather than a guarantee.

'Shout if you're stuck for anything,' Liam said. 'We're in and out past your mother's the whole time. It's no bother to keep an eye.'

'I appreciate it,' Ciarán said.

They moved away then, into their own conversations about slurry and regulations and some new broadband scheme that may or may not ever arrive. Their talk blurred into the general hum.

An old pop song came on the radio – something from the late eighties, all synth and yearning. Without thinking, Ciarán found himself silently counting along to the bassline, his fingers moving just slightly on the glass as if fretting invisible strings. The muscle memory made his hands tingle.

He'd played that song once, years ago, in a cover set in a small student bar in Rathmines. He remembered the feel of the bass strap digging into his shoulder, the vibration of the strings against his stomach, the drummer's cymbal slightly cracked. There had been maybe fifteen people in the place, mostly friends of the guitarist, but when they'd hit the chorus, the whole room had sung along, loud and drunk and momentarily united.

He'd gone home that night with his ears buzzing and his heart thrumming, convinced that this – *this* – was what he was meant to be doing. That it would grow into something, that the shapeless ache he carried would be filled with sound and applause and at least a modest record deal.

Instead, he'd become a teacher.

He took another drink.

Halfway through his pint, his bladder pinched. The now-familiar ache low in his pelvis made itself known, insistent, like a child tugging at a sleeve.

He put down the glass and made his way to the gents.

The toilets were narrow and badly lit, a rectangle of damp tiles and condensation. Graffiti climbed the cubicle doors – phone numbers, county colours, declarations of love and hate. He chose a urinal, stood, waited.

The stream came reluctantly, stopping and starting, the relief incomplete. A dull burn at the end.

He stared at the wall, at a sticker half peeled off that read *Support Your Local Team*, and thought of the GP's office three weeks ago. The quiet way the doctor had said, 'We'll just do some bloods,' and the almost offhand suggestion of a PSA test. 'Given your age,' he'd said. 'Just to be on the safe side.'

He'd nodded, trousers hitched up, part of his mind still in the taxi where he'd left Joan after the hospital appointment, the smell of antiseptic still in his nostrils.

He hadn't gone back for the follow-up. Things had been 'busy'. His father's health had dipped. Joan's chemo cycle had intensified. His mother had started ringing more often at night. There was always something.

He'd convinced himself that if it were truly serious, the surgery would have called him.

Now, standing in the half-dark of Dolan's toilets, he felt that conviction wobble.

He zipped up, washed his hands in water that never seemed to rise above lukewarm, and looked at himself in the mirror. The harsh strip light flattened everything, turning his skin grey, making his eyes look like someone had taken an eraser to them and scrubbed out the colour.

He looked like a man who could be ill. The thought startled him, as if until now he'd thought of illness as something that belonged to other people: parents, patients, the anonymous figures in hospital adverts.

He splashed water on his face and dried it with paper that scratched.

Back at his stool, his pint had settled. A crescent of foam clung to the glass. He drank, feeling the liquid slide down into a body he no longer fully trusted.

As the evening thickened, the pub grew busier. A young couple came in – maybe in their early twenties, close together, carrying a quiet warmth between them. They sat at a high table and leaned into one another as they talked, the woman's hands moving in small, excited gestures, the man nodding, eyes never leaving her face.

Watching them, Ciarán felt something like nostalgia, but wider and more blurred – not just for youth or romance, but for a time when the future had felt like a field of open gates, any of which he might walk through without thinking about what lay on the other side.

He thought of himself and Joan when they'd first met – both teaching in Dublin, both convinced that they'd leave the country within a few years for somewhere else, anywhere else, just to see. They'd shared cheap wine and long evenings in cafés, arguing about books and films and politics, both secretly delighted to have found someone who knew the same poems by heart.

Somehow, without ever quite deciding it, they'd ended up back here instead.

The two young teachers who had once promised themselves

cities had bought a semi-detached near the town where he'd grown up. They'd painted the kitchen themselves, bickered over tiles, learned the names of the neighbours' dogs.

Life had shrunk and deepened at the same time.

He finished his pint more quickly than he'd meant to. When he set the empty glass down, Joe appeared at his elbow.

'Another?' Joe asked.

Ciarán considered. The ache in his back had sharpened slightly. The thought of another trip to the toilet, with its stuttering relief, was suddenly unappealing.

'I'll leave it at the one,' he said. 'You'll be closing the doors in a minute if I start another.'

'Going soft in your old age,' Joe said, but there was no judgement in it, only the casual affection of someone who measured lives in the intervals between Friday nights.

'Something like that,' Ciarán replied.

Outside, the air was sharper than when he'd gone in. The cold seemed to have found new teeth. He zipped his coat to his chin and stood for a moment under the weak yellow light above the door.

The main street glowed in small pockets – the chemist's still lit, the Chinese takeaway doing a slow trade, the newsagent's shutter halfway down. Above, on wires strung between lamp posts, the town's Christmas lights trembled in the slight breeze. They were the same set they'd been using for as long as he could remember – a reindeer with a missing antler, a star that flickered unreliably, a string of bulbs that always had one dark patch in the middle. Every year the council promised new ones. Every year, these returned from whatever shed they were stored in, hung out again like a tired hope.

He walked slowly toward the car. The pavement gleamed

in places where frost had begun to form, turning the street lights' reflections into smears of white.

Passing the bookmaker's, he saw a man standing alone outside, cigarette cupped in his hand, coat collar turned up. It took him a second to recognise him.

'Is that you, Dev?' the man said, squinting slightly.

It was Brendan Byrne – once the thin, intense drummer from the band Ciarán had played in, now heavier around the middle, his hair cut brutally short, a deep groove between his eyebrows that hadn't been there before.

'Brendan,' Ciarán said. 'Jesus. How are you?'

'Above ground,' Brendan said. 'Can't complain. Well, I could. But no one listens.'

They laughed.

For a second, seeing him, Ciarán was back in a different evening, in a cramped rehearsal room that smelled of sweat and dust and borrowed amps, Brendan counting them in, his sticks clicking together, the thrill of that first joint chord.

'You're still around?' Ciarán asked.

'Couldn't escape,' Brendan said. 'Came back when the recession hit. The city spat me out. You?'

'Same,' Ciarán said. 'School. Mam. Joan.'

'I heard about your wife,' Brendan said, his face softening. 'Sorry, man. That's rough.'

'How did you— '

'Word gets around,' Brendan said. 'My sister works up in the hospital. She says it's like half this town is on a rota up there.'

They fell into a short silence that wasn't entirely comfortable, each aware of the things they weren't saying.

'You still playing?' Ciarán asked.

Brendan snorted. 'Only my knees. You?'

He shook his head. 'The bass is in the attic. Probably grown mould by now.'

'Shame,' Brendan said. 'You were good. Better than you thought you were, anyway.'

'Doesn't pay the bills,' Ciarán said.

'Neither does teaching,' Brendan countered. 'At least with music you get to sweat.'

They smiled, and for a moment something of the old easiness returned.

'Do you remember that night in Portobello?' Brendan said. 'When the power went and you kept playing anyway? Like some kind of gobshite unplugged monk.'

'I remember you throwing your sticks at the landlord,' Ciarán said.

'He'd cut the power. He deserved it.'

They laughed again, the sound briefly warming the cold street.

'Well,' Brendan said, flicking the last of his cigarette into the gutter and grinding it with his heel. 'We'll get a reunion gig going for the over-50s. Chairs provided. Exit doors clearly marked.'

'I'll bring the defibrillator,' Ciarán replied.

Brendan clapped him on the shoulder. 'Mind yourself, Dev. And mind that wife of yours.'

'I will,' Ciarán said.

As he watched Brendan go, shoulders hunched against the cold, Ciarán felt a strange double sensation – as if he were both walking with his old bandmate down the street and standing where he was, watching them leave. Past and present brushing quietly against one another.

There were versions of himself that had never left Dublin, that had gone on tour in battered vans, that had played to indifferent crowds in German basements. There were versions that had moved to Canada, to Australia, followed friends who'd gone chasing work and weather. He'd stayed. Taught. Married. Come back to this town that was both too small and too big.

He unlocked the car and sat for a moment with his hands on the wheel, the key not yet turned. His breath fogged the windscreen.

In the reflection in the rear-view mirror, his face floated faintly over the street behind, half there, half not.

The Invisible Man, he thought. Present in every room and yet somehow transparent, his edges smudged by other people's needs and tragedies.

He turned the key.

At his mother's house, the light in the front window was on, the net curtain glowing like thin paper. He parked at the gate and walked up the path, the gravel crunching under his feet.

Inside, she was in the sitting room, cardigan buttoned wrong again, the television now showing a crime drama in which a handsome detective strode through a city at night, always framing the right question, always arriving in time.

'You weren't long,' she said.

'Only the one,' he replied. 'I met a fella I used to play music with. Brendan Byrne.'

'I remember him,' she said. 'Your father used to say he'd end up in prison or parliament.'

'Still time for both,' Ciarán said.

She smiled. 'Did you enjoy it? The pint?'

'It was … all right,' he said, sitting. 'Nice to be somewhere I'm not needed.'

She gave him a sideways look. 'You're needed everywhere you go. That's half your trouble.'

He didn't argue.

‘I’ll make you a cup of tea,’ he said instead.

In the kitchen, as the kettle boiled again, he felt the ache in his back flare, a hot pressure that radiated down toward his hip. He pressed his hand against the worktop and breathed through his teeth.

Tomorrow, he thought. I’ll ring the doctor tomorrow.

He pictured the surgery – the plastic chairs, the leaflets about prostate health and diabetes, the smell of hand sanitiser. He pictured sitting in the waiting room, just another man in a line of men, each of them carrying a quiet dread no one would speak aloud.

For a moment he saw himself as if from above – moving between his mother’s house, his own house, the school he would soon return to, the pub, the hospital. A pinball ricocheting off obligations, lighting up small parts of each place but never resting.

He poured the tea, carried the tray through.

His mother had dozed off, her head tilted back, her mouth slightly open. On the TV, the detective had just solved the case, standing in a floodlit car park with an air of weary satisfaction.

He put the cups down quietly and turned down the volume.

In the muted light, watching his mother breathe, Ciarán felt himself sink into the chair, into the room, into the web of two houses and a town that held him firmly but not unkindly.

The tea steamed between them, cooling slowly in the soft, ordinary dark.

Invisible or not, he thought, this was where he was.

Chapter Three

The Long Night

The road out to the yard was one his body knew better than his mind. He could have driven it blindfolded: out past the GAA pitch, where the floodlights rose like silent sentries; past the old schoolhouse with its broken gutters and faded mural of a smiling sun; then down the boreen that narrowed with every bend, hedges closing in until the car seemed to squeeze between hawthorn and briars.

The sky that morning was the colour of a bruise. Low cloud sagged over the fields, and the frost that had silvered everything at dawn was already retreating into the shadows. The potholes were full of thin water, reflecting uneven fragments of sky.

He hadn't meant to come here. Or that was what he told himself. He'd left his mother's after breakfast with a vague list – petrol, bread, see if the butcher had any of the good sausages left. But when the junction came, instead of turning right toward town, his hands had turned the wheel left. By the time he noticed, the car was already bumping down the narrow lane, the decision made somewhere below language.

The gate to the yard hung slightly open, as if the last person who'd gone through it – his father – had always meant to come back out again. The paint on the bars had long since surrendered, rust bloomed in patches, and there was a familiar squeal as he pushed it wide enough for the car. Gravel crunched under the tyres. Oil-stained puddles reflected the grey sky in broken circles.

He cut the engine and sat for a moment, letting the silence of the place arrive. It wasn't real silence, not quite: he could hear a crow somewhere beyond the trees, a tractor faintly on a distant road, the slow drip of water from a roof. But compared to the tightness of his mother's house, the cluttered hum of his own, the yard felt like a space set aside, a pause in the middle of the day.

The machinery shed loomed ahead, a long, low building of corrugated iron and block, the roof bowed slightly like the back of an old animal under a load it had carried too long. Moss streaked the gutters; ivy had begun its slow, sure climb up one corner, tendrils slipping between rusted nails.

He pulled his collar up against the bite of the air and walked across the yard. His boots slipped once in a patch of years-old diesel, still slick. The smell hit him as he neared the door: oil, grease, damp metal, the ghost of cutting fluid. It was the scent of his childhood Saturdays, of summer evenings when he'd been dragged along to 'give a hand', and of winters when he'd sat in the office with his homework while his father worked on into the dark.

The big sliding door resisted his first pull, the wheels sitting reluctant in their track. He leaned into it with his shoulder and felt it jerk, then whine along, opening a mouth of dimness.

He flicked the light switch just inside out of habit. Nothing. The bulbs that had hung from the rafters like bare moons were dark, dust-dulled. Of course – the electricity had been cut off months ago, when it became clear that there'd be no more work booked in, no more calls about broken diggers or tractors that wouldn't start.

His eyes adjusted slowly. The shed's interior emerged in layers: the workbench under the far window, cluttered with tools and rags; the old compressor in the corner, silent now; the red Massey Ferguson half-sunk in its own dust, tyres slack, bonnet streaked. Chains hung from a beam, looping down in great steel parentheses around the empty space where the last customer's machine had once stood.

Nothing had moved. That was his first thought. Nothing had changed since the last time he'd been here, sometime in the spring, when his father had still been well enough to come out and stand in the doorway, hands in his pockets, looking at the empty yard without comment.

Ciarán stepped inside, the cold going through his clothes at once, as if the shed refused to acknowledge the weak heater in his bones.

In the old office cubby at the side, he could just make out the outline of the small desk where his father used to sit with his books, peering at figures under the yellow glare of a lamp. A calendar from a fertiliser company still hung on the wall, stuck forever in a March from two years ago, a glossy photo of a green field in some hypothetical better weather.

He moved toward the workbench.

Here the evidence of his father was at its most concentrated: spanners laid out in a rough order, from the big ones down to the small; jam jars full of bolts and washers, the lids streaked with old fingerprints; a chipped blue mug with a tide-mark of long-evaporated tea inside. On the shelf above, an ancient plastic radio sat mute, its aerial bent, the tuning dial fixed somewhere between stations for the rest of time.

He reached out and ran his hand along the benchtop. A thin film of dust came away on his fingers, though under it he could feel the familiar dints and gouges, the scars of years of work. He wiped the dust on his jeans automatically and stood there, not sure where to look.

He had hated this place when he was small. The smells had seemed overwhelming (burnt oil, hot metal, the sweet chemical tang of primer), the noise violent – grinders and hammers and the sudden crack of something releasing. He'd resented the way the yard claimed his father's time and attention, the way the phone could ring at any hour and pull him away from the kitchen table, the TV, the game.

Later, as a teenager, he'd envied it. Not the work itself – not the cold mornings and the heavy parts – but the sense of certainty it seemed to give his father. He knew things. He could stand in front of a machine, listen to it cough or fail to start, and identify the fault immediately. *It's the fuel line; it's the starter; the clutch needs replacing*. There was comfort in that kind of knowledge, the comfort of diagnosis and remedy.

Ciarán's knowledge had always been of softer, less useful things: dates and poems and political movements; chords and counterpoint; the way light fell in certain rooms. None of it, he'd been told often enough, would fix a broken PTO shaft.

And yet here he was, the one left to decide what to do with the yard.

He opened drawers and found ledgers – rows of names and numbers in his father's small, controlled hand. McTiernan – pump seals – paid. F. Flynn – clutch kit – outstanding. Receipts from parts suppliers. A dog-eared manual for a JCB from the 1980s. A cracked plastic tub containing a dozen keys, all unlabelled, each one once essential to something.

In one drawer, under a stack of old envelopes, he found a biscuit tin. For a foolish second he thought of money – some secret stash, notes folded and hidden, his father hedging against bad days. Instead, when he prised the lid off, there were photographs. Loose, unprotected, curling at the edges.

He sat on the old wheeled chair and spread them on his lap.

His father, younger, standing beside a freshly painted digger, the bucket gleaming yellow. A group shot of men in overalls, lined up in front of the shed in some long-gone summer, all squinting into the light. His father and mother at some wedding, his father in a suit that didn't quite sit right on him, his mother's hair impossibly dark and tall.

One photo caught him: the yard in winter, snow on the ground, a boy of eight or nine – himself – standing by the open door, wrapped in a too-big jacket, his cheeks pink with cold. His father in the background, not quite in focus, glancing toward the camera, his expression caught between irritation and amusement. He tried to remember the day. A snowman, maybe. Hot chocolate after. Or had there been an argument? The memory wouldn't sharpen.

He slid the photos back into the tin, closed the lid and placed it on the desk as if it belonged there, as if time might yet circle back and find his father's hand reaching for it.

In the far corner, the coat rack held his father's jackets, hanging in a row as though waiting their turn. The waxed one for bad weather, the faded brown for every day, the heavy winter one that smelled of turf smoke and damp dog, though they'd never owned a dog. Ciarán lifted the brown jacket off its hook and slipped it on.

It was almost the right fit, but not quite. The sleeves were a shade too short, the shoulders sitting differently, the weight unfamiliar. The lining smelled of oil and the faint ghost of his father's aftershave, that cheap Old Spice he'd worn all his life.

He looked at himself in the small mirror by the door, the one his father had used to check that the grease on his hands hadn't climbed all the way to his face. For a moment the resemblance took his breath.

He looked like a version of his father from some parallel

timeline – a man who had stayed in England, maybe, or who had never opened a yard, who had taken up teaching, who had learned to talk more.

'It doesn't suit you.'

The words landed in his mind in his father's voice, so clearly that he half turned before remembering.

He shrugged the jacket off and folded it over his arm. He would bring it to his mother, he decided. Let her decide what was to become of it. The thought of leaving it here, hanging on a dead man's peg, was suddenly unbearable.

Outside, the light had shifted. The grey sky had paled further, thinning toward a kind of reluctant brightness. Low clouds scudded over the hills, the wind picking up just enough to worry the top branches of the ash trees by the gate. A squall of rain blew through, fine and slanting, the drops cold on his face.

He locked the shed door out of habit, even though there was nothing inside to steal that anyone would want.

Standing in the middle of the yard, he turned slowly, taking it all in: the oil stains, the broken pallets stacked by the wall, the pile of scrap metal his father had always meant to 'sort out one of these days'. He tried to imagine it sold, cleared, turned into some neat concrete yard where someone else might park a caravan or a row of cars. The idea made his stomach knot.

A crow landed on the top of the shed, tilted its head at him, then hopped twice and flew off.

On the drive back, he took the long way, through narrow roads hedged in on both sides, past fields he could have named the owners of in his sleep. He rolled the window down a crack and let the air in. It smelled of wet earth, slurry from some distant tank, wood smoke. Familiar, and yet slightly altered, as if some note in it had gone missing.

At a crossroads he stopped without meaning to. The

signposts pointed in three directions: TOWN, BYPASS, LAKE. For several seconds he sat there, the car idling, the wipers squeaking once across the windscreen.

A car came up behind, its driver giving a small, polite tap of the horn.

He indicated left, toward town, and went on.

The day rolled itself out in small tasks. He called to McEntee's for bread and milk, endured two more rounds of *Sorry for your trouble*, bought extra teabags without quite knowing why. At home, he made lunch for Joan – thin soup, bread – and stood by the kitchen window while she dozed on the sofa, the television muttering. He put on a wash, hung shirts on the rack in the utility room, the domestic motions soothing in their simplicity.

Once, as he reached up to pin a sleeve, a sharp pain shot through his lower back into his groin. It was so sudden he had to catch himself against the wall, the world narrowing to a bright, mean point.

He stood there, breathing shallowly, waiting for it to subside.

It did, slowly, leaving behind a dull, throbbing ache.

He thought of the leaflet the GP had pressed into his hand after that last appointment. *Men's Health After 50*. It was probably still in the glovebox, folded and unread, its clip-art diagrams and bullet points waiting patiently for his attention.

'Tomorrow,' he said aloud.

But there was always tomorrow.

By the time he drove back out to his mother's, the sky had already tilted toward evening. A veil of fine rain had begun to fall again, turning the road into a blurred ribbon of reflections. The hedges, dark and glossy, leaned in.

His mother's house shone at the end of the lane, every downstairs light on, the kitchen window a square of yellow against the grey. It looked, he thought fleetingly, like an illustration from a children's book – a cottage in a half-wild landscape, promising warmth and safety.

Inside, however, the warmth felt thinner.

She was at the table, her hands resting on either side of a plate with a single digestive biscuit on it, untouched.

'You're late,' she said, though when he looked at the clock it was barely half six. Her face softened a fraction. 'How is Joan?'

'Wrecked,' he said. 'Maeve's calling in on her later.'

'I don't know how the girl does it,' she said. 'All that driving, back and over. Costing her a fortune in petrol.'

Ciarán didn't point out that he was doing the same, or that Maeve's car and job were both better equipped for such things.

Instead, he filled the kettle, reached for the tea caddy, pulled two cups from the press. The motions were becoming a rhythm between them, a language of their own.

'Did you go up to the yard?' she asked, watching him.

'I did,' he said. 'This morning.'

'How was it?'

He shrugged. 'The same. Empty.'

She nodded, as if that confirmed something she already knew.

'Did you see his jacket?' she asked.

'I did,' he said. 'I brought one of them with me. It's in the car.'

A flicker passed through her eyes – hurt, perhaps, or gratitude. 'Bring it in later,' she said.

She smiled faintly. 'We can hang it there,' she said,

gesturing vaguely toward the back hall. 'For a while. Till we decide what to do with it.'

When the tea was poured, he took his cup to the sitting room. The electric fire was on, its red coils glowing, the fake embers shifting mechanically. She followed, carrying a plate of biscuits.

They watched the news without taking any of it in. Politicians at podiums, floods in other counties, footage of shoppers in busy cities. His mother tutted at a story about a fight outside a nightclub, shook her head over the price of housing in Dublin, and fell silent again.

When *Fair City* came on, she perked up slightly, making small comments about characters whose names he couldn't keep straight. He let the familiar theme tune wash over him. It had been playing in this room, in some form, for as long as he could remember – through his own adolescence, through his father's years of late returns from the yard, through his mother's quiet evenings alone while he'd been away in college.

He stayed till ten. Made sure she'd taken her tablets. Checked that the back door was locked, that the immersion was off, that the key was turned in the side door. The old rituals of rural fear.

'I'll ring you if I need anything,' she said, standing in the hallway in her dressing gown, the tartan blanket over her shoulders.

'I'll be back in the morning,' he replied.

She reached up and straightened his collar, a gesture so familiar it almost undid him.

'You're a good lad,' she said.

He kissed her cheek and left.

The road home was empty. The rain had thickened into a fine, soaking mist that the wipers barely disturbed. The town's lights glowed ahead, a small cluster in the half-dark. As he drove into it, passing closed shopfronts and the black rectangles of upstairs windows, he felt a wave of tiredness so sudden he had to grip the wheel.

By the time he pulled into his own driveway, all he could think of was bed. He was woken by the phone, its harsh ring slicing the dark.

For a few disorienting seconds he had no idea where he was. The room was a familiar blur – the wardrobe's silhouette, the darker shadow of the window, the soft sound of Joan's breathing beside him. The red numbers of the alarm clock said 11:14.

He fumbled for the phone on the bedside table, the screen briefly blinding him.

'Mam,' he said, before he'd fully answered, seeing her name.

'There's someone in the yard,' she said.

Her voice wasn't hysterical, but there was a tightness there that sharpened every syllable.

'In the yard?'

'I heard them,' she said. 'Just now. Walking around. I could hear the gravel.' She took a breath that shuddered. 'I know the sound, Ciarán. Your father's boots. But it's not him.'

He sat up, keeping his voice as level as he could. Beside him, Joan shifted slightly, murmuring.

'Are the lights on?' he asked.

'I turned on the kitchen one,' she said. 'And the hall. I looked out, but I couldn't see anyone. But I heard it, I swear to God. The back step creaking. You know the way it does? And the latch. As if …'

She didn't finish.

He swung his legs out of bed, his feet hitting the cold floor.

'Okay,' he said. 'Okay. I'll come over. It's probably a fox. Or the wind.'

'There's no wind,' she said.

He glanced toward the window. The branches of the rowan tree outside were very still.

'I'll be there in twenty minutes,' he said. 'Put the chain on the door. Don't open it for anyone until you hear my knock. All right?'

'I shouldn't have rung,' she said, suddenly uncertain. 'It's late. You've your own troubles. But I got a fright ...'

'You did the right thing,' he said. 'I'm coming now.'

He hung up and sat for a moment, the phone in his hand, the dark humming.

Joan's hand found his arm. 'Your mother?' she asked, sleep roughening her voice.

'Yeah,' he said. 'She thinks there's someone in the yard. She's scared. I'll go over, have a look around. I won't be long.'

She sighed, the sound neither approval nor complaint. 'Be careful,' she said. 'The roads will be greasy.'

He dressed quickly – jeans, jumper, the first pair of socks his hand hit. His back protested as he leaned to pull on his boots, the ache flaring, then settling into a throb.

Downstairs, he grabbed his coat and keys, then stepped out into the night.

The cold hit him sharp in the face. The mist had thickened; visibility was poor, the world reduced to a few metres of glistening tarmac and the faint suggestion of hedges beyond. His breath hung in the air, then vanished.

He drove quickly, the headlights carving narrow tunnels through the dark. The whiteness at the road's edge seemed to move, tricks of light that suggested figures where there were none. The radio stayed off. The only sound was the engine and the wet hiss of tyres.

As he turned in to his mother's lane, his stomach clenched. All the downstairs lights were on again, the house glowing too brightly, like a ship adrift.

He parked at the gate and walked up the path, gravel loud under his boots now that he was listening for it. At the door, he knocked three times in their old pattern: two quick, one slow.

The chain rattled. The door opened a crack, the chain still on.

'Who is it?' his mother's voice, close.

'It's me,' he said. 'Ciarán.'

She peered through the gap, then slipped the chain and opened the door.

'I told you,' she said. 'I heard them. Just now.'

He stepped inside. The house smelled of boiled milk and the faint singe of something that had been forgotten on a ring and then rescued.

'Stay here,' he said. 'I'll have a look around.'

He went through the rooms one by one, switching lights off as he left them, the old automatic reflex. The back door was locked; the bolts were on. In the utility room, the cat flap (long unused; the last cat had died a decade ago) rattled slightly in the draught.

He stood at the back kitchen window and looked out. The yard beyond was an indistinct smear of grey and black. The security light failed to come on.

He opened the back door, stepped out, listened.

Nothing. Just the sound of his own breathing, and, far off, the faint whoosh of a lorry on the bypass.

He checked the gate, the shed door. Both were closed, the locks stiff under his hand. The gravel lay undisturbed, its damp surface unmarked.

He went back inside. His mother was sitting at the kitchen table now, hands wrapped around a mug of tea, untouched.

'Well?' she asked.

'No one there,' he said gently. 'Everything locked up tight.'

She pursed her lips. 'I know what I heard,' she said. 'I heard the step. I heard the gravel. That's not nothing.'

'I'm not saying it's nothing,' he said. 'Could have been a fox. Or the wind moving something.'

'There was no wind,' she insisted. 'And a fox doesn't sound like boots.'

She looked at him then, a flash of anger in her eyes – anger that softened almost at once into something else. Fear, maybe. Or shame.

'I'm not going mad,' she said, quieter. 'I can tell the difference between a fox and a man.'

'I know,' he said. He pulled out the chair opposite her and sat. 'I know you can. It gave you a fright. That's reason enough to call.'

Her shoulders dropped a fraction, as though something in her had been waiting for permission.

'Would you stay?' she asked, after a moment, her voice small. 'Just tonight. It's worse in the dark.'

'Of course,' he said. 'I'll text Joan. She'll be all right. She's probably asleep already.'

He made another cup of tea. They sat drinking in the bright kitchen, the clock ticking too loudly over the sink. On the fridge, held by a magnet from Knock, was a photograph from Christmas five years before – himself and Joan and his parents, all in paper hats, his father mid-laugh at some forgotten joke.

His mother's gaze flicked to it, then away again.

'I was talking to him,' she said, staring into her cup.

'To Dad?'

She nodded. 'Before I rang you. I said to him, "If that's you, Sean Devlin, you'll have to do better than that. I don't like these creeping games."'

He smiled despite himself. It was exactly the tone she used to take with his father when he'd track muck into the hall.

'And did he answer?' he asked, keeping his voice light.

She shook her head. 'Not yet.'

She looked up, and for a second he saw how thin the line was between her and the raw edge of things.

'It's worse at night,' she said. 'The house … it changes. You hear every sound. Every pipe. I keep thinking he's in the yard. Or at the back door. Or in the hall, leaving his boots.'

'He was never that quiet coming in,' Ciarán said. 'You'd hear him a mile off.'

'I know,' she said, a ghost of a smile. 'Banging and slamming and whistling his daft tunes. But now … I don't know. The mind plays tricks.'

She rubbed the heel of her hand against her chest, slow circles. The gesture made him think of heartburn, of a knot that would not go down.

'I'll sleep in the spare room,' he said. 'Leave the light on at the top of the stairs if you want. That way if you wake, you'll know I'm here.'

She nodded, relief softening her face.

'You're a great comfort,' she said.

He didn't feel like much of anything. Comfort, or otherwise. He felt tired, thin, stretched. But he smiled, because she needed him to.

The spare room looked exactly as it had the night after the funeral, and the hundred nights before that: the same floral curtains, the same faded wallpaper with its pattern of climbing roses, the same crucifix above the bed, casting its small wooden shadow.

He changed into the old tracksuit bottoms and T-shirt he kept in the wardrobe here, folded his clothes over the chair, and slid under the covers. The sheets were cold but clean, the smell of his mother's fabric conditioner rising – a faint, artificial lavender.

For a while, he lay on his back and listened to the wind whistling through the guttering outside.

He was almost asleep when he heard it.

A voice.

So faint he wasn't sure at first if it was real or a dream. He sat up, heart thudding, ears straining.

It came again. Not from outside, but from down the hall.

He got out of bed and padded barefoot into the corridor, the lino cool underfoot. His mother's bedroom door was slightly ajar. Light from the bedside lamp spilled into the hallway in a narrow wedge.

He edged closer and, feeling like a thief in his own house, glanced in.

She was lying on her side, facing the empty half of the bed, her hand resting lightly on the hollow where his father's body had been for nearly sixty years. Her mouth moved; the words, at his distance, were only a murmur.

He stepped nearer, just enough to hear.

'... you've left me with all of it,' she was saying. 'The bins and the bills and that old boiler. You never thought about the boiler. You just banged it when it made a noise. That's no use to me now.'

There was a pause. Her fingers smoothed the sheet as if reassuring it.

'You were supposed to go after me,' she went on. 'That was the arrangement. I always said it. "You'll have to bury me, Sean. I won't be able for burying you." But here we are. You've gone off and left the mess.'

Her voice cracked on the last word.

He stood in the doorway, invisible, knowing he had intruded on something intimate and entirely private.

'I'm doing my best,' she whispered. 'The boy is worn to a shadow. Back and over like a yo-yo. It's not right. It's not fair. You should have stayed to mind him. Or taken me with you.'

She fell silent then, whether because she'd run out of words or because sleep had claimed her, he couldn't tell.

He stepped back, careful not to let the floorboard outside her room creak, and returned to the spare bed.

Lying in the dark, his chest ached, but not in the physical way he'd first feared. It was a deeper kind of ache, down in the place where all the unsaid things were stored.

The boy is worn to a shadow.

He thought of himself as his mother saw him: not a man approaching sixty, with his own failing body and regrets, but still 'the boy' – the youngest, the one who had stayed close, the one who was expected to be elastic, stretching to fit whatever shape was needed.

He thought of Joan asleep alone in their bed. Of the students who would be waiting for him in a few weeks, their essays half-finished, their questions about treaties and rising movements. Of the yard, sitting empty under a dull sky, the tools waiting for hands that would not return.

Sleep, when it came, was full of small, disjointed images: his father standing at the back door, wet coat dripping; his mother at the sink, washing the same cup over and over; Joan by the sea, her scarf whipping in the wind.

He woke just after five, his body still on some internal early shift. The house was quiet, the particular pre-dawn silence that felt neither like night nor morning. He dressed and went downstairs, moving carefully, not wanting to wake his mother yet.

In the kitchen he filled the kettle, set it to boil, got out the porridge pot. The motions were the same as they'd been yesterday, and the day before that, and the decade before that when his father had sat at this table with his newspaper, not yet old, not yet ill.

Through the small window, the garden was a grey smudge. The bird table was empty. Somewhere beyond the hedge, a rooster crowed, its sound oddly distant.

He warmed the porridge, added salt, stirred. Steam rose, fogging the glass.

As he stood there, spoon in hand, he realised that this – these early mornings, this moving quietly in cold kitchens, this balancing of two houses and two lives – wasn't a temporary state. It wasn't a rough patch to be got through before things 'went back to normal'. This was the new normal. This was the shape his life had taken, slowly, without his consent, like ivy creeping.

He poured the porridge into bowls, set them on the table, and sat for a moment, hands around his mug, watching the slow light begin to form at the edges of the window.

The long night, he thought, doesn't always end with a sunrise. Sometimes it just thins, a fraction at a time, into a different kind of dark.

Upstairs, a floorboard creaked. His mother's steps made their careful way toward the bathroom.

He stood, readying his face to meet her day.

Outside, somewhere beyond the hedges and the half-seen fields, the world kept turning, indifferent and unstoppable, pulling all of them along on its slow, unhurried spin.

Chapter Four

The Milk Run

'You're up,' his mother said, entering the kitchen in her dressing gown, hair flattened on one side.

'Habit,' he said. 'How'd you sleep?'

'On and off,' she said. She sat slowly, like someone lowering herself into water. 'Once I knew you were in the house, it was better. He didn't come back.'

She said it simply, without irony. He didn't correct her pronoun.

They ate their porridge in silence, the spoons scraping gently.

'Will you be back tonight?' she asked when the bowls were empty.

'I have to see how Joan is,' he said. 'She had bloods yesterday. If she's all right, I'll come over. If she's not, I might need to stay with her.'

She nodded, considering. 'Of course,' she said. 'She's your wife. I'll be grand. But if I get a fright, I'll ring.'

'Do,' he said. 'Even if it's late.'

She reached over and patted his hand. 'You're a good lad,' she repeated.

He flushed, as he always did when she said it, the compliment sitting awkwardly on him. He didn't feel like a 'good lad'. He felt like someone constantly stepping from one sinking stone to another.

The town looked half-awake when he drove in. Children with heavy school bags trudged along footpaths, their breaths small ghosts in the cold air. A delivery van was parked outside the supermarket, its back doors yawning, crates stacked on a trolley. Christmas lights dangled disconsolately between lamp posts, waiting for darkness so they could pretend at magic again.

He pulled in outside McEntee's and sat in the car for a moment, watching the condensation on the inside of the windscreen bloom and fade with each breath. He wiped it with the heel of his hand, leaving a smear.

Across the street, a refrigerated truck from the creamery was parked halfway up on the kerb, hazard lights blinking. A young man in a hi-vis jacket and wool hat was unloading plastic crates of milk, moving with an easy, unhurried rhythm: lift, step, stack, straighten. His headphones were tucked under his hat; the thin thread of wire disappeared into his pocket. Every so often he would pause, grin at something only he could hear, and shake his head, shoulders loosening to some private beat.

The world was simple for him, Ciarán thought. Or at least, it looked that way from across the street. Shift work, a wage packet, a body that didn't argue with stairs. Music in his ears. The weight of other people's mornings in his hands.

The young man glanced up and caught him looking. He gave a brief nod – acknowledgement without invitation – then turned back to his crates.

Inside McEntee's, the bell above the door gave its familiar jangle. The air was warmer than outside, smelling of bread, newspapers, and the faint, artificial fruitiness of cheap sweets.

'Morning, Ciarán,' said Mary from behind the counter, her

glasses perched halfway down her nose. 'I was only saying to Pat you'd be in early. Your mother rang for the *Western*.'

'She likes the death notices,' he said.

'Sure, where else would you get the news?' Mary replied. 'How is she?'

'Holding her own,' he said. 'Same as.'

'And yourself?' she asked, in that half-joking tone people used when they knew the answer wouldn't be simple.

'I'm here,' he said.

She nodded, pursed her lips, and rang up his bread, milk, teabags, rashers. As she put them into a brown paper bag, she paused.

'You've a bit of post as well,' she said. 'Aoife left it in when she was opening the office.'

She bent behind the counter and emerged with three envelopes held together by an elastic band.

Two were official-looking: one with the logo of the HSE in the corner, the other from the Department of Education. The third was smaller, addressed by hand, the envelope thinner and cheaper.

His stomach dipped in that small, conditioned way it always did when he saw his name in unfamiliar handwriting. The mix of hope and dread that belonged to his younger self more than to the man he was now.

He slid the letters into his coat pocket without looking at them.

'Thanks, Mary,' he said.

'Tell your mother I was asking for her,' she said. 'And tell Joan I lit a candle for her in the chapel yesterday. Doesn't do any harm.'

'I will,' he said.

Outside again, the milk crates had been stacked by the shop door. The young man was closing the back of the truck, breath puffing in short bursts. He hopped down to the road, turned, and for a moment the morning light caught his face – barely any stubble, clear skin, eyes still with that unclouded readiness for whatever the day might throw at him.

Ciarán thought of himself at that age. Not unloading milk but stacking books in a warehouse off the Quays, scribbling lines on the back of invoices between runs, head full of songs and poems, heart full of other people's cities.

He watched the truck pull away, the hazard lights blinking off as it merged into the thin traffic, and felt an odd tenderness for the boy he had been and the boy at the wheel now – two strangers sharing nothing but an age, separated by decades and decisions.

He didn't open the letters until he was parked at the lake.

It wasn't planned that way. He could have gone straight home, straight back to the house on the hill where Joan would be at the kitchen table, cup in hand, waiting for the clock to move toward the next appointment or the next nap. But when he reached the junction at the edge of town, his hands turned the wheel almost of their own accord.

The road out to the lake climbed gently, hedges giving way to open fields. Sheep grazed in scattered groups, their wool dirty from weather and muck. The sky was trying its best – a few half-hearted breaks in the cloud, a faint suggestion of blue – but the main impression was still of a lid, low and unyielding.

He pulled into the small gravel car park, killed the engine, and sat for a moment. The lake lay ahead, a sheet of pewter, its surface unbroken. Reeds marked the edges in shaggy lines. A single swan moved slowly near the far shore, white against the dull water.

On summer days, the place would be dotted with cars, families lifting picnic baskets from boots, children running toward the water with that particular heedless energy that makes adults wince. Today, in the thin cold, he was alone.

He took the letters from his pocket and laid them on the passenger seat.

The Department of Education first: a bland circular about professional development opportunities and new inspection guidelines. He scanned it, took in none of it, and put it back in the envelope.

The HSE next.

He hesitated a fraction longer before opening this one. The paper was heavier, the logo in the corner crisp.

He slit it along the top with his thumb and unfolded the single sheet.

Dear Mr Devlin,

We are writing to remind you that you recently had blood tests taken at our clinic, including a PSA test. We would like to discuss the results with you. Please contact reception at your earliest convenience to arrange a follow-up appointment.

There was a phone number beneath, and a bland closing line: *Yours sincerely, Dr T. O'Malley.*

He read it twice.

His mouth was dry.

They didn't send reminders for nothing, he thought. If it was all fine, they'd send out a standard 'results normal, no further action required'. This – this nondescript invitation to 'discuss' – held in its neutrality both the possibility of something minor and the shadow of something not.

He folded the letter carefully, too carefully, and slid it back into the envelope.

For a few seconds he simply sat, the paper heavy in his hand, the sound of his own breathing suddenly loud in the car.

Later, he told himself. Not now. Today was already full – Joan, his mother, the yard that still sat in the back of his mind like an unopened room. He couldn't add the contents of that envelope to the list, not yet.

He put it back on the seat, as if distance would make it lighter.

The third letter – the hand-addressed one – waited.

He knew what it would be even before he opened it. He recognised the weight, the feel. Thin paper. A single page. The kind of envelope that had fallen through his letterbox at intervals for the last thirty years.

He slipped his finger under the flap and pulled out the page.

Dear Mr Devlin,
Thank you for submitting your work to The Heron Review. *We are sorry to inform you that on this occasion we will not be able to include your poems in our upcoming issue. We received a large volume of excellent submissions, and competition was exceptionally strong …*

He stopped reading. The phrasing, though politely varied from magazine to magazine, was always the same. He could have written it himself by now.

He looked at the by-line at the bottom – *With best wishes, the Editors* – and felt a flicker of the old sting. It wasn't the fierceness it had once been, more a kind of dull familiarity, like the ache in his back. Ah yes, this again.

He crumpled the letter slightly, then smoothed it out with his hand, as if regretting the momentary violence.

He'd sent those poems off six months ago, in a burst of

momentum during one of Joan's better weeks. Sitting at the kitchen table with the laptop open, the sense of purpose almost exhilarating. Picked four from his notebook – winter hedges, his father's hands, Joan's scarf, awakening – and pressed 'send' with something like faith.

The faith had been small, but it had been there.

Now, holding the paper, he felt … not quite foolish, but old. The game, he thought, might not be for him any more. The world of 'upcoming issues' and 'exciting new voices' seemed to belong to another generation – one that knew how to take rejection as fuel rather than proof.

He folded the letter and slipped it into the glovebox, where others like it already lived – a small archive of his disappointments, rustling every time the car hit a pothole.

From the shore, a gull cried once, the sound shredded by the wind.

He got out of the car and stood at the low wall, hands in his pockets, the cold air biting his cheeks. The lake lay before him, flat and opaque. A skein of ducks cut across, leaving a narrow V of disturbance that closed slowly behind them.

He had brought Joan here once in late spring, between treatments, when her energy had rallied enough for a short walk. They'd sat on this very wall, sharing a flask of tea and a packet of biscuits, her wool hat pulled down over the half-grown fuzz of her hair. The gorse had been in bloom then, the yellow bright and somehow vulgar against the blue.

'This is all I need,' she'd said, sipping from the flask. 'You, the lake, and something sweet. We don't really need the rest of it, do we?'

He'd nodded, agreeing, and at the time he'd meant it.

Now, standing in the bare version of that day, he felt the edges of that memory, the way it glowed slightly in his mind, separate from what was happening now. That day had felt like a reprieve; this one felt like a reckoning.

He took his notebook from his coat pocket. The wind riffled the pages as he flicked to a blank one. His pen hovered.

The lines came slowly, like a weak signal searching for a mast.

The milk van comes in the dark
while the town pretends to sleep.
Crates on wet ground,
white mouths waiting on doorsteps.
We wake to glass,
to cold kettles,
to letters on thin paper
explaining what we are not.

He paused, pen at the end of the line, the last words hanging.

It wasn't good, not yet. It was raw, too direct, the image of the milk boy and the rejections jammed together without subtlety. But there was something there – the rhythm, maybe, the way the mornings stacked on one another. He circled 'explaining what we are not' and scribbled 'telling us what we are' above it, then crossed that out too.

The wind lifted the corner of the page, impatient.

He wrote again.

We wake to glass,
to cold kettles,
to small sorrows folded
and waiting in the hall.

Better. Or at least, less on the nose.

He closed the notebook and tapped it lightly against his palm, as if that might set the words more firmly.

Back in the car, the two official envelopes lay on the passenger seat like quiet accusations. The HSE one in particular seemed to press at his peripheral vision.

'Not today,' he said aloud, feeling vaguely foolish. 'I'll ring tomorrow.'

He started the engine, turned the heater up a notch, and drove back toward town.

Joan was at the kitchen table when he came in, a cardigan over her nightdress, a book open in front of her, spine down. The radio played low on the counter – a presenter talking about some scandal in Dublin, his voice full of manufactured outrage.

'Busy man,' she said. 'Your mam rang to see if you'd landed alive.'

He set the brown paper bag on the table. 'You two are worse than the parish newsletter.'

'We're worried about you,' she said, but the reprimand in it was gentle. 'How is she this morning?'

'Fragile,' he said. 'She heard him in the yard again, or thinks she did.'

'And you?' Joan asked.

He shrugged. 'I heard pipes, and the fridge, and her talking in her sleep.'

He put the milk and rashers in the fridge and the bread in the breadbin. His movements were quick, nearly brusque. He was aware of her watching him.

'You have post,' she said, staring at the envelope he placed on the table.

'Yes,' he said.

'The hospital?' she asked.

'HSE,' he corrected. 'They want me to ring about the bloods.'

'And will you?'

'Tomorrow,' he said.

She gave him a look then – not angry, not nagging, just steady. 'You're not doing yourself any favours,' she said. 'You know that.'

He sighed, leaning back against the counter. 'I know. It's just … between you and Mam and the funeral and school starting back …' He trailed off, aware of how feeble it sounded.

'And you think your prostate will wait patiently till things calm down?' she said, a brief edge to her voice.

He opened his mouth and closed it again.

She softened. 'Ring them this afternoon,' she said, more gently. 'Even just to make the appointment. You don't have to go today. Just put your name on the list. That way it's not hanging over you.'

He looked at her, at the dark circles under her eyes, the pallor of her skin, the thinness of her wrists resting on the table. It felt obscene to be talking about his own possible illness when she was already so obviously in the middle of hers.

'What if it's …' he began, then stopped.

'What if it's nothing?' she said. 'Then you'll sleep. And if it's something, better to know when it's small than when it's big. Isn't that what you'd tell one of your students if you weren't the one in the chair?'

He managed a half-smile. 'You're very wise for your years.'

'Side effect of chemotherapy,' she said. 'Makes you sound like your own mother.'

He boiled the kettle. The comforting hiss filled the small space between them.

'Did you write?' she asked, nodding toward the notebook peeking from his pocket.

'A bit,' he said.

'Any good?'

'I don't know yet,' he said. 'But I did it. That counts for something.'

She reached across the table for his hand. He took it, felt the coolness of her fingers, the slight tremor that hadn't been there a year ago.

'It counts for a lot,' she said. 'You're still you in there somewhere. Not just the courier between two houses and a waiting room.'

He looked at her and felt, for a moment, something like solidity. Then the kettle clicked off and the spell broke.

He rang the doctor's surgery mid-afternoon, while Joan was dozing and the house was briefly still.

The receptionist – a woman whose voice he recognised but whose name he never remembered – was brisk but not unkind.

'Yes, Mr Devlin,' she said. 'We were going to ring you if we didn't hear back. Dr O'Malley would like to see you. There's an opening on Friday at half nine.'

'Friday,' he said. 'Half nine is perfect.'

'No problem,' she said. 'We'll see you then.'

He wrote it on the back of an electricity bill on the table. *Friday 9.30 Doc*. The smallness of the letters made the appointment look less significant, as if, reduced to shorthand, it might be reduced in power too.

For the rest of the afternoon, the knowledge that the appointment existed sat in his chest like a stone. He didn't feel better for having made it, exactly, but there was a tiny sense of something shifted. The dread had a shape now, a date. It would come and it would pass. What lay beyond it was still a blank.

He didn't tell his mother about it when he called in later with her bread and milk and the *Western People*. She was in her armchair, cardigan buttoned wrong as usual, the TV showing a quiz show where contestants guessed the price of washing machines.

'You're doing great,' she said when he placed the groceries on the counter. 'You're run off your feet. I don't know how you do it.'

He smiled, took the cup she offered, listened as she talked about the neighbour's new car and the priest's sermon and the rising price of stamps. There would be time, he told himself, for his own news. Later. When there wasn't already so much sorrow in the house.

On the drive home in the early dark, the milk truck passed him again on the narrow road, its headlights bright, its driver a pale blur behind the wheel. Somewhere in town, people would be lifting bottles and cartons from doorsteps and shop shelves, not thinking about the boy who had carried them, not thinking about the man who had watched him.

The errands, he thought, never ended. Milk and bread and teabags and forms and bloods and prescriptions. A constant small circulation of necessities, moving between houses and hands, keeping everyone going in the most literal sense.

The big things – death, illness, regret, poems no one wanted – floated above all that, like weather systems.

But it was the milk run that got done.

Chapter Five

The Things We Keep

Wednesday came in low and colourless, as if the week had been wrung out and this was what was left.

Ciarán woke before the alarm, the dull ache in his back like a hand pressed steadily into him. Beside him, Joan was still sleeping, her breath shallow but even, the duvet pulled up to her chin. In the half-light her face looked younger, the shadows under her eyes softened.

He lay for a minute, watching the rise and fall of her chest. On the bedside locker, the digital clock glowed 6:12. His appointment with Dr O'Malley was still two days away; the knowledge of it sat somewhere at the edge of his thoughts, a distant outline. Today, though, was already spoken for.

His mother had asked him – no, not asked, suggested, in that way she had – that they might 'start at your father's things'. The phrase had stuck with him all week: *your father's things*, as if the man had dissolved into his shirts and jackets and account books.

'They're no use to him now,' she'd said, hands worrying the corner of a tea towel. 'They're only looking at me.'

He'd agreed, because there seemed no other answer.

Now, in the early dimness, the prospect of it felt heavier than he'd expected. It was one thing to sit in his father's yard among the tools and machines; quite another to open drawers and wardrobes, to move through the private geography of the man's clothes and small hoards.

Joan stirred, her eyelids fluttering. 'You up?' she murmured, voice roughened by sleep.

'Nearly,' he said. 'Go back over.'

She blinked a few times, focusing. 'What time is it?'

'Too early,' he said. 'Saturday early.'

She shifted onto her back, winced, then settled. 'You're going out to your mam's?'

'I am,' he said. 'She wants to start on … things.'

'His stuff,' Joan said, more blunt. 'The clear-out.'

He grimaced at the phrase. 'Some of it. Clothes, maybe. We'll see.'

She looked at him properly now, eyes sharper. 'You don't have to do it all today.'

'I know,' he said. 'But if we don't start, it'll hang over her. And me.'

'She could always leave it,' Joan said. 'Some people do. They leave the wardrobe as it is. Twenty years later, the coat's still hanging where it always hung. There's no rule that says it has to be cleared.'

He thought of his mother's face when she'd said *They're only looking at me*. The unease there, the way she'd flinched at the sight of his father's boots by the back door.

'She wants to,' he said. 'Or thinks she does. I'll go for a few hours, anyway. I'll be back for lunch.'

'I'll be fine,' she said.

He knew she would say that even if she could barely stand, but today she seemed better than she had last week. The chemo fog had lifted a little. Her colour, though still too pale, had a hint more life in it.

He leaned over and kissed her forehead. Her skin was cool, faintly dry.

'Ring me if you need anything,' he said.

'Same,' she replied. 'If you find any old love letters, bring them home. I'll judge them for scandal.'

He smiled despite himself, the knot in his chest easing a fraction.

By the time he reached his mother's, the sky had settled into a flat, unpromising grey. The lane was slick from overnight drizzle, mud peeking through the gravel where tyres had worn it thin. A stray hen from the neighbour's field pecked at the verge, jittering at the sound of the car.

His mother had the front door open before he reached it, as if she'd been standing in the hall listening for his engine.

'You're early,' she said, though it was nearly nine.

'You said you wanted to get started,' he replied.

She stepped back to let him in. 'I made scones. You can't work on an empty stomach.'

The kitchen smelled of baking and something slightly burnt, probably the first batch sacrificed to distraction. On the table, a plate of scones cooled beside the butter dish, the butter softened into that particular state between fridge-hard and melt.

He poured tea while she fussed with plates. They ate in near-silence, the quiet between them not unfriendly, just occupied. He watched her hands as she cut her scone: the knuckles enlarged, the fingers slowed but precise. Her wedding ring, now loose on her thinner finger, flashed dully in the light.

'Where will we start?' he asked, when the second cup of tea was poured.

'The wardrobe, I suppose,' she said. 'Upstairs. There's no

point in keeping suits. He hated the sight of them. And the shirts.'

They went up together, the stairs creaking in familiar protest.

His parents' bedroom felt smaller than he remembered. The big bed dominated the space, its wooden headboard scarred with the faint indentations of decades, each mark a reminder of nights that had long since slipped away. The photograph of the Sacred Heart still hung opposite the bed, the tiny red bulb beneath it unlit. On the dresser, his father's comb lay where it always had; a comb without a head to accompany it.

The wardrobe took up most of one wall: three doors, the varnish dulled by time, handles polished bright where hands had gripped them over and over. His mother stood in front of it for a second, her fingers resting on the middle handle.

'I don't know where to begin,' she said, almost to herself.

'Open it,' he said gently. 'We'll see.'

She pulled the door. The smell hit him at once – stale clothes, old cigarette smoke, a faint trace of his father's aftershave. The jackets hung in a close row: the good suit in the plastic cover from the last time it had been dry-cleaned; the grey sports jacket he'd worn to weddings; two cheaper ones bought in a sale, never really liked; a procession of shirts, their collars frayed to varying degrees.

His mother reached in and ran her hand along them, fingertips brushing the cloth as if it might respond.

'This one is no use to anyone,' she said, touching the old brown sports coat with the shiny elbows. 'It's held together with wishes.'

'We can bag it for the recycling,' he said.

She nodded. 'The good suit … I suppose that should go somewhere decent. He was always proud of that one.'

'He wore it to my graduation,' Ciarán said, the image rising unbidden: his father standing awkwardly in the courtyard at Maynooth, tie too wide, shoes too shiny, his hands restless with nowhere to go. The suit had looked almost new then. Now, it bore the faint sheen of fabric that has done its time.

'Your brother Peter wore it to his wedding as well,' she said, reaching for the hanger. 'He never said it, but your father was fit to burst that day. "Two wives in one suit," he said to me. "Sure that's value."'

Her mouth twitched, grief and humour tangling as she pictured the day Peter left home and emigrated to Australia over thirty years ago. Ciarán thought of Peter then the way he always did now – briefly, without anger. Peter had left early, learned another life, and in doing so had lost the knack of returning. There were messages, careful and kind, and money sent at the right moments, but some things could not cross an ocean without becoming awkward or false. Ciarán understood this more than he admitted. Someone had to stay. Someone always did.

They worked slowly. She took each item off its hanger, examined it, made a small decision, and handed it to him. He folded the shirts onto the bed in separate piles: good enough to give away, too far gone even for that. Every so often he came across a shirt he recognised from a particular day: the pale blue one with the faint paint splatters from when they'd redecorated the kitchen in the late nineties; the checked one he'd worn in the photograph at the lake, Joan in her navy coat beside him.

'You can keep any you want,' his mother said, watching him.

He fingered the cuff of the blue shirt, imagining himself wearing it. The fabric was thinner than his own shirts, the cut slightly different, the ghost of his father's shape still in the shoulders.

Behind the row of shirts, on the top shelf, there were boxes. Old shoe boxes, a biscuit tin, a shallow cardboard tray that had once held oranges. His mother reached up for one, then stood on tiptoe, fingers just grazing the edge.

'I'll get it,' he said, stepping forward.

He took down the first box. It was heavier than it looked. Inside, envelopes lay in a loose stack, some tied together with brittle string, others free. The top one, yellowed and soft at the corners, bore a London postmark from 1963.

His mother's breath caught.

'Your father's letters,' she said. 'From when he was in England.' She took the box from him, her hands suddenly careful. 'And some from his brothers. They used to send him scraps. News from home, who'd died, who'd had a child. We wrote the odd time when we were courting.' She smiled faintly. 'Courting. That's what we called it. As if writing three letters in six months was a big romance.'

'Do you want to look at them now?' he asked.

She shook her head, closing the lid gently. 'No. Not yet. If I open that box, we'll never get anything else done. Put it over there.' She nodded toward the dressing table. 'We'll keep them. They're part of the story.'

The next box held nothing more romantic than socks, neatly rolled, some with careful darns at the heel. She turned them over in her hands, appraising. 'The done ones we can keep for cleaning rags,' she said. 'The rest … the bin.'

He set them aside.

The biscuit tin was familiar. It was the one that had once held chocolate biscuits, the fancy kind they'd only had at Christmas or when the priest called. He'd seen his father take it down occasionally to retrieve receipts or stamps.

Inside, however, it wasn't receipts this time. It was photographs – and something else.

On top lay a faded snapshot he recognised: the yard in winter, himself as a boy in an oversized jacket, his father in the background. Similar to the one he'd discovered in his father's workshop. Beneath it, others: his parents at dances and weddings; a younger version of his mother with a beehive of hair and a shy grin; his father in London, standing with two other men outside a prefab, all three in short jackets and narrow ties, their eyes wary but hopeful.

As he lifted the photographs, a folded sheet of notepaper slid free and fell to the floor.

He bent to pick it up.

The paper was lined, torn from an exercise book, the edges frayed. The handwriting was his father's, smaller and more careful than in the ledgers.

He recognised the first line at once.

It was one of his own.

Or almost.

The mornings are slow here now,
no engines breaking the dark,
just the crows in the field across
and her cup, rattling in the saucer.

He read it twice, the words familiar and unfamiliar together. It was his poem – one he'd written a year ago, in the first months of Joan's chemo, about waking early and hearing the house before it fully rose. He'd called it 'First Light'. He'd shown it to no one except Joan and, later, sent it off in a batch to a magazine that had never replied.

But this wasn't in his own hand. This was his father's, each letter pressed into the page as if he'd been afraid of making a mistake.

Underneath the last line, there was a note in brackets: *(From the paper, Feb 12)*.

He frowned, trying to remember. Then it came.

He had been asked, months back, to give a reading at a small arts evening in town, a fundraiser for the hospice. The local paper had done a piece, a little sidebar with his photograph and one of his poems printed beside it. He hadn't thought anyone much had read it.

Apparently, his father had.

'Is that more bills?' his mother asked, seeing the paper in his hand.

'Not exactly,' he said. 'Look.'

He passed it to her.

She peered at it, squinting. 'I'll have to get my glasses,' she said, reaching for the pair on the bedside locker. She settled them on her nose and held the page closer.

'Well now,' she said, after a moment. 'Would you look at that.'

'He copied it,' Ciarán said. 'From the paper.'

She nodded. 'He was very proud of that. Of you. He brought the paper into the kitchen and read it to me. Twice. "Our lad in the paper with the poems," he said. "Not everyone can say that."'

Ciarán felt his throat tighten. He hadn't known. His father had never mentioned it beyond a gruff, 'Saw you in the *Herald*,' and a nod.

'He never said,' he managed.

'He wouldn't,' she said. 'He wasn't great at saying. But he kept it. That's saying something.'

She folded the page along its existing crease, smoothing the fold with her thumb, and handed it back.

'You should keep that,' she said. 'That's yours now.'

He slipped it into his wallet, the paper stiff against the soft leather.

In the bottom of the tin, beneath the photographs, there was a postcard. A black-and-white image of a London street in the sixties, all boxy cars and men in long coats. The writing on the back was again his father's, untidy, rushed.

Mary,
The work is grand. Long days but sure that's what we came for. The digs are clean. There's a pub round the corner does good bacon. I'll be home when I can get the fare. I dreamt last night I was back on the lake road with no shoes on me. Tell Mam I remembered to say my prayers. Tell the boy—

It cut off there. The line ended halfway across the card. No signature.

'The boy?' he said aloud, turning it over. The postmark was smudged, the year unreadable.

His mother looked over his shoulder. 'That would be Peter,' she said. 'He was only a baby when your father went first. He missed his first steps. Broke his heart.'

'Why didn't he finish it?' Ciarán asked.

She shrugged. 'He probably started talking to someone and never went back to it. Or he ran out of space. He wasn't great for endings. I got plenty that just said, "We're grand. Hope you are too."'

She took the card from him, reading the half-sentence again.

'He kept it, anyway,' she said. 'It mustn't have been posted. That or it came back to him somehow. Maybe he didn't want to send me a card with it half wrote. God forgive him, he could be very fussy about daft things.'

'It's strange,' Ciarán said. 'Seeing his writing like this. Not numbers. Not bills. Just … words.'

His mother smiled, a little sadly. 'He had more in him than he let on,' she said. 'Same as yourself.'

They went back to the wardrobe.

The work was slow and stopping. Every object seemed to carry a story, or at least the possibility of one. A tie unearthed from the back of a drawer would lead to ten minutes on someone's wedding in 1983. A pair of cufflinks, still in their box, became the springboard for a recollection about the day his father had been talked into buying a dress suit he'd never worn again.

At one point, his mother pulled a battered shoebox from the floor.

'That'll be rubbish,' she said, handing it to him.

He lifted the lid. Inside lay keys, dozens of them, in a tangle of metal. Keys to tractors long scrapped, gates long replaced, locks that had been changed.

'The kingdom of heaven,' he said. 'If we only knew which door they opened.'

His mother snorted. 'He'd never throw a key out,' she said. 'You'd never know when you might need it. "The day you throw it, that's the day you'll find what it does," he used to say.'

They looked at the heap for a moment, two generations of Devlins defeated by potential.

'We'll keep them for now,' she decided. 'We've enough decisions to make today.'

By noon, three black bags stood in the hall, full of worn shirts and socks, the weight of years compressed into crinkling plastic. A smaller pile of what she called 'the good stuff' was stacked on the bed, waiting to be offered to sons and grandsons.

His mother sat on the edge of the mattress, her back to the window, the light behind her making a faint halo of the flyaway hairs around her temples.

'That's enough for today,' she said. 'I'm only half here now as it is.'

'We can leave the rest,' he agreed. 'There's no hurry.'

She looked around the room, her gaze passing over the now half-empty wardrobe, the quiet bedside locker, the comb on the dresser. 'There is and there isn't,' she said. 'He's gone whether we do it or not. But it's like … every shirt you fold, you fold a bit of him away. You'd be tempted to leave them swinging there just to pretend.'

He thought of Joan's comment that morning, about some people never touching anything, letting rooms become shrines.

'What will you keep?' he asked.

She considered. 'The good suit, maybe, for someone in the family. The jacket he wore to Mass. His cap. I couldn't bear to throw that. And a few of the old jumpers. For the smell.'

She said it without self-consciousness. He understood. There were things you kept not because they were useful, but because they held something of the person, some last trace that hadn't yet faded.

'Will you keep his comb?' he asked, nodding toward the dresser.

She looked at it as if seeing it afresh. 'I might,' she said. 'It's silly, but sure what harm? It doesn't take up much space. Not like him.' She smiled faintly.

He glanced at his watch.

'I'd better head,' he said. 'Joan will be waiting on her chef.'

'Go on,' she said. 'You've done enough. More than enough.'

He bagged the rubbish, tied the tops. She insisted on walking him down the stairs.

At the bottom, in the hall, his eye fell again on the peg where his father's cap had hung. The peg was still bare, the pale oval on the varnish a little less stark than the week before but visible.

'Would you like me to bring the cap down?' he asked.

She shook her head. 'Not yet,' she said. 'Let the peg be empty a while. I'll know he's gone every time I see it.'

He thought of arguing – gently, kindly – but something in her face stopped him. Grief had its own logic.

Outside, the cold hit him anew. The sky had darkened further, a thin rain falling now, almost too fine to see but enough to dampen the shoulders of his coat.

He loaded the bags into the boot, the black plastic rustling. They felt heavier than they were.

As he drove away, he glanced once in the rear-view mirror.

His mother stood in the doorway, one hand on the frame, watching the car until it turned at the bend. The house behind her looked both smaller and more solid, as if his father's absence had made its edges sharper.

At home, the kitchen was filled with the smell of onions and something frying. Joan stood at the stove, apron on over her jeans and T-shirt, stirring a pan with slow, deliberate movements.

'I thought you were the one who needed minding,' he said, setting the shopping bags on the counter.

'I got bored waiting,' she said. 'And hungry. And you can't be the only one who cooks just because I've a few rogue cells.'

She turned and he saw the sheen of sweat on her forehead, the slight drag in her movements. The effort had cost her something.

'You should sit,' he said. 'I'll finish.'

'I'm nearly done,' she replied. 'You can do the heroic job of plating.'

They fell into the familiar choreography of their marriage: him setting the table, her bringing the pan, their movements close but practiced enough not to collide. He poured water, cut bread. She ladled stew into bowls.

Over lunch, he told her about the wardrobe, the letters, the biscuit tin.

'He copied your poem?' she said, eyes widening. 'Sean?'

'Yes,' he said, still tasting the surprise. 'In his neatest writing. You'd laugh if you saw the effort he made at the loops.'

"It's … sweet. In his own … reticent way,' she said softly. 'Will you show it to me later?'

'I will. He kept it in the tin with the photos,' he said. 'As if it belonged to the family archive.'

'Well, it does,' she said. 'You think your poems just live in little journals no one reads. But they live in people's heads too. Even men who'd rather fix a gearbox than say "well done".'

He toyed with a piece of bread. 'It made me think,' he said, slowly. 'About what we keep. Him, I mean. The things he chose to keep. Old keys. Letters. My poem. That stupid postcard from London that he never finished.'

'What about you?' she asked. 'What do you keep?'

He considered. 'Not enough,' he said. 'I keep the wrong things in my head and not enough of the good stuff on the page.'

'You keep me,' she said lightly. 'That's a start.'

He looked at her, at the way she held her spoon, the slight tremor in her hand. 'That's not a thing,' he said. 'That's a person.'

'People are things too, in their own way.' She smiled to soften it. 'We're made of all the bits we hold on to.'

He thought of his father's jacket in the hall, his poem in the biscuit tin, the unposted postcard. Thought of the HSE envelope in the glovebox, his upcoming appointment folded into a small square of dread.

'We're drowning in bits,' he said.

She reached across the table and brushed a crumb from his jumper. 'Then maybe we need to decide which ones to let go of,' she said. 'And which to copy out in our best writing and fold into tins.'

In the afternoon, after he'd washed up and Joan had gone to rest on the couch, he went to the small room they jokingly called his 'study' – a corner of the spare room with a desk, a sagging bookshelf, and a chair that complained in a familiar way when he sat down.

He took his wallet from his pocket, removed the folded page in his father's handwriting, and laid it on the desk.

Reading his own lines in someone else's hand felt like looking at himself in a distorted mirror – recognisable but altered.

He took a fresh sheet of paper and uncapped his pen.

At the top he wrote, slowly, *The Things We Keep*.

Then, beneath it, a first line suggested itself, tentative.

In the wardrobe, his shirts still face the door,

He paused, listening to the words in his head. It didn't sound right. He crossed it out and tried again.

In the wardrobe, his sleeves still wait for arms,

Better. There was space in it.

He wrote on, the poem trying to form itself around the morning's images: the three black bags in the hall; his mother's fingers on the coats; the biscuit tin; the half-written postcard.

He found himself thinking of his students, his past selves – the band days, the city nights. The things he had kept and the things he had lost without even noticing he'd let them go.

After a while he stopped and read back what he had.

It wasn't finished, but it was a start. A scaffolding.

He thought of his father sitting in the office at the yard, copying lines of his poem onto a scrap of paper, brow furrowed, the radio muttering in the background. The image was both funny and piercing.

He smiled, unexpectedly.

For the first time in weeks, he felt something like alignment: his life, his grief, his words – even his father, the taciturn mechanic – and the page before him all seemed to be part of the same thing, not separate compartments he had to visit in turn.

He smoothed the paper, capped the pen, and slid the poem-in-progress under the blotter, safe from spills and drafts.

Manuals. Instructions. Letters from London. Poems copied by hand. The things that told you how to manage when you had no idea what you were doing.

The things you kept because, without them, you might forget who you'd been.

That night, after they'd eaten a simple supper and watched a documentary neither of them really followed, they went to bed early.

Joan fell asleep quickly, the chemo fatigue pulling her under like a tide. Ciarán lay awake longer, staring at the ceiling.

His mind drifted to Friday's appointment. Dr O'Malley's

neat beard, his careful phrasing. The words Ciarán expected to hear – 'nothing to worry about', 'a bit elevated but we'll keep an eye'. The words he feared – 'biopsy', 'treatment', 'options'.

Beside that, his father's voice floated up from memory, the gruff encouragement when he'd first gone to college. *You're the first of us in a cap and gown,* he'd said, embarrassed by the sentiment. *Don't waste it.*

He wondered what his father would say now, if he could see the mess of obligations and appointments and half-finished poems his son was juggling.

He suspected it would be something simple.

Go to the doctor. Mind your wife. Don't let your mother move on her own. Keep your head. Take your time with the bolts. They'll come if you don't force them.

He turned onto his side, fitting his body carefully around Joan's, not wanting to wake her, and reached for her hand under the duvet.

Her fingers curled around his without waking.

In the dark, he pictured the biscuit tin, the folded sheet with his own words in another hand, the postcard with the unfinished line: *Tell the boy–*

He completed it silently.

Tell the boy to hold on to what matters and let the rest go.

Whether his father would have agreed with that wording, he didn't know. But lying there, listening to the night gather at the window, it felt like as good a start as any.

The things we keep, he thought, are not always the ones we expected.

Sleep came eventually, not as an escape this time, but as a kind of storing away: the day folded carefully and placed alongside all the other days, in a box somewhere inside him, waiting for whatever use he might someday make of it.

Chapter Six

Sisters

It was one of those days that seemed to hover between weather conditions and intentions – not quite wet, not quite bright, not quite restful. The sky lay low over the town, a lid of pale wool, and the air had that raw edge that made you think of fires without actually lighting one.

Ciarán woke late for once, close to nine, the room already a soft grey. Joan was awake beside him, propped up on pillows, reading glasses perched on her nose, a book open in her hands. The lamp was still on, though the light from it now seemed unnecessary.

He blinked. 'What time is it?'

'Late for the industrious,' she said. 'Early for the lazy. Quarter to nine.'

He reached for his watch on the locker, as if he didn't believe her. 'How long are you awake?'

'An hour,' she said. 'You were doing your snoring symphony. I didn't have the heart to interrupt the third movement.'

He groaned softly. 'I don't snore.'

'You do,' she said. 'Gently. Like a small tractor in the distance.'

He rolled onto his back, stretched, and immediately

regretted it as his lower back protested. The ache had settled into a kind of background hum now, a presence he was never entirely unaware of.

'Any plans for today?' she asked, closing the book on her finger.

'I thought I might do nothing very badly,' he said. 'Mam will be all right for a few hours. We could … I don't know … watch something that doesn't involve autopsies.'

'We could,' she said. 'Except Maeve is coming down.'

He turned his head. 'Today?'

'She rang the other night after you were at your mother's,' Joan said. 'She wants to "check in" and "have a proper chat". Her phrases, not mine.'

He felt a small tightening in his chest. 'You didn't tell me.'

'You were knackered,' she said. 'And it was late. I knew if I told you, you'd lie awake rehearsing arguments.'

He couldn't deny it. 'What does she want to chat about?'

'You, me, Mam Devlin, her. The usual. Logistics. Options.'

He knew what 'options' meant. It had been skirting the edges of every conversation for months now: the question of where Joan should be if – when – the treatments did what they could and then no more.

He sat up slowly, the sheet falling to his waist. The room felt colder suddenly.

'What do you want?' he asked.

She looked at him, her gaze steady. 'Today, I want a cup of tea and two slices of toast,' she said. 'And maybe for you to do the good sausages. Beyond that, I'm open to suggestions.'

He didn't push. They both knew there were some questions that couldn't be answered lightly before breakfast.

Maeve arrived just after twelve, in a car that looked as if it had never seen a muddy boreen in its life. Sleek, dark, the kind of vehicle that seemed more at home in office car parks and underground shopping centres than outside houses on the edge of small towns.

Ciarán saw it pull up from the kitchen window, the kettle just starting to murmur. He watched her get out – tailored navy coat, ankle boots with a heel that made him nervous on their gravel, hair pulled back in a way that suggested both control and expense.

He opened the door before she could knock.

'Well, if it isn't the big smoke,' he said, stepping back to let her in.

'Very funny,' she replied, but she smiled as she said it. She kissed his cheek, quick, her perfume a brief, foreign note in the hallway – something sharp and citrusy that didn't belong to turf smoke or boiled cabbage.

'You look wrecked,' she said, taking his face in for half a second.

'You're a ray of sunshine as always,' he said. 'Come on. She's in the sitting room.'

Joan was on the couch, a blanket over her legs, a mug cupped in her hands. She brightened visibly when Maeve entered.

'Look at you,' Maeve said, crossing the room in quick steps. 'You're thinner again. You're going to vanish altogether.'

'Yes, but I'll be very chic about it,' Joan said, smiling. She raised her face for a kiss. Maeve bent, hugged her more gently than she hugged anyone else, aware of bones and lines and tubes that weren't visible but might as well have been.

Ciarán hovered for a moment, then retreated to the sanctuary of the kitchen. The kettle clicked off. He busied himself making fresh tea and setting out cups.

From the sitting room, he could hear the high, bright register that meant Maeve was doing her first round of questions: *How are you? Really? How was the last cycle? Any side effects? What did Dr Murphy say?* He recognised the pattern; he'd heard it enough in hospital corridors and over the phone.

He carried the tray in and set it on the coffee table. Maeve was perched on the edge of the armchair, coat off now, legs crossed, a notebook on her knee that she closed when he entered.

'You're very official,' he said, nodding toward it.

'Occupational hazard,' she said. 'I like lists.'

'She has a list for everything,' Joan said. 'Birthdays, appointments, Christmas presents, grudges ...'

'Grudges are for amateurs,' Maeve replied. 'I prefer "long-term strategic memories".'

They laughed, but Ciarán felt the humour skim over the surface of something more solid.

He poured tea. Maeve took hers black, two sugars. Joan had started taking hers weaker since her stomach turned easily these days. He'd learned to pour, watch, add milk, pour again, the gradient of colour becoming its own language.

'So,' Maeve said, once everyone had a cup. 'How's Mrs Devlin Senior?'

'Talking to ghosts and listening to Mass,' Ciarán said. 'Same as ever, only more so.'

Maeve's face tightened briefly. 'Is she sleeping?'

'On and off,' he said. 'She rang the other night thinking there was someone in the yard. I stayed over.'

Maeve smiled, but the line between her brows remained. 'She's on her own now,' she said. 'It's a lot.'

'I know,' he said. 'I'm with her most days.'

Joan shifted the blanket, as if adjusting herself for a meeting she hadn't entirely agreed to attend.

'Well?' she said. 'Let's have it. What's in the notebook?'

Maeve glanced at the closed cover, embarrassed. 'It's

nothing dramatic,' she said. 'I just thought … we should talk about … the next few months.'

'Define "talk",' Joan said. 'Little talk? Big talk?'

'Somewhere in between,' Maeve said. She turned to Ciarán. 'How are you fixed with school? After Christmas, I mean.'

He rubbed the back of his neck. 'I talked to the principal,' he said. 'He's been decent. I'm going to work a few days next week. Reduced timetable for January, maybe February. Senior classes only. Less contact, more correction. But it can't go on forever. The Leaving Cert won't wait for us to get our act together.'

'You've two people to mind,' Maeve said, ticking points off on her fingers. 'Your mam and Joan. Plus yourself, though you won't. Your mam is … settled in her own way. She can't be lifted. She won't leave that house unless it's in a box. Joan…'

She paused and looked at her sister.

'Joan is in the middle of treatment and needs someone with her most of the time,' she went on more gently. 'That can't just be you running back and forth on your own. It's not sustainable. We need a plan that doesn't involve you collapsing in the middle of a classroom.'

'I'm not collapsing,' he said, more sharply than he intended.

'Not yet,' she said. 'But you're on your way.'

Joan put a hand on his knee. It was both a comfort and a warning.

'What are you suggesting?' he asked.

Maeve took a breath. 'I've been thinking,' she said. 'About Dublin.'

'Oh Jesus,' he said.

'Hear me out,' she said quickly. 'My place is too small, but there are apartments near the hospital. Short-term lets. We could get yous into one for a few months. You'd be near St James's. No more five-hour round-trip for every appointment. I could be there in twenty minutes if there was a crisis. You'd have proper oncology support, hospice services if – when – you need them. You wouldn't be doing this run between town and school and hospital on your own.'

Her words came out quicker now, as if she'd rehearsed them.

Joan was very still beside him. He could feel the tension through the blanket.

'And Mam?' he asked. 'Does she get an apartment near St James's too? She won't even come up for a weekend. She gets hives if she crosses the M50.'

'You can arrange home help for her,' Maeve said. 'She could get a carer in the mornings and evenings. Meals on Wheels. Neighbours are good. She's not helpless.'

'She's eighty,' he said. 'She talks to the hallway as if Dad's still hanging his coat there.'

'I know how old she is,' Maeve said, a flicker of irritation. 'She's also not alone in the world. You can't all revolve around her like satellites forever. She's not the only patient in the family.'

Joan shifted again, her hand pressing down slightly on his knee.

'I don't want to live in Dublin,' she said quietly.

Maeve softened. 'I know,' she said. 'I know you love it here. The town, your house, your lane, all the little birds you've named. But this isn't about preference, Joanie. It's about … the practicalities.'

'The practicalities of dying, you mean,' Joan said, a hint of steel in her voice.

Maeve flinched, then recovered. 'The practicalities of being very sick,' she said. 'Sorry. Bad phrasing.'

Joan looked at her for a long moment. 'I don't want to finish up in a flat over the Luas lines,' she said. 'I want to hear the wind off the trees and the neighbours' kids kicking a ball and the bin lorry on Tuesdays. I want to look out the window and see your man walking his ridiculous dog with the yellow jacket. I want ...' She faltered, swallowed. 'I want to be where my life is. Where our life is.'

She nodded slightly at Ciarán.

'And I want to be able to get to you quickly if something happens,' Maeve said. 'If he ends up in a bed of his own. Which, let's be honest, could be on the cards.'

Ciarán bristled. 'We don't know that yet.'

'No, but we know enough not to pretend it's impossible,' Maeve shot back.

Joan's hand tightened on his leg. He could feel the fine bones of her fingers.

'Maybe we deal with that when we get to it,' he said. 'Rather than relocating everyone in a panic because of things that might happen. Joan shouldn't have to uproot herself on the off-chance I'll fall apart.'

'It's not an off-chance,' Maeve said. 'It's a likelihood. Look at you.'

He flushed, anger and shame mixing. 'What does that mean?'

'It means you look ten years older than you did last Christmas,' she said. 'You jump every time your phone rings. You smell like an old hospital waiting room half the time. You're living on tea and biscuits and worry. That's not sustainable.'

Joan laughed once, unexpectedly. 'You do smell like a waiting room,' she said, trying to defuse. 'Disinfectant and guilt.'

He smiled despite himself.

Maeve saw the crack and stepped back a little. Her voice softened. 'I'm not saying move permanently,' she said. 'I'm not trying to steal you away. I'm saying … consider it. For the rough bit. It might be a relief, not having to drive the same bit of road till you can do it in your sleep.'

He thought of the lane to his mother's, the familiar bends, the pothole near the crossroads that he'd stopped registering years ago. Of the road to the hospital, the petrol station where he always stopped, the coffee he never quite finished.

'I hate Dublin,' he said, but there was less heat in it now. 'The traffic, the noise. The way no one looks where they're going.'

'You loved it once,' Maeve said.

'I loved being twenty-two in it,' he said. 'There's a difference.'

They fell silent. The clock on the mantel ticked too loudly. Outside, a car passed, its tyres hissing on the damp road.

Joan broke the quiet.

'I don't want you two to be at each other over this,' she said. 'The last thing I want is to turn into a disputed territory.'

'You're not land,' Maeve said at once. 'You're not an asset to be allocated. I know that.'

'But you're talking about me like a problem to be solved,' Joan said gently. 'Which I probably am, fair enough. But I'm still here. I still get a say.'

'Of course you do,' Maeve said. 'I'm just … trying to get ahead of the wave. That's my job. I see people who leave everything to the last second and it's carnage. Families at each other's throats in corridors because they never sat down and had the hard talk.'

'We're half having it,' Joan said. 'That's something.'

Ciarán looked at his wife, at his sister-in-law, and felt an odd sense of being in two places at once: the boy sitting at the edge of the grown-ups' table, listening to adults talk about mortgages and weather, and the man whose life they were now sketching in outlines on a mental whiteboard.

He cleared his throat. 'Here's where I'm at,' he said. 'Today. It might change. Joan wants to stay here. Near her friends. Near the sea. Near my mam, even. I want that for her. For us.' He looked at Maeve. 'I also know you're right about the practical stuff. The driving. The support. I don't know how long I can keep juggling it all without dropping something. Probably myself.'

Maeve said nothing, but relief flickered across her face at the admission.

'So,' he went on. 'We split the difference. We talk to the hospice team here. See what options there are locally. We see what home help Mam can get realistically.' He forced a half-smile. 'And we keep Dublin as a card in the deck. If things get unmanageable here, if Joan needs something that only the big guns can provide, we pull it. Short-term. But we don't move like we're evacuating ahead of an air raid.'

Joan nodded slowly. 'I can live with that,' she said.

Maeve frowned, thinking. 'I … can work with that,' she said. 'On the condition that we actually talk to the hospice team. Not just say we will.'

'I'll ring them,' he said. 'After I see O'Malley. I'll be in the mood for hard truths anyway.'

Joan squeezed his knee again, quietly.

Maeve exhaled, some of the tension leaving her shoulders. 'Okay,' she said. 'That's something. And I'm not the enemy, you know. I'm not trying to drag you all into the Big Smoke because I love the M50. I just … I hate the thought of you two drowning quietly in a place no one can reach.'

'We're not drowning yet,' Joan said. 'We're … up to our chests, maybe. There's a difference.'

'You always were good at metaphors,' Maeve said.

'Occupational hazard,' Joan replied.

They smiled at each other, the old sisterly warmth reasserting itself for a moment.

Later, when Maeve had gone – her car reversing carefully out of the narrow drive, her hand raised in a last brisk wave – the house felt both emptier and heavier.

Joan lay flat on the couch, eyes closed, the conversation having cost her more than she'd let on.

Ciarán stood at the kitchen sink, washing the cups, staring out at the small square of garden. A robin hopped along the low wall, its chest absurdly bright against the dull hedge. Somewhere down the road, a dog barked three times, then stopped.

He dried his hands and made two hot-water bottles, one for Joan's feet and one for his own back. When he brought hers in, she opened her eyes.

'Truce?' she asked.

'Between who?' he said, settling the bottle at her feet.

'You and Maeve. Me and Maeve. You and yourself.'

He smiled. 'Working on it.'

He sat on the armchair, his own hot-water bottle wedged behind him. The heat seeping into the sore muscles was almost narcotic.

'You know she's only like that because she loves you,' he said.

'I know,' Joan said. 'It's just … exhausting sometimes. Being loved by efficient people.'

He laughed. 'Imagine being loved by useless ones.'

'I married one,' she said, eyes twinkling.

He placed a hand over his heart in mock offence. 'Harsh.'

'You know what I mean,' she said. 'You're not useless.

You're … porous. You soak everything up. Hers is a different kind of love. Sharp. Strategic. She wants to get ahead of the pain. You … you sit in it with me.'

He wasn't sure if that was a compliment or a diagnosis.

'Which do you prefer?' he asked.

'Both,' she said. 'On different days. Today … I'm glad she's thinking about the practical stuff. I haven't the energy. But I'm also glad you're here, not drawing up spreadsheets of my decline.'

He winced slightly at the bluntness of the last word. She saw it.

'Sorry,' she said. 'The euphemisms get tiring. "Journey", "battle", "rollercoaster". It's all bollocks. I'm getting sicker, slowly. That's what's happening.'

He looked at her thin wrists, the way the blanket lay almost flat over her legs.

'I know,' he said quietly.

She reached for his hand. 'If the doctor says something bad tomorrow,' she said, 'I need you to tell me. Straight. Don't be noble and spare me. I can't be managing two unknowns.'

He swallowed. 'We don't know he'll say anything bad.'

'No,' she said. 'But you're already half living in that eventuality. I can hear it in your voice. Whatever it is, we'll handle it better if it's not a secret between us.'

He nodded, throat tight.

'Okay,' he said. 'I promise. No secrets.'

She held his gaze. 'Good,' she said. 'Because I can usually tell when you're lying. You get this little twitch near your eye. It's very endearing and very annoying.'

He laughed weakly. 'I'll work on my poker face.'

'Don't,' she said. 'I married you without one. No point developing it now.'

That evening, as the light faded and the street lights blinked into life one by one, he drove down to his mother's with the Sunday dinner plates they'd promised to bring – slices of roast chicken; potatoes; carrot and parsnip mashed together the way she liked.

She met him at the door, cardigan buttoned wrong, slippers flapping a little. He followed her into the kitchen and they both sat down.

'You've had visitors,' she said, sniffing the air as if she could smell Maeve's expensive perfume still lingering in his jacket.

'Maeve,' he said. 'She says hello. And she lit a candle for you in some fancy Dublin church that probably has a coffee shop in it.'

His mother snorted. 'They all have coffee shops now,' she said. 'You'd miss your Mass queueing for a cappuccino. How's Joan?'

'Tired,' he said. 'We had a long talk. About … arrangements.'

His mother's face changed, something wary passing through it. 'What kind of arrangements?'

'Hospice, maybe, down the line,' he said. 'Support. Help. Not yet. Just … thinking.'

His mother tightened her grip on the back of the chair. 'She won't be going into a home,' she said, sudden, fierce. 'Not while I'm above ground. I promised her mother we'd mind her.'

'She's not a dog,' he said gently. 'And it's not about putting her somewhere and washing our hands. It's about having people who know what they're doing nearby. Nurses. Doctors. Counsellors. People who can help when we can't.'

His mother's eyes shimmered. 'I know,' she said, after a moment. 'I'm just … old-fashioned. In my day, you died at home. In your own bed. With the priest and the relations. That was that.'

‘In your day, they didn’t have half the things they have now,’ he said. ‘You also went to school in bare feet and thought it was a character-building exercise. Times change.’

She huffed, a reluctant smile. ‘You have an answer for everything,’ she said.

‘Not for this,’ he replied.

He put the plates in front of her, watched her eat. She talked about the Mass, about the woman two doors down who’d got a new satellite dish, about the priest’s announcement about the roof fund.

He said nothing yet about Dublin. Or about tomorrow’s appointment. One conversation at a time, he thought. The rest could wait the span of one more night.

Driving home in the dark, the road a familiar corridor of his own headlights, he felt the three lives he was trying to hold – his mother’s fear and stubbornness, Joan’s humour and clarity, Maeve’s efficiency and worry – pressing in on him from three directions.

He thought of the book he’d read with the students when he had to cover a Geography class and teach about tectonic plates, about pressure building unseen over years, until one day the ground shifts and cracks.

Chapter Seven

The Waiting Room

Friday morning was the kind of cold that slipped in under doors and up sleeves, the kind that seemed to come from the ground rather than the sky. A low, colourless light lay over the estate when Ciarán stepped out to the car, his breath showing in small clouds that vanished almost as soon as they formed.

The dashboard clock read 9:02.

'Plenty of time,' he said aloud, though there was no one to hear him. The surgery was only a ten-minute drive. Thirteen if you got caught at the town's single set of traffic lights.

He sat for a second with his hands on the steering wheel before turning the key. The engine coughed into life, the radio snapping on at a volume that made him wince. Some DJ with too-bright cheerfulness was talking about 'beating the Monday blues'.

He turned it off.

The silence in the car felt heavier.

From the kitchen window, he could see Joan, a pale shape behind the glass, the mug in her hand dark against the light. When she saw him glance back, she lifted the mug in a small, mock-toast. He raised his hand in return and reversed slowly out of the drive.

The road into town was familiar and utterly new at the same time. He had driven it in all kinds of weather, in all moods. Today, though, each bend seemed to have acquired a subtle threat. The frost that still lingered in the hedgerows looked sharper. The pothole before the garage seemed deeper.

The car's heater wheezed, pushing out lukewarm air that smelled faintly of old dust and the pine air freshener his mother had insisted on attaching months ago. He cracked the window a fraction, letting in a thread of cold that stung his eyes and made him feel more awake than the tea had.

He thought of the appointment like an exam, one of those oral Irish tests he'd dreaded in school, where you sat in a classroom with a teacher and tried to dredge up phrases you knew you'd once known.

Except this time there were no phrases to rehearse. Only questions. *How long have you noticed this? Any pain? Any blood? Any family history?*

He stopped at the lights at the bottom of Main Street. A woman in a padded coat crossed in front of him with a small child tugging at her sleeve, the boy's school bag almost as big as he was. The woman's face was turned away, but he could see the tight set of her shoulders, the way she held her jaw. Another Monday, another start.

The lights changed. He drove on.

The surgery sat just off the square. He parked around the side, in the patients' car park. The place was half-full already: a battered van with a plumber's logo, a small red hatchback with a baby seat visible in the back, a silver saloon he recognised as belonging to Tom McHugh, who had been telling anyone who'd listen for the last year about 'this dose on my chest that won't shift'.

Ciarán killed the engine and sat for a moment, listening to

the tick of cooling metal. His hands were damp on the steering wheel. He wiped them on his jeans, took a breath, and got out.

The surgery was a squat building that had once been a bank. Now the old teller windows had been replaced by a reception desk, the vault turned into a records room. A ramp with a cold metal rail led up to the glass door. A sign beside it reminded people gently to cancel appointments if they weren't attending.

Inside the surgery, the air was warmer, overlaid with the familiar bouquet of such places: disinfectant, paper, the faint tang of hand sanitiser. The reception desk had a low Perspex screen, smudged at the edges. Behind it, the receptionist looked up, her hair piled on top of her head with a pencil stuck through it as if she'd stabbed it there in a moment of exasperation.

'Morning, Ciarán,' she said. 'You're here to see Dr O'Malley?'

He nodded. 'Half nine.'

'You're grand,' she said, her tone implying he might not be but that this was the phrase they used. 'You're on time. If you take a seat, he shouldn't be too long.'

He glanced at the waiting room. The chairs were arranged in a loose U, upholstered in a pattern of muted swirls that might once have been reassuring. A low table in the centre held a collection of magazines – old copies of *Hello!*, a gardening one with last year's date – and leaflets about flu shots, fanned out like a pack of cards.

He took a seat in the corner, where he could see both the door to the doctors' rooms and the one back out to the car park. He held his hands together, fingers laced, and tried not to tap his foot.

There were five other people waiting.

An elderly man he knew only by sight sat directly opposite,

his stick upright between his knees, both hands resting on it. He wore a tweed cap even indoors, his coat buttoned to the top. His gaze rested somewhere in the middle distance, unfocused but not unkind.

Beside him, a young woman in sports leggings and a fleece scrolled on her phone, earphones in, her thumb moving with a speed that suggested she was somewhere else entirely.

Near the window, a father with a child on his lap, the boy's face flushed and damp with some small fever. The man murmured to him in that half-soothing, half-bargaining tone all parents adopt in public places: 'Nearly there now. Then we'll get a treat.'

Every so often, the door to the inner sanctum opened and a name was called. *Mrs O'Hara? James? Philomena?* A person stood, gathered coat and bag and whatever courage they had, and disappeared into the corridor.

The clock on the wall above the reception desk ticked loudly, though the seconds hardly seemed to move.

He tried to distract himself by reading the posters. *Know the Signs of Stroke. Men's Health Matters. Are You Depressed?* Each question seemed to require a more thorough answer than a waiting room allowed.

The Men's Health one caught his eye: a silhouette of a man's body with red circles highlighting areas of concern. Prostate. Bowel. Heart. The text beneath, in friendly bullet points: *Don't ignore symptoms. Speak up. Early action saves lives.*

He wondered how many men had sat in this room, read that poster, and still gone home without saying a word.

'Mr Devlin?'

He hadn't heard the door open. He looked up.

Dr O'Malley stood there, wearing his habitual checked shirt under a white coat that didn't quite fit his shoulders. He was in his forties, with a beard that seemed permanently a day away from needing a trim, and eyes that managed to be both kind and clinical.

'Come on in,' he said.

Ciarán stood, his knees cracking louder than he'd have liked, and followed him down the short corridor. The doctor's room was at the end, on the left. There was a frosted glass pane in the door, the etched GP sign slightly crooked.

'Take a seat,' O'Malley said, gesturing to the chair beside the desk.

The room was both familiar and foreign. He'd sat here for sore throats, for prescription renewals, for the occasional student travel vaccine. Today, it felt smaller.

On one wall hung a framed print of a lake at dusk, all blues and greys. There was a poster of the human circulatory system, arteries picked out in bright red. The desk was tidy, for a doctor's desk, but still had the scatter of a busy life: notes, a stethoscope, a mug that proclaimed *World's Okayest Doctor*.

'How are you keeping?' O'Malley asked, clicking onto the computer.

'Grand,' Ciarán said automatically, then heard how ridiculous it sounded and added, 'Tired. Busy. You know yourself.'

'I do,' O'Malley said, giving him a brief smile. 'You've had a lot on, between your wife and your father.'

The words stung, the casual summation of the last year. He nodded.

'We'll talk about you today,' the doctor said. 'If that's all right.'

'Joan made me promise I would,' Ciarán replied.

O'Malley's expression softened. 'She's a wise woman.'

He clicked a few things on the screen, scanning.

'So,' he said. 'You were in with me a few weeks ago for

that urinary trouble. We did some bloods, including a PSA test. We sent you a letter, but … you missed it.'

'I saw it,' Ciarán said. 'I just … didn't rush to ring.'

O'Malley's eyebrows lifted slightly, but he didn't comment. 'Well, you're here now. That's the main thing.'

He turned the screen slightly, as if sharing a secret.

'Your PSA is elevated,' he said. 'Not sky-high, but higher than I'd like for a man your age.'

The phrase *your age* landed heavier than it should.

'What does that … mean?' Ciarán asked.

'It doesn't mean you have cancer,' O'Malley said at once, as if anticipating the leap. 'PSA can be raised for lots of reasons – prostate enlargement, infection, even recent activity. But it is a marker for prostate cancer, and in your case, given the urinary symptoms you described, I'd be happier if we had a closer look.'

'Closer how?' he said, though he suspected he knew.

'We can repeat the bloods to see if it continues to rise,' O'Malley said. 'But I'd also like to refer you to a urologist in Sligo. They can do further tests – an MRI, possibly a biopsy if they feel it's warranted.'

The word *biopsy* sat in the air like a cold object.

'Right,' Ciarán said slowly. 'And … what's the … likelihood?'

'We don't deal in likelihoods at this stage,' O'Malley said, a hint of weariness in his voice. 'We deal in possibilities. Your PSA is moderately raised. You're having urinary symptoms. It could be benign prostatic hyperplasia – a fancy term for an enlarged gland that comes with age. It could be prostatitis, an infection. Or it could be something more. We won't know until the specialist has a look.'

He paused, letting that sink in.

'Do you have any family history?' he asked. 'Brothers, father, uncles … prostate issues? Cancer?'

'Not that I know of,' Ciarán said. 'My father had a dodgy heart. My mother has knees that are like rusted hinges. But no one talked about … that.'

'They rarely do,' O'Malley said dryly. 'It's the curse of Irish men. We'll tell you everything about our tractors and nothing about our bodies.' He tapped a few keys. 'How are your waterworks now? Any worse than when you first came in?'

'The same,' Ciarán said. 'Up and down half the night. Slow to start. More … urgency than there used to be. No pain as such. Just … pressure.'

'Any blood? In urine or semen?' O'Malley asked, matter-of-fact.

He flushed. 'No.'

'Any pain in your hips, back? Weight loss you can't explain?'

He thought of the ache in his lower back. The way his trousers sat a bit looser on him these days, though that could just as easily be down to poor eating.

'Back is sore,' he admitted. 'Has been for a while. But sure that could be anything. Lifting boxes. Stress. Age.'

'It could,' O'Malley agreed. 'But we'll mention it in the referral.'

He clicked again, printing something.

'I'm going to send this letter through marked "urgent",' he said. 'That doesn't mean I think you're at death's door. It just means I don't want you waiting six months to be seen. With Joan's situation, you've enough on your plate without uncertainty dragging on.'

Ciarán swallowed. 'How long are we talking?' he asked. 'Weeks? Months?'

'Hard to say,' O'Malley said. 'The system is what it is. But marked urgent, I'd hope within six to eight weeks. We can ring and chase if it goes longer.'

Six to eight weeks. The phrase spread out in his mind, not as a finite span but as a terrain to be crossed, full of small days and nights.

'In the meantime,' O'Malley said, 'we'll put you on some medication to help with the urinary symptoms. It won't fix the underlying cause, but it may give you better sleep. I'd recommend cutting back on evening fluids – tea, especially – and alcohol.'

He thought of the single pint in Dolan's, of the comfort in it. 'Right,' he said.

O'Malley leaned back slightly in his chair. 'How are you doing … apart from this?' he asked. 'Really.'

He hesitated. The instinct was to say *Grand, fine, sure you know yourself*. But Joan's voice floated up in his mind: *I need you to tell me. Straight.*

'Tired,' he said. 'Worried. For Joan. For Mam. For the students. Now for myself, I suppose. I feel like I'm … standing in the middle of a yard with too many machines running and no one at the controls.'

O'Malley smiled, an expression that was more sad than amused. 'That's a good image,' he said. 'I might borrow it for myself someday.' His face grew serious. 'You're under extraordinary strain,' he said. 'Carers often are, but you've had more than your share. It's no wonder the body starts shouting.' He steepled his fingers, a habit Ciarán had noticed before when he was about to make a suggestion. 'I can sign you off work for a period if you want,' he said. 'Give you time to deal with Joan's treatment, your mother, this investigation. You don't have to be in the classroom on top of everything.'

The thought of not going back to school in January – of

letting go of that structure, that identity – filled him with a mixture of relief and panic.

'I don't know,' he said slowly. 'I feel … guilty when I'm not there. The students … the exam classes. It's their last year.'

'Students will always have exams,' O'Malley said. 'You only have one nervous system. If it breaks, you're no use to them or anyone else. We can do a review – with you, the principal, maybe occupational health – see what's viable.'

He nodded, the words washing over him. Part of him filed them away. Another part wanted to flee back to the simplicity of timetables and lesson plans, where cause and effect were clearer.

'I don't want to be … dramatic,' he said. 'Other people have it worse.'

O'Malley's gaze sharpened. 'This isn't a competition,' he said. 'You're allowed to be tired. You're allowed to be frightened. You're allowed to need help.'

Ciarán looked down at his hands. The knuckles were reddened from the cold, a faint smear of ink near the thumb from the poem he'd been drafting the day before.

'Will you tell Joan?' O'Malley asked.

'Yes,' he said. 'She made me promise.'

'And your mother?'

He hesitated. 'Eventually,' he said. 'Maybe after the specialist. She has enough ghosts without lending me one of mine.'

O'Malley nodded. 'Fair enough. One disclosure at a time.'

He printed a prescription, signed the referral letter with a quick, practiced flourish, and handed Ciarán a slip of paper with the hospital's number on it.

'If you don't hear anything in six weeks,' he said, 'ring this. If you're worried in the meantime – new symptoms, pain, anything – ring us. Don't ignore it. You're not a tractor. You don't have to keep going until something falls off.'

'I'll try to remember that,' Ciarán said.

He stood. His legs felt oddly unsteady, as if the floor had shifted a few degrees.

At the door, O'Malley added, almost as an afterthought, 'And one more thing – try not to let the word "cancer" swallow everything. It's a possibility, not a certainty. Most elevated PSAs I see turn out to be benign. Hold that in mind on your walks between here and the hospital.'

The phrase *on your walks* made it sound almost leisurely, like an afternoon ramble, not a crossing over some invisible line.

'Right,' Ciarán said. 'Thanks.'

As he stepped back into the waiting room, the air felt different. The chairs were the same, the elderly man still staring into the middle distance, the young woman still scrolling, the father still murmuring to the dozy child. But he felt as if he were observing it all from behind glass.

He nodded to the receptionist, signed whatever needed signing, and stepped out into the cold.

The sky had lowered further. A fine drizzle had started, the sort that made more noise on the car roof than it seemed to account for in actual droplets.

He sat in the driver's seat, closed the door, and let his head fall back against the rest.

For a moment he did nothing. Didn't turn the key. Didn't reach for the radio. Just stayed there, feeling the tightness in his chest, the slight tremor in his hands.

PSA. Elevated. Urgent referral. Six to eight weeks. Biopsy. Benign. Cancer.

The words jostled in his head like people in a too-small doorway.

He lifted his hand and traced a small circle on the fogging windscreen with his thumb. Outside, the surgery door opened and closed, releasing patients in ones and twos. Life went on. People had things to do. Prescriptions to fill. Groceries to buy.

He took out his phone.

Joan would be waiting. She had said she wanted honesty, not protection.

His thumb hovered over her number, as if it might be a threshold.

He pressed call.

She answered on the second ring. 'Well?' she said, bypassing any greeting.

'Well,' he echoed.

There was a brief pause. 'Give me the short version first,' she said. 'Then we can expand into the long, torturous one.'

'PSA's up,' he said. 'Not through the roof, but up. He's referring me to Sligo. Urologist. Maybe MRI. Maybe biopsy. Six to eight weeks, if the system is feeling generous.'

'And?' she asked.

'And it might be nothing. Or something small. Or not,' he said. 'He doesn't know yet. He says don't panic. But he would say that.'

Another small pause. He could imagine her, sitting at the kitchen table, the light on her hair, her hand around the mug.

'Okay,' she said carefully. 'How do you feel?'

'Like I've been told I might be sick in an interesting way in two months' time,' he said. 'And that in the meantime, I should carry on as normal.'

She made a small sound that was half a laugh, half a breath. 'That's a very you answer,' she said. 'On a scale of one to ten, how terrified are you?'

'Seven,' he said, surprising himself with the honesty. 'Fluctuating. Sometimes four. Sometimes … eleven.'

'Valid,' she said. 'We'll call it seven for now. Did he give you anything for the waterworks?'

'He did,' he said. 'Tablets. Less tea at night. Less beer, which in my case is hardly a sacrifice.'

'Any talk of … time?' she asked. 'Probabilities? Winnable battles?'

'He avoided percentages,' he said. 'Which I'm grateful for. I've enough numbers correcting essays.'

'Good,' she said. 'They're only sticks to beat yourself with later.'

He felt some of the tightness ease. Her voice, steady and wry, was like a hand on his shoulder.

'We'll take it one step at a time,' she said. 'Sligo letter. Appointment. Test. Result. No jumping ahead to the scene where you're in a bed beside me and we're reenacting some tragic indie film.'

'Wasn't that one of your fantasies once?' he asked, managing a weak smile. 'Us in adjacent rooms, communicating in bad poetry?'

'That was when we were twenty-five and idiotic,' she said. 'I've since revised my ambitions down to a quiet life and a functioning bladder for my husband.'

'I'll do my best,' he said.

She was quiet for a moment.

'Do you want to come straight home?' she asked. 'Or do you need a walk or a coffee or a shout at the sea?'

He looked at the sky. The idea of walking by the bay in this wet, raw light, the wind whipping around him, was both appealing and exhausting.

'I'll come home,' he said. 'We can shout at *The Chase* together.'

'Grand,' she said. 'Drive carefully. You're precious cargo now.'

'I was before,' he protested.

She laughed, and the sound made something loosen in his chest.

On the way home, he took the longer road, skirting the edge of town, past the industrial estate and the new houses that all looked like they'd been cut from the same catalogue. A flock of starlings moved as one over a field, their shifting shape like thought made visible.

At a red light, he caught sight of himself in the rear-view mirror. The angle flattened his features, made his eyes look darker, his mouth downturned. He pulled his face into a ludicrous smile, baring his teeth, then let it go. The expression didn't reach his eyes either way.

At home, Joan had the kettle on. The house smelled of toast and that faint, clean scent that came from the washing powder they'd always used – cheap, but oddly comforting.

She was at the table, dressing gown over leggings, hair tied back loosely, a pen in her hand. A crossword lay open in front of her.

'Eight down,' she said, as soon as he stepped in. 'Six letters. "Unwelcome visitor". I was going to put "mother-in-law" but I thought, out of respect, I'd leave it blank.'

'"Cancer",' he said automatically, then winced. 'Too dark?'

'Funny you should say that,' she replied dryly. 'It actually fits.'

He sat opposite her. She watched his face with that directness that had always both unnerved and steadied him.

'You all right?' she asked.

'I'm ... upright,' he said. 'I made it to the car without collapsing dramatically in the waiting room. That's something.'

She reached across, took his hand. The warmth of her palm surprised him every time. He'd expected her to feel colder, somehow, as if illness should have cooled her from the inside out.

'Welcome to the club at the edge of the cliff,' she said. 'Membership is free, coffee is crap, and the view is terrifying.'

'I preferred your book club,' he said.

'That had its own terrors,' she said. 'Remember the woman who cried because you said *Brooklyn* was "grand"?'

He laughed, the memory briefly eclipsing the present.

'So,' she said. 'We wait. We have bacon. We watch pointless television. We ring your mother at some point and tell her you're going to Sligo for your "waterworks". We don't use the word "cancer" yet. Deal?'

'Deal,' he said.

'And you ring the hospice team tomorrow,' she added. 'Not as a surrender. Just as an enquiry. Information is ammunition.'

'Joan Devlin,' he said, 'you'd have made a terrifying general.'

'I'm too fond of naps,' she said. 'I'd lose the war because of a duvet.'

After lunch, when Joan went to lie down, he found himself standing in the small room they called his study again, the waiting room of his own thoughts.

He took out his notebook, flicked to the poem he'd started about the things they kept. He read the lines he'd written, the ink slightly smudged where his hand had rested.

In the wardrobe, his sleeves still wait for arms,
buttons patient as saints in a quiet chapel.

He added nothing. Instead, he turned the page and wrote at the top, without thinking, *The Waiting Room*.

The lines came more slowly now, each one an effort.

Fragments of the morning flickered: the old man with the cap, the young woman's scrolling thumb, the father's murmur, the poster with red circles.

The chairs are all the same disease-colour,
muted swirls that don't belong to any field.
Names are called like raffle tickets,
no one cheering when they win.

He paused, tapped the pen against the page.

Too easy, he thought. The kind of poem that got written a hundred times a day in a hundred waiting rooms.

He crossed out the last line and tried again.

Names are called into the bright corridor,
and we stand, one by one, to be weighed.

Better. The weight of it closer to what he felt.

He wrote until his hand cramped, then stopped. The page wasn't finished, but the act of writing had shifted something in him. Given the morning a shape outside his skull.

He put down the pen, flexed his fingers. His back complained when he straightened, the ache flaring along his spine.

In the quiet of the room, he became acutely aware of the sounds in the rest of the house: the washing machine's low churn, the distant murmur of a radio from a neighbour's, the faint, rhythmic wheeze of the central heating.

His phone buzzed.

A text message from Michael Lally, the school principal: *Hope you are okay. No rush, but when you're up to it, we should talk about a reduced timetable. Take care of yourself.*

He stared at the screen. The words *Take care of yourself*

looked odd coming from a man whose main relationship with him had been through exam timetables and discipline reports.

He typed back: *Happy to call in next week. Thanks.*

The day drifted. In the afternoon, he drove down to his mother's with a few messages and the vague intention of telling her something, though he wasn't yet sure what.

She was in the sitting room, as always at that hour, cardigan buttoned wrong, the television showing a quiz show she wasn't really watching.

'How did you get on at the doctor?' she asked, almost before he'd taken his coat off. News travelled fast in small houses.

'Fine,' he said, then checked himself. 'Well. Half-fine. He's referring me to Sligo. For the waterworks. Just to be sure.'

Her face creased. 'Sligo?' she said. 'What's wrong with here?'

'They don't have the machines,' he said. 'It's routine. Men my age.'

He tried to keep his voice light. The last thing he wanted was to see his own fear reflected in her.

She pursed her lips. 'Your father never went near a hospital unless they carried him,' she said. 'And look where that got him.'

'Dead,' he said.

She blinked, then nodded slowly. 'Dead,' she agreed. 'You're wise to go. If they tell you you're fine, you'll have peace. If they tell you you're not, at least you'll know where you stand.'

He sat, the familiarity of her phrasing a comfort.

'Don't be letting them fob you off,' she added. 'Ask the questions. You're good at that. Always were. You drove me mad with the "why" of everything when you were small. Use it on them now instead.'

He smiled. 'I will.'

She looked at him then in that assessing way mothers have. 'You look tired,' she said.

'I am,' he said. 'But I'm all right.'

'Get your sleep,' she said. 'Drink water. Eat vegetables. And mind Joan. She'll be worrying more about you now than herself.'

'There's some competition for that title,' he said.

She smiled faintly. 'We'll share it.'

When he left, the light was already going from the day. The sky had taken on that washed-out tone that meant rain again before nightfall. The road was wet, the hedges dark.

Driving home, he felt the day settle on him like a coat: the waiting room, the doctor's voice, Joan's hand, his mother's insistence.

He didn't feel braver. Or wiser. Or especially stoic. He felt … suspended. As if the ground beneath him were solid for now but with a tremor running quietly somewhere deep down.

At a bend near the GAA pitch, he saw a boy in a tracksuit kicking a football against a wall, his dog watching with rapt attention. The ball hit the wall with a satisfying thud, came back, was trapped, kicked again. A simple loop of action and reaction.

He envied that simplicity, the clear cause and effect. Kick, return. Question, answer.

Life, he thought, was more like a waiting room. You sat in it with your own quiet fear, watching others go ahead of you, hearing snatches of information and pain and relief, and when your name was called, you walked into a corridor you couldn't see the end of.

Back at the house, Joan was in the sitting room, the lamp

on beside her, a blanket over her knees. *The Chase* was indeed on, the host's eyebrows doing their familiar dance.

'Did the lads beat the Chaser?' he asked, hanging up his coat.

'They had no chance,' she said. 'One fella thought Yeats wrote *Dubliners*. I lost interest.'

He sat beside her, the couch springs sighing under his weight.

They watched the rest of the quiz without really seeing it, and then he turned the TV off.

In the quiet that followed, the house seemed to lean in, listening.

'Well,' he said. 'We're officially a two-patient household.'

'We always were,' she replied. 'You were just undiagnosed.'

'Do you regret it?' he asked suddenly. 'Us coming back here. Leaving Dublin. Buying this house. Booking in to this life.'

She thought for a moment. 'Sometimes,' she said. 'When I see friends posting pictures from Berlin or Barcelona. When I get an email about a job I would have killed for ten years ago. When the rain comes in sideways for the fourth week in a row.'

She shifted, looked at him.

'But then there's this,' she said. 'This stupid couch. This street. Your mother's boiled cabbage. The lake. The kids in your class who'll never forget that you explained the Treaty to them in one diagram. The way we can see the stars from the back step when the clouds lift. It's … ours. I don't regret that.'

He exhaled, something easing.

'Do you?' she asked.

He thought of the band in the Rathmines basement, the half-written postcards from London in his father's biscuit tin, the poems copied in a neat, unexpected hand.

'Sometimes,' he said. 'In both directions. I regret the roads I didn't take and the ones I did. If I'd stayed in Dublin, I'd regret not coming home. If I'd never gone, I'd regret that too. There's no clean version.'

She smiled. 'That's very philosophical for a Friday,' she said.

'Doctor's orders,' he replied. 'Severe case of existentialism. Take two poems and ring me in the morning.'

She laughed.

Later, when they went to bed, he lay awake longer than she did. The appointment with the urologist in Sligo was still theoretical, a date not yet inked in. The future felt like one of those hazy weather forecasts beyond three days – *unsettled, with a chance of showers*.

He thought of the waiting room again, the hush, the rustling of paper, the way people avoided each other's eyes.

He wondered how many of them, like him, went home and opened notebooks, or letters, or bottles. How many of them sat in kitchens telling their news in the simplest possible words. How many kept it to themselves, letting it harden inside.

He turned onto his side, careful not to jostle Joan. In the dark, he could hear the faint murmur of a match commentary from a neighbour's house, the steady tick of the clock in the hall.

Somewhere, in a hospital he hadn't yet visited, his name would soon be written on a list. A file would be started. A number assigned.

For now, though, he was still just a man in a bed in a small house on the edge of a small town, the long night stretching ahead, divided as always into a series of small, ordinary breaths.

Chapter Eight

Teaching

While he waited for a letter from Sligo, life did what it always did: it went on. Days leaned into one another, shaped by small routines that, taken together, looked suspiciously like a plan.

On Tuesday morning, the sky over the town had the faintest hint of blue in it, as if the clouds had tired of their own weight. The frost was light, the grass edged in white that would be gone by ten. Ciarán drove to school in that narrow band of time when the sun was still low enough to be in his eyes, but not yet high enough to offer warmth.

He hadn't been back since before the funeral, apart from a quick visit to drop in a sick cert. As he parked in his usual space at the back – between the caretaker's van and the head of Maths' hatchback – he felt the slight shift inside him that always came with this place. It was like stepping onto a stage he knew by heart, even if he no longer trusted his lines.

The building looked as it always did in December: tired, functional, streaked with the damp of too many winters. A string of wilting tinsel hung around the office window – an attempt at cheer that only highlighted the dullness of the glass.

He grabbed his bag from the passenger seat, slung it over his shoulder, and walked in through the side door. The corridor smelled of floor polish, wet coats and teenage bodies waking up. A clatter of lockers being shut, voices rising and falling, the particular nervous energy of a Monday transferred wholesale to a Tuesday because the week hadn't yet fully settled on them.

In the staff room, the kettle was already on. Someone had left a plate of biscuits on the central table, half demolished – the good chocolate ones gone, the plainer ones soldiering on.

'Look what the tide brought in,' said Barry Keane from over by the photocopier. Barry taught maths and coached the senior team. He had the relaxed saunter of a man who had never quite accepted that he was no longer twenty.

Ciarán set his bag down on a chair. 'I heard there was free tea,' he said.

'Free is a strong word,' Barry replied. 'We pay with our souls. And supervision duty.' He moved closer, lowering his voice. 'How are you?' he asked. 'I was sorry about your dad. And Joan ... I heard bits. From O'Shea. His wife saw her at the hospital. How's she doing?'

'Up and down,' Ciarán said. 'She's ... in the middle of it. Tired. But still giving out about the newsreader's hair, so that's a good sign.'

Barry huffed a small laugh. 'And yourself? You look ... grand,' he said, in the peculiar way Irish men had of using the word to mean anything from 'wonderful' to 'on the verge of collapse'.

'I've had better months,' Ciarán said. 'Doc wants to have a look under the bonnet. Sligo. Prostate stuff. Could be nothing. Could be more. We're in the raffle.'

Barry's face sobered. 'Ah, Jesus,' he said. 'I didn't know. Sorry, man.'

'There isn't a notice up yet,' Ciarán said. 'We'll see. I'm on the "urgent" pile. Which in HSE terms means maybe before Easter.'

'The joys,' Barry said. He hesitated, then put a hand briefly on Ciarán's shoulder, an awkward pat. 'If you need cover, shout,' he said. 'I can yell about the Treaty at your crowd for a few days. Scare them straight.'

They both smiled, the momentary warmth easing the air between them.

The principal, known to the students as 'The Pope' for his slow, deliberate way of speaking and his tendency to clasp his hands as if about to deliver a homily, appeared in the doorway.

'Ciarán,' he said, spotting him. 'Good to see you. Have you a minute?'

As if he could say no.

In the principal's office, the blinds were half drawn against the low sun. Files sat in neat stacks on the desk. A small Christmas tree blinked in the corner, its lights struggling against the daylight.

'How are things?' Lally said, motioning to the chair. He was a big man who had somehow managed to make his presence gentle rather than dominating; he always gave the impression of someone who had been heading for the priesthood and changed his mind at the last minute.

'Flying it,' Ciarán said. 'Tired. Like everyone.'

'I won't insult you by pretending I don't know you're carrying more than everyone,' Lally said. 'I was very sorry to hear about Sean. He was a good man. Kept half the parish moving.'

'He kept us in clutches,' Ciarán said.

'And Joan ...' Lally's face shifted. 'My wife said she saw ye up in the unit one day. If there's anything ...'

'Thank you,' Ciarán said, cutting gently across. 'We're managing. One day at a time.'

Lally folded his hands. 'That's actually what I wanted to talk to you about,' he said. 'Next term.'

Here it comes, Ciarán thought. The timetable. The question of whether he was a teacher or a ghost.

'We'd like to support you,' Lally said. 'But I also know you. I know if I say "take the year off", you'll ignore me. You'll feel guilty. You'll worry about the students. So I'm trying to find the middle ground.'

He slid a sheet of paper across the desk: a version of the timetable with highlighter on certain blocks.

'This is what we're proposing,' he said. 'Keep you on with the two sixth-year History groups – they need the continuity, and frankly, you're the one they'll listen to about Parnell and Collins. Drop your junior classes for now. We'll redistribute them. No Transition Year module. No after-school study. How does that sound?'

It sounded, Ciarán thought, like someone quietly pulling stones out of his pockets while he wasn't looking.

'You don't have to,' he began. 'If it's too much of a headache to— '

'It is my job to have headaches,' Lally said. 'Let me do it. And if, mid-term, you decide it's too much, we sit down and adjust again. You're not chiselled into stone.'

Ciarán looked at the sheet. The blocks looked manageable. Two double periods of Leaving Cert a day. Some free time. Enough structure to stop him unravelling entirely.

'It might be good to have something ... else,' he said. 'That's not hospitals and boiled potatoes.'

'I thought so,' Lally said. 'I know when my father died, the only thing that kept me from climbing the walls was having to explain quadratic equations to a room full of teenagers. Their lack of perspective is oddly grounding.'

They talked logistics for a while longer – dates, exams, parent-teacher meetings. The normality of it, the familiar small irritations (no, he didn't want his double with 6B moved to a Friday afternoon), felt like walking briefly on firm ground.

At the end, Lally said, almost as he opened the door, 'And

if you need to step out of a class someday because the world is too much, you step out. We'll catch you. We're good at catching. Better at that than at Throwing Them In At The Deep End, despite what the papers say.'

'I'll keep my flailing discreet,' Ciarán said.

Back in the staff room, the bell went for first class. The room emptied in a flurry of mugs grabbed and seats vacated.

He took his battered folder from his bag – the one with *Europe 1870–1970* written on the front in a student's messy marker – and made his way to his sixth-year room.

They were already half in their seats when he arrived, the particular mixture of tired and wired that characterised seventeen-year-olds in December. School bags slumped on the floor. One lad in the back had his hood up. Another girl had her head on the desk, face obscured by hair.

As he stepped in, there was a fractional change in the air. Conversations dropped a notch.

'Sir,' someone said.

'Morning,' he replied, closing the door behind him. 'Everyone surviving?'

A mutter of assent. One voice: 'Barely.'

He wrote the date on the board in his neat, precise hand. Beneath it: *The Treaty Negotiations – Key Issues*.

'We're going to talk about men in suits arguing in smoky rooms,' he said. 'Which, I'm aware, sounds like the worst Netflix series ever. But bear with me. By the end of this, you'll hate the word "plenipotentiary" as much as I do.'

A small ripple of laughter. It was enough.

'Sixth December 1921,' he said. 'Downing Street. What's on the table?'

Hands went up. Not as many as in September, but enough.

'Dominion status,' said Anna in the front row, her plait chewed at the end. 'Like Canada.'

'The oath,' said another. 'They have to swear to the king.'

'The ports,' from the back. 'They keep the ports.'

'And what does that tell us?' he asked. 'About what each side cares about? About what they're willing to lose to get what they think they need?'

They talked. Halting at first, then more freely. He moved among the rows, prodding, coaxing, occasionally letting a silence stretch just long enough that someone rushed to fill it.

He found, to his surprise, that the rhythm of it came back. The call and response. The sense of a room thinking together, even if some were only thinking about lunch.

'Is there a right answer, sir?' asked one lad, frowning. 'Like … were they right to sign it?'

'That, Doyle,' he said, 'is the question that kept people awake at night for about ten years. And then some. There isn't a Leaving Cert mark scheme answer to it. There are arguments on both sides. That's what we're trying to see today. The complexity.'

He paused, knowing that somewhere inside that explanation there was an echo of his own morning.

'Sometimes,' he went on, 'you're given a choice where both options are bad, and you pick the one you think you can live with. And then you spend the rest of your life wondering if the other one would have been better. And there's no way to know, because you only get to live the version you chose.'

'Like going to UL instead of Galway,' muttered someone. A few laughed.

'Exactly,' he said. 'Or marrying someone who supports Mayo.'

A bigger laugh at that. He saw a few eyes flick toward the back, where a girl in a Mayo hoodie grinned and stuck her tongue out.

He wrote key phrases on the board. *Stepping stone. Freedom to achieve freedom. Document No. 2.*

As he spoke, part of his mind stood aside and watched himself, curious. Here he was, talking about historical men in crisis, about compromise and pressure and the long echo of decisions, while his own life sat as a kind of parenthesis outside the classroom door.

The forty minutes passed quicker than he would have liked. The bell cut across his sentence about de Valera's absence.

'Make sure you can explain three reasons for signing and three against,' he said as they gathered their books. 'No lists. No headlines. Sentences. Thought. There will be an exam question. There is always an exam question.'

As they filed out, a few lingered.

'Sir,' said one girl, shyly. 'Sorry about your dad.'

'Thanks, Aoife,' he said.

'And your wife,' another offered. 'My mam said she saw you in the ward. She's … you know. She's there as well.'

They looked at each other, an odd moment of recognition.

'How's she doing?' he asked.

The girl shrugged. 'Grand some days,' she said. 'Wrecked others. Same as.'

'We're in the club,' he said softly.

She nodded, relieved at the acknowledgement, then followed her friends.

He sat for a moment in the empty room, the fading smell of cheap body spray and markers hanging in the air. On the board, *Freedom to achieve freedom* looked suddenly like a phrase from a different language.

He wiped it away.

The rest of the schoolday was a blur of small things: a staff meeting where the vice-principal talked about mock exam schedules; a corridor duty where he broke up a trivial scuffle over a hat; a visit from the guidance counsellor who left him a leaflet about 'teacher well-being' that he slid, unread, into his bag.

By four, the building had emptied of students, the echo of their presence lingering in scuffed floors and discarded worksheets.

He drove home with the sense of having visited an old country and returned with its dust on his shoes.

Joan was in the kitchen, the small table covered in leaflets and a notebook. A woman sat opposite her, in a navy fleece with a logo on it, a clipboard on her lap.

'This is Deirdre,' Joan said, as he stepped in. 'From the hospice team.'

The woman stood, smiled, held out a hand. Early forties, maybe, with short hair that looked like it had been grown out of practicality rather than fashion. There was something grounded about her, an ease that didn't feel performed.

'We were just talking about you,' she said, shaking his hand. 'All good. Mostly.'

'That's worrying,' he said. 'People only say that when it isn't.'

She laughed. 'I was telling Joan we're here for both of you,' she said. 'And for your mother, if needs be. We cover a lot of ground. Sit down. I promise I'm not here to sign you up to anything you don't want.'

He took a chair, aware suddenly of the weariness in his limbs.

On the table, he saw pamphlets with titles like *Living with Serious Illness* and *What Hospice Means*. The word 'hospice' still made his stomach clench, the association too tightly bound to endings. But the woman in front of him did not look like a grim reaper. She looked like someone who spent her days in other people's kitchens, listening more than speaking.

'I know people hear "hospice" and think "death house",'

she said, as if reading his mind. 'We get that a lot. But what we really are is a support service. For the long road. Not just the last bit.'

Joan agreed. 'I was telling her we're not there yet,' she said. 'Not ready to talk about beds in other buildings. But open to ideas about how to cope in this one.'

Deirdre nodded. 'That's most of my job,' she said. 'Helping people stay where they want to be, as long as possible, with as much comfort as we can manage. Sorting practical things. Pain management. Equipment. Bits of counselling if you fancy it. Respite. Advice for family. Sometimes we even do the old-fashioned thing of listening to people complain about the news.'

'Are you trained for that?' Ciarán asked. 'That's advanced work.'

She smiled. 'We have a special module,' she said.

They talked logistics for a while. Deirdre asked about Joan's pain levels, her medications, what the oncologist had said about the next cycles. She asked about stairs, bathrooms, handrails. She made notes in a neat, unhurried script.

'And yourself, how are you?' she asked at one point, turning to Ciarán.

'I'm fine,' he said.

'We have a carers' group. Men and women. Some cry. Some don't. Some just sit and drink bad coffee. No pressure to share. Think about it.'

He nodded, non-committal. The idea of sitting in a circle talking about his feelings with strangers made his skin itch. But the thought of being in a room full of people who understood the particular exhaustion of loving sick people had its pull.

Before she left, Deirdre stood and looked around the small kitchen as if taking its measure. 'We'll get you a proper shower chair,' she said to Joan. 'And maybe a rail for that step.

It's begging to catch you out. We'll send someone to assess your mother's place too, if you like. No obligation.'

'My mother will fight anyone who tries to take away her rickety mat,' he said.

'We're used to that,' Deirdre said. 'We're very good at losing arguments gracefully and coming back later with biscuits.'

When she had gone, leaving behind a rustle of paper and the faint smell of hospital soap, the house felt oddly bigger. As if another layer of air had been added.

'What do you think?' Joan asked.

'She seems … sane,' he said. 'Which is more than can be said for some people in the system.'

'I like her,' Joan said. 'She didn't flinch when I said "dying". Most people change the subject. Or look at the floor. Or start talking about miracles.'

'Maeve would approve,' he said. 'She loves a woman with a plan.'

'We have a plan now,' Joan said. 'Sort of. Or at least a woman with a clipboard who'll help us make one.'

He poured tea, the kettle's hiss a background note to their thoughts.

On the table, one leaflet lay open. A line in bold caught his eye: *Hospice is about living as well as possible, for as long as possible.*

He thought of his father's biscuit tin, of his poem in another hand. Of his students wrestling with the Treaty question. Of his mother talking to the empty half of the bed.

As well as possible, for as long as possible.

It wasn't a bad phrase, he thought. Slightly vague, slightly hopeful. Like a treaty negotiated between the living and the dying.

The letter from Sligo arrived on Thursday.

He found it when he came in from his mother's, lying on the hall mat between a takeaway menu and a catalogue no one had asked for. The envelope had the hospital's crest in the top corner.

He picked it up slowly, as if it might go off in his hand.

In the kitchen, Joan looked up from the crossword as he came in.

'White smoke?' she asked.

He held up the envelope. 'Sligo,' he said.

He sat opposite her, the paper cool between his fingers, and opened it.

Dear Mr Devlin,

We have received a referral from your GP, Dr T. O'Malley, regarding your recent PSA test and urinary symptoms. An appointment has been scheduled for you at the Urology Clinic, Outpatients Department, Sligo University Hospital, on Friday 26th January at 10:15 a.m. …

He scanned the rest quickly. Instructions about fasting (not necessary), medications (continue as normal), what to bring (a list of current prescriptions, an empty bladder, an open mind).

'Twenty-sixth January,' he said. 'Ten fifteen.'

Joan did quick mental arithmetic. 'Five weeks,' she said. 'More or less what he said.'

'Plenty of time to panic in,' he replied.

She reached for his hand. 'Plenty of time to live in,' she corrected. 'Five weeks of ordinary things. Classes. Walks. Tea. My terrible jokes. Hospice leaflets. We'll fill them.'

He looked at the date again. End of January. The far side of Christmas. A time still painted in his head with tinsel and bad television, but now tagged with another colour entirely.

He folded the letter carefully, too carefully, and placed it on the table. He pushed it away, just far enough that it wasn't in his immediate line of vision.

Outside, it had started to rain again, fine and steady, the kind that seemed to fall from the very air rather than the clouds. The street lights had come on, halos in the damp.

He stood, went to the kettle, filled it.

On the counter, his notebook lay open from that morning, a fragment of a line visible: *Names are called into the bright corridor …*

He picked up the pen and, without quite deciding to, wrote beneath it:

Some days the door stays closed,
and we are left to mind the coats,
making tea, marking copies,
learning the weight of waiting.

It wasn't perfect. It barely scanned. But as he wrote it, something inside him settled, just a fraction.

Five weeks, he thought. Long enough for another chapter. Long enough for a few more mornings in the yard, a few more lessons on the Treaty, a few more cups of tea with his mother talking to ghosts, with Joan making jokes about death on the crossword.

As well as possible, for as long as possible.

He capped the pen. The kettle sang.

For now, there was milk to fetch from the fridge, cups to set out, and the small, fierce comfort of Joan's presence across the table, the two of them living in the space between appointments, making what peace they could with both the light that remained and the evening that was, inevitably, coming.

Chapter Nine

The Carol Service

By the time the school broke up for Christmas, the town had given up trying to look cheerful and settled for looking less miserable than in November.

Tinsel drooped in shop windows. A plastic Santa clung wearily to the front of the hardware shop, his red-suited legs flapping whenever the wind got up. The fairy lights strung across Main Street were looking worse by the day, one in three bulbs had already surrendered, leaving gaps in the constellations. The big tree in the square looked better at night, when you couldn't see the bald patches.

On the Friday afternoon, the corridors of the school echoed with that peculiar hysteria that comes when teenagers can sense freedom but haven't quite been released yet. Teachers moved through the noise with the resignation of zookeepers on feeding day.

'Once more with feeling,' Barry muttered beside Ciarán as they stood outside the hall, supervising the flow of students going in for the end-of-term assembly. 'This is what we trained for.'

'I trained for teaching,' Ciarán said. 'Not crowd control.'

They watched as the students filed into the hall, some moving quickly to get the good seats at the back, others dragging their feet as if the assembly were a punishment rather than a reprieve from classes.

On the small stage, the principal stood with a stack of papers in his hand, the chaplain beside him. A cluster of first-years sat with borrowed instruments, a makeshift band tuning up in tentative coughs of sound.

'Are you staying for this?' Barry asked.

'I'm reading something,' Ciarán said. 'Apparently my "calming presence" is required between the tin whistles and the raffle.'

'Oh God,' Barry said. 'Poetry?'

'Worse,' Ciarán replied. 'The school prayer.'

Barry clapped him on the back. 'You're a braver man than me,' he said. 'Don't go full Latin on them. They'll riot.'

As the last stragglers found seats, the doors at the back were pulled shut. The murmuring dimmed to a low simmer.

Lally stepped up to the microphone. 'Right,' he said, in that slow, carrying voice that always made them listen whether they meant to or not. 'We'll keep this short. I know your minds are already on mince pies and bad jumpers.'

There was a ripple of laughter. The chaplain led a short prayer that half the hall murmured along with, the other half mouthing 'watermelon' in rough unison. The first-years played 'Silent Night' at a tempo that sounded frightened but made it to the end without anyone actually stopping.

Then it was Ciarán's turn.

He moved up to the lectern, paper in hand more for something to do than because he needed it. He could have said the words in his sleep. In some ways he had, over the years.

He looked out at the sea of faces – bored, amused, distracted, earnest. The sixth-years sat near the back, trying to look like they were too old for all this, but their eyes betrayed them; this was their last Christmas here and part of them knew they would miss it.

He cleared his throat.

'We gather today,' he began, 'at the end of a long term, at the end of a long year ...'

His voice sounded strange to his own ears at first: too loud, too formal. But as he went on, something loosened. He spoke not just the prayer as it was written, but the things behind it: the hope that the students would get home safe; that they would not go into ditches or fights or worse over the holidays; that they would, in their own messy ways, be all right.

'... and we remember those who aren't with us,' he said, stumbling slightly over the last line of the text and adding the clause almost without thinking. 'Those we've lost this year. Those who are in hospital. Those who are far away.'

There was a small shift in the room. A girl in the third row glanced down; somebody in the back row coughed too loudly. The chaplain looked at him, surprised, then nodded, almost imperceptibly.

'Amen,' he finished.

A murmur went up. He stepped back, letting the next item take over: the raffle for the enormous hamper that everyone pretended to despise but secretly coveted.

As he returned to his seat at the side of the stage, he caught sight of Anna in the front row, one of his sixth-years, wiping at her eyes with the heel of her hand. He remembered, belatedly, that her grandmother had died in October. Death wasn't an abstract word in this hall. It lurked in uniforms and hoodies and staff-room mugs.

After the assembly, the students poured out into the cold air, scattering in all directions – toward buses, parents' cars, town. The staff room filled briefly with the rustle of coats and the hiss of the kettle. Someone put a tin of Roses on the table. The blue ones went first.

'You got them with the grief line,' Barry said to Ciarán, unwrapping a sweet. 'They didn't know what hit them.'

'It slipped out,' Ciarán said. 'I didn't mean to depress the whole school.'

'They could do with the odd reality check,' Barry replied. 'Anyway, half of them were only thinking about their fake IDs.'

On the drive home, the road had that quiet it gets when school is out, a slightly less frantic pace. The daylight was thin but brighter than it had been in weeks. Patches of blue showed between strips of cloud, a reminder that there was sky above the lid after all.

He felt a strange buoyancy. Not joy exactly, but a sense that for a few weeks at least, the rhythm would change. No school bell. No registers. A different kind of timetable, made up of visits and phone calls and whatever small rituals they could still manage.

At home, the boxes of decorations had already made their way from the attic to the sitting room. Joan sat on the couch, a blanket over her legs, one of the boxes open beside her. The place smelled of dust and old paper and the faint citrus of the cleaning spray she'd insisted on using yesterday in a burst of energy.

'You've started without me,' he said, shrugging off his coat.

He looked at the array on the carpet: tangled fairy lights, a three-legged Rudolph whose fourth leg had gone missing years ago, a nativity scene missing one of the kings.

'The survivors,' he said.

'The chosen,' she corrected.

He sat cross-legged on the floor, picking up the fairy lights and beginning the familiar process of trying to detangle them without losing his temper or his religion.

'How was the assembly?' she asked.

'The same,' he said. 'Different faces, same yawns. I traumatised them by mentioning mortality.'

'Excellent,' she said. 'Consider it your small contribution to their character building.'

He held the coil of lights up. 'Will we even bother with these?' he asked. 'Half of them will be gone. We'll have a dark patch in the middle of the tree like last year.'

'We'll use the good ones for the front,' she said. 'And the dying ones at the back. Like a parish choir.'

He laughed.

They worked slowly. He tested bulbs, she directed placements from the couch. The tree itself – a modest artificial one, bought the year he'd finally given up on dragging a real tree home on the roof of the car – stood in the corner, a little hunched, its branches needing to be coaxed into shape.

As he fitted the bottom section into the stand, he felt the now-familiar pull in his lower back. A flash of sharpness, then the dull ache.

'Go easy,' Joan said, watching his face.

'I am,' he said. 'This thing weighs less than your handbag.'

'That's because my handbag contains everything you own,' she replied. 'Including most of your dignity.'

He straightened carefully, rolled his shoulders.

'Are you all right for the carol service?' he asked, changing the subject.

He meant the town service on the Sunday evening – the ecumenical effort in the church where the choirs from all three denominations squeezed themselves into a single programme.

It was one of those events that could be grim or unexpectedly lovely, depending on the year.

She considered. 'If I pace myself,' she said. 'And if we sit at the back. And if you don't make me stand up for too many verses.'

'I can arrange chairs like an old man,' he said. 'Your throne awaits.'

They hung the first few decorations together, their movements slowed by commentary and pauses.

'Do you remember where we got this one?' Joan asked, holding up a small wooden angel with one wing chipped.

'Galway,' he said. 'The Christmas market. You insisted on haggling.'

'I did not,' she said. 'I simply asked if that was their best price.'

'That's haggling,' he said.

'That's survival,' she replied.

He watched her fingers on the angel. They were thinner than they used to be, the veins more pronounced. The chemo had left her nails ridged, the skin dry. But her touch was still delicate, careful with small things.

After an hour, the tree looked finished enough to pass. They stepped back – he literally, she figuratively – and appraised it.

'It's grand,' Joan said.

'High praise,' he replied.

'It's not what it was,' she added, 'but neither are we. We'll call that even.'

On Saturday evening, he drove his mother to the carol service.

The sky was already dark at half four, the street lights casting orange pools on the wet road. His mother was waiting in the hall when he arrived, coat on, scarf wrapped too tightly around her neck, hat perched at an angle that suggested haste.

'You're early,' she said, checking her watch.

'You're ready,' he replied. 'That's a dangerous combination.'

She sniffed and grabbed her handbag from the sideboard. 'I'm not missing my carols for anyone,' she said. 'They'll only do the same ones as every year, and I'll give out, but sure it's not Christmas without giving out.'

In the car, she held her hymn book on her lap, the edges worn soft from years of being taken out and put away.

'Will Joan be there?' she asked.

'If she's up to it,' he said. 'She said she'd see how she was after her nap.'

His mother pursed her lips. 'She's very good,' she said. 'The way she keeps at the jokes. I don't know I would have it in me.'

'She has days,' he said. 'Same as the rest of us.'

'Yes, I suppose you are right.' His mother sighed.

'Have you made your mind up about coming to us for Christmas Day?' Ciarán asked as he steered the car.

'Well, yes, of course, if Joan doesn't mind.'

'We will both be delighted to have you with us,' Ciarán said as he gave his mother a reassuring tap on her shoulder.

'Thank you, son,' his mother said with a teary-eyed smile.

At the church, the car park was already half full. People made their careful way up the steps, collars up against the cold, breath clouding. The stained glass in the windows glowed from the light inside.

He helped his mother out of the car, offered his arm for the steps. She took it, not quite heavily, but more firmly than she would have a year ago.

Inside, the air was warm and smelled of candle wax, perfume, damp wool. The Christmas crib had been set up to the side of the altar, the baby still missing, waiting for its official entrance. The altar itself was still bare of full decoration, a wreath and a few red candles hinting at what was to come.

They found seats halfway down, on the aisle. The church slowly filled around them: neighbours, school parents, people he hadn't seen since the funeral nodding awkwardly from a distance.

Joan slipped in just before it started, a little flushed from the effort of getting there, scarf wrapped around her neck, hair tucked under a woollen hat. Ciarán had tried to convince her that he would drive her to the church and bring her along with his mother. However, Joan being her usual headstrong self she had insisted it was only a short walk and she needed to get some fresh air.

'You made it,' he whispered, relief stronger than he'd expected.

'On a wing and a prayer,' she whispered back. 'Mostly the wing. How's your mother?'

'I'm here,' his mother whispered across him. 'You can talk to me, you know. I'm not in the Belfast confessional.'

They smiled at each other, then looked toward the altar as the organist began the first slow notes of 'Once in Royal David's City'.

The service had its own ritualised shape. One carol, one reading. Another carol, another reading. Local worthies stepping up to the ambo to proclaim the familiar words in unfamiliar voices. A nurse from the hospital. A man from the GAA. A girl from the secondary school, her voice trembling at first and then steadying as she found the rhythm.

Ciarán let the words flow over him. He'd never been particularly religious, not in the way his parents' generation had been. But something in the cadence of the carols, the old phrases, the communal breathing in and out, tugged at a part of him that had nothing to do with belief and everything to do with belonging.

The hopes and fears of all the years are met in thee tonight.

He glanced at Joan on that line. Her eyes were closed, her lips moving around the words. His mother's voice, thin now but still true, wove under the rest of the congregation, finding harmonies where none were written.

Between carols, his gaze wandered around the church. The memorial plaques on the walls. The statues. The familiar faces aged another year. His father's absence was almost a presence of its own; there were certain spots where he should have been, standing with his cap in his hands, or walking up for communion, or sitting in the car afterwards complaining about the length of the sermon.

During 'O Little Town of Bethlehem', he felt a sudden sharp pain shoot from his lower back down into his groin. It was so quick and fierce that he had to grip the pew in front of him.

'Are you all right?' Joan whispered, catching the movement.

'Just a twinge,' he whispered back, the word too small for the feeling. 'I'm grand.'

He breathed through it, the pain receding into its usual dullness. He could feel his mother's gaze on him, but when he glanced at her she was looking straight ahead, her lips moving steadily on the words.

Afterwards, in the porch, there were the usual small shufflings of social obligation. People shook hands, wished each other a happy Christmas, smiled with varying degrees of sincerity.

'How are you keeping at all, Ciarán?' asked Mrs Farrell, who had taught him in primary school and now seemed to know every bit of news that passed through the parish.

'Ah, you know yourself,' he said. 'One day at a time.'

'And herself?' Mrs Farrell nodded toward Joan, who was talking to a woman from her book club. 'She's very brave, God love her. I light a candle every morning.'

'She'd appreciate that,' he said. 'You don't have to call her brave to her face. She hates it.'

'It's hard to know what to say,' Mrs Farrell admitted. 'You don't want to say the wrong thing. You don't want to say nothing. We're very bad at it in this country. We talk around everything.'

'We're getting better,' he said. 'Slowly. The hospice woman came to the house the other day. She said sometimes the kindest thing is to say, "This is awful, isn't it?" and leave it at that.'

Mrs Farrell considered this. 'She's not wrong,' she said. 'I'll try that next time my Larry starts talking about the government.'

He laughed. They moved on.

His mother stood near the door, talking to a neighbour, her hymn book clutched like a passport. When he came up behind her, he heard the tail end of the conversation.

'... well able for it,' she was saying. 'You'd never know, looking at him, only that he's a bit pale. But sure he was always a grey child. Came out looking worried.'

The neighbour, a woman with chronic curiosity and no malice, patted her arm. 'He's a good lad,' she said. 'He'll mind you. And she'll mind him. And we'll all mind each other. That's all we can do.'

On the way back to the car, his mother linked his arm again.

'That was nice,' she said. 'Not as good as when Father Larkin was here. He knew how to sing. But nice.'

'High praise,' he said. 'Your standards are impossible.'

'At my age,' she said, 'you're allowed to be fussy.'

He helped her into the passenger seat, closed the door carefully.

As he walked around to his side, he saw Joan a few cars away, talking to a woman with a pram. The woman leaned in, showing her the baby. Joan bent, smiling, her hand reaching out to touch the tiny foot. Her face in that moment – soft, open, full of something he couldn't name – made his chest ache in a way that had nothing to do with any physical symptom. The fact that they were never fortunate enough to have children cut deep at moments like these.

On the drive back up the hill to her house, his mother hummed bits of the carols under her breath. It was slightly off-key, but he recognised each fragment.

'Will you be lighting the candle?' he asked, as they turned in to the lane.

'Of course,' she said. 'Same as always. You'll have yours in the window?'

He nodded. 'Joan has the good one ready,' he said. 'We even cleaned the sill.'

His mother sniffed approvingly. 'Your father would be glad of that,' she said. 'He hated a dirty window.'

The candle in the window had always been a quiet, unquestioned ritual. A single candle on Christmas Eve, lit at dusk, left burning till midnight. A sign for the Holy Family, his mother had said when he was small. A sign for people coming home, she'd added when he was older: emigrants, lost souls, anyone who needed a bit of light.

Now, the thought of it took on another layer. A light for the living and the dying. For those waiting on letters from hospitals. For those who had been reduced to names on plaques and prayers.

'I'll call down tomorrow,' he said, as she gathered her bag

and hymn book from the footwell. 'We'll get your house ready for the big day.'

'You'll have enough to be doing in your own house,' she said. 'Anyway, there'll be no "big day" this year. Not without your father.' She shifted, the words making her face harden for a moment.

'There'll be some kind of day,' he said. 'We'll get through it. We always do.'

She looked at him, her eyes suddenly sharp. 'You're very good at the "getting through it" talk,' she said. 'Where did you learn that?'

'Teaching,' he said. 'It's all I have between me and a nervous breakdown in front of the Leaving Certs.'

She laughed, but when she opened the car door, she held on to it a moment longer than usual, as if steadying herself.

'Mind yourselves,' she said. 'Both of you. And tell Joan I liked her hat.'

'I will,' he said.

He watched her walk up the path, the porch light coming on as she opened the door. The house looked the same as it always had at this time of year. And yet.

At home, the tree lights were on, the room bathed in their gentle, uneven glow. Joan had taken off her hat, her hair flattened, the fatigue of the outing beginning to show now that the adrenalin of getting there and back had gone.

At some point, his hand found hers on the cushion between them. Their fingers tangled, the contact almost unconscious.

They sat like that for a while, the television on in the background showing something neither of them were watching. Outside, the wind got up, rattling the branches of the trees at the back. The window reflected their shapes back at them, ghosted by the lights of the tree.

‘Do you ever think about next Christmas?’ Joan asked suddenly, her voice so quiet he almost missed it.

He hesitated. The question had been crouching somewhere behind them all evening, but he hadn’t expected it to emerge so baldly.

‘I try not to,’ he said, eventually. ‘Not in any definite way. It’s like staring at the sun. You can’t do it for long without doing yourself harm.’

She nodded. ‘Me neither,’ she said. ‘But it keeps poking at me. The thought that this is the last time for certain things. The last carol service. The last time I’ll see the tree in that corner. The last time I’ll buy too many selection boxes and regret it.’

He swallowed. ‘You don’t know that,’ he said, the reflex answer.

She tilted her head, not unkindly. ‘We both know the odds,’ she said. ‘I don’t need you to soft-focus them. I’m not asking for reassurance. I’m just … saying it aloud. Naming it. So it doesn’t sneak up on me.’

He looked at her, the curve of her cheek, the way the light from the tree picked out the hollows at her temples.

‘I hate that you’re thinking like that,’ he said. ‘I hate that these are the questions in your head.’

‘I hate that yours are about Sligo and biopsies and percentages,’ she said. ‘But here we are.’

They sat with that for a moment, letting the discomfort lie between them without covering it.

‘Maybe,’ he said slowly, ‘instead of thinking “last”, we think “this one”. This tree. This candle. This carol service. This year. And we squeeze it.’

She smiled, a little crookedly. ‘Trust a teacher to rephrase the homework,’ she said.

‘It’s all I know,’ he replied.

'All right,' she said. '"This one", then. We'll give this one welly.'

They sat in silence for a while longer, the room gently breathing around them.

Later, before bed, he stood for a moment at the front window, looking out at their cul-de-sac. Lights glowed in other windows. He could see the vague shape of a Christmas tree in the house opposite, the silhouette of someone moving in the kitchen next door.

In two nights, they would put the candle in the window, same as his mother, same as half the town. A small stick of light against the dark.

He thought of his father's hand, once, guiding his small one to the matchbox. *Mind your fingers,* he'd said. *The flame will catch you if you're not careful.*

Now, the flame was elsewhere. In blood tests and scans and appointments. In conversations with hospice nurses and sisters who came with notebooks. In the quiet bravery of a woman who could joke about crosswords and death in the same breath.

He turned off the tree lights, the room dipping into shadow, then followed Joan up the stairs, his back protesting each step. In the bedroom, the air was cooler. He could hear the faint hum of the heating pipes, the occasional gust against the window.

As he lay down, careful with his back, Joan turned toward him.

'Read me your waiting-room poem tomorrow,' she murmured, already half asleep.

'It's not finished,' he said.

'Neither are we,' she replied.

He lay awake for a while after her breathing had settled, the words of half-remembered carols drifting through his mind.

Yet in thy dark streets shineth
The everlasting light …

He didn't know about everlasting. But he knew about the small, temporal ones: candles, fairy lights, hospital-corridor fluorescents, street lamps on wet tarmac. The way they held back the dark, not entirely, but enough to make faces visible.

Enough to see each other by, for another night.

Chapter Ten

The Candle in the Window

Christmas Eve arrived the way most big days did in that house now – quietly, without fanfare, slipping into the spaces between medication times and the morning news.

Ciarán woke to the sound of the bin lorry grinding its way up the estate road, the familiar hydraulic hiss and clank oddly comforting. Pale winter light seeped around the edge of the curtains. Beside him, Joan was awake, propped on one elbow, her hair flattened into an improbable peak on one side.

'You were talking in your sleep,' she said.

'Was I?' His voice came out hoarse. 'Who was I annoying this time?'

'You were giving out about footnotes,' she said. 'Very passionately. Something about "If you won't reference properly you don't deserve a Leaving Cert".'

He groaned and pulled a pillow over his face. 'That sounds like me,' he admitted. 'I'm sorry you have to live with this level of glamour.'

She lay back, the pillow creasing under her head. 'It was almost soothing,' she said. 'Better than you shouting "De Valera wasn't at the talks" at three in the morning.'

He shifted carefully, feeling the now-familiar ache in his back stretch and complain.

'Christmas Eve,' she said, staring at the ceiling. 'We made it.'

'For certain values of "made it",' he said. 'But yes. We did.'

There was a small pause.

'And how are you in yourself, Mr Devlin?' she asked, slipping into the mock-formal tone she used when she was trying to get him to tell the truth.

He thought about it.

'Like someone who has an exam in a month and hasn't started revising,' he said. 'Pretending it's still the mid-term. Slightly sick. Slightly relieved. Slightly hungover from dread.'

'Accurate,' she said. 'On the plus side, you're very prepared for similes.'

'That's my only transferable skill,' he replied.

He swung his legs out of the bed and sat for a moment, waiting for the vertigo that sometimes came with standing too fast. When the room stayed mostly in the right place, he got up.

In the kitchen, the early news grumbled from the radio – travel updates, last-minute shopping mania, an item about hospital overcrowding, the words *trolley crisis* now as much a part of the seasonal vocabulary as *stocking filler*.

He turned it down and put the kettle on.

On the table, Joan's notebook lay open, a short list written in her compact hand:

Bread (decent)
Cream
Cranberry sauce (if you insist)
Fresh veg – carrots/parsnips/sprouts
Batteries for lights
Candle for window (thick, reliable, no-nonsense)

When he brought her tea, she was sitting up in bed, glasses on, flicking through channels with the remote even though the sound was muted.

'Shopping list,' he said, handing her the notebook.

'Don't go mad,' she said. 'It's only the three of us for Christmas Day.'

'I'll get enough so we can pretend we're entertaining hundreds and then eat leftovers till New Year,' he said. 'Tradition is tradition.'

Town was madness.

Cars nudged too close to each other, parking in places that weren't really spaces. People in padded jackets walked faster than they usually did, shoulders hunched, expressions set in that particular festive grimness that came with last-minute errands.

He found a spot down near the river and walked up, the wind cutting at his ears. The decorations looked better now, in the winter light, than they had in the flat greys of earlier weeks. Shop windows were crowded with displays – naïve, hopeful, a bit desperate.

Inside Kelly's supermarket, the heat hit him like a damp blanket. Christmas songs played just low enough to be ignored until an especially tinny note caught the ear. The smell of oranges, ham and something sugary hung in the air.

He moved through the aisles slowly, taking the list item by item. Bread (the decent kind). Cream. Vegetables. Batteries. He remembered, at the last minute, the cranberry sauce 'if you insist' and put a jar in the basket just to annoy Joan.

At the candle shelf, he stood and considered. There were red ones in gaudy shapes, scented ones promising cinnamon or pine, small tealights in plastic cups. He reached for a plain, thick, white candle in a glass holder. Reliable. No-nonsense. It looked like it would burn straight and steady.

'Good choice,' said a voice beside him.

He turned. A woman in her fifties stood there, a basket on her arm. She wore a coat he vaguely recognised from funerals.

'You always want the ones in the glass,' she went on. 'Less mess on the sill. And they don't fall over if the cat gets ideas.'

'Noted,' he said. He couldn't remember her name, but he remembered her son from school – a quiet lad, good with numbers, bad with eye contact.

'How are you keeping at all, Ciarán?' she asked. 'We were sorry to hear about Sean. And your wife … I see her name on the intentions nearly every Sunday.'

'We're … managing,' he said. 'She's tired. But still giving out about the programmes, so she's not gone yet.'

The woman smiled. 'That's half the battle,' she said. 'My sister is up there too. The chemo. She says the worst thing is people pretending it's grand. I'll not do that. It's awful. But the nurses are saints. And she likes the biscuits.'

He found himself relaxing, slightly. 'Our nurse is lovely and kind,' he said. 'She has a clipboard and the patience of Job.'

'Ah, you're lucky,' the woman said. 'We had a nurse called Mary. She terrorised the consultants and made them get their act together. You want a good nurse on your side.'

He smiled. 'You are right,' he said.

At the till, the girl scanned his things with early-acquired efficiency.

He put his card in, the small beep of approval oddly reassuring.

Outside again, the air felt sharper. He loaded the bags into the boot, feeling his back complain with each lift, and stood for a moment, breath clouding, looking up the street.

He could see the church spire, the crooked cross silhouetted against the sky. A few people bustled in and out of shops, hatted and scarved, their arms heavy with bags. The town wasn't beautiful in any conventional sense. But it was his. Their lives were threaded through its small streets like wire through a hedge.

On an impulse, he pulled out his phone and rang his mother.

'Are you all right for the messages?' he asked.

'I have the turkey in since 1978,' she sniffed. 'It's grand. Just bring your own bits. And yourself. And her.'

'We'll be down later to peel,' he said.

'I have the peeler,' she replied. 'You have the back. Don't be going mad.'

He smiled, still holding the phone to his ear after she'd hung up, listening to the faint crackle as if something else might come through.

Back at the house, Joan was at the kitchen table, a pencil in her hand, peering at a list.

'Santa's workshop?' he asked, putting the bags on the counter.

'I'm delegating,' she said. 'Trying to decide which jobs are actually important and which are just habit. There is, apparently, a difference.'

'Shocking,' he said. 'My whole personality is built on habit.'

She began unpacking slowly, examining each item as if it were a specimen. When she pulled out the cranberry sauce, her eyebrows rose.

'You insisted,' he said.

'I said *if* you insist,' she replied. 'That's not the same.'

'It's in the conditional,' he agreed. 'We're beyond grammar now.'

She picked up the candle, turned it in her hand.

'That's a good one,' she said. 'Your mother will approve. No fragrance. No-nonsense. No glitter.'

'We're a no-glitter household,' he said. 'Medical reasons.'

The phone rang just after noon, while the kettle was coming to the boil. Ciarán looked at the screen for a long second before answering.

'Hello?'

There was a pause, a faint echo on the line. 'Ciarán. It's … it's Peter.'

Another pause, both of them adjusting to the sound of a voice that still knew their names.

'Happy Christmas,' Peter said, too brightly, then corrected himself. 'Or – well. You know.'

'Yes,' Ciarán said. 'Happy Christmas.'

'How are things there?' Peter asked. 'Cold, I suppose.'

'Wet,' Ciarán said. 'Same as ever.'

They sat with that. Somewhere in the background Ciarán could hear gulls, traffic, a life continuing at a different pitch.

'I was thinking of him this morning,' Peter said at last. 'Dad. I kept seeing him out in the yard. That old jacket. Do you remember it? The one with the torn cuff.'

'I remember,' Ciarán said.

'I should have—' Peter began, then stopped. 'I was sorry I couldn't—' He stopped again, the words stumbling over themselves awkwardly. 'You did right by him.'

Ciarán watched steam rise from the kettle and fade into nothing. 'We managed,' he said.

'And Mam?' Peter asked. 'How is she holding up?'

'Some days better than others,' Ciarán said. 'She doesn't like the nights.'

'No,' Peter said quietly. 'She was always worse at night.'

Ciarán said nothing. He wondered if Peter realised he'd said *was*.

'And Joan?' Peter went on, more carefully now. 'How is she?'

'She's tired,' Ciarán said. 'But she's still herself.'

'That's good,' Peter said. 'She always was the strong one.'

There was relief in his voice, and something like gratitude, as if Ciarán were minding more than he'd been asked to.

'I'll come home one of these days,' Peter said, not quite promising. 'When things settle.'

'Of course,' Ciarán said.

They spoke a little longer – about weather, about nothing – until the conversation thinned and began to fray. When they said goodbye, it was gentle, almost tender.

Afterward, Ciarán stood alone in the kitchen with the kettle cooling beside him, thinking how strange it was that a voice could travel halfway around the world and still stop short of what mattered.

After lunch, he loaded the bags for his mother's into the car: potatoes, carrots, a portion of sliced ham he'd cooked the night before, a box of mince pies. The candle for their own window he left on the hall table, where they wouldn't forget it later.

Joan walked him to the door.

'Tell her I said I'll ring after *It's a Wonderful Life*,' she said. 'We can compare traumatic childhoods.'

He kissed her, quick, the hallway cold around them.

'Take it easy,' he said. 'If anyone calls, pretend I'm making you work.'

'I'll tell them you're up the chimney,' she replied.

His mother's kitchen smelled like every Christmas of his childhood at once: roasting ham, the sharp steam of potatoes on the boil, an undernote of washing powder from the clothes horse in the corner.

She had the radio on to some station playing a muddle of hymns and carols and bland pop. The table was already half covered with bowls and utensils, her system impenetrable to outsiders.

'You're late,' she said, though he was ten minutes early.

'I brought reinforcements,' he replied, holding up the bag of potatoes as if they were munitions.

He took his place at the sink, the peeler familiar in his hand. The rhythm of slicing skin from flesh, dropping the peeled potatoes into the bowl of cold water, soothed something in him. It was a job that required just enough attention to distract without exhausting.

His mother fussed with the ham, basting, muttering.

'Did you get your candle?' she asked, without turning around.

'I did,' he said. 'A good one. Glass case.'

She nodded, satisfied. 'Your father always insisted on the beeswax ones,' she said. 'As if God was up there sniffing, saying "That's not proper candle I smell."'

'He was picky,' Ciarán said. 'For a man who smoked in the shed.'

She sniffed, half a laugh, half a sound of grief.

They worked in parallel for a while, the silence between them comfortable enough. Outside, he could hear the wind picking up, a rattle at the kitchen window.

'Did you ever get word from Sligo?' she asked suddenly, her tone light but not casual.

He rinsed a potato under the tap, buying himself a second.

'Letter came Thursday,' he said. 'End of January. Twenty-sixth.'

She put the roasting pan down with a clatter. 'That's ages away,' she said. 'You'd be dead twice by then.'

'I intend to disappoint them,' he said.

'What did he say?' she persisted. 'Your man. O'Malley. You gave me the half-story the last time. I'm not an eejit.'

He wiped a hand on the tea towel, turned to face her.

'He said the PSA is up,' he said. 'He said it could be a few things. One of them is the thing we don't say at the dinner table. He wants the experts to look. That's where we are.'

She watched him, eyes sharp, mouth pressed in.

'And how are you?' she asked. 'Not your bladder. You.'

He hesitated. 'I don't know yet,' he said. 'Somewhere between "I'll be fine" and "this is it now". Depends on the weather. And the time of day.'

She nodded slowly, as if this answer met some internal standard.

'You should have told me,' she said.

'I did,' he said. 'Just not … all at once.'

She wiped her hands on her apron, a habitual, nervous gesture.

'When your father went in for his heart,' she said, 'the first time, he didn't tell his own mother. "Sure what good would it do her," he said. "She'll only worry." And she found out off a neighbour. I never forgave him for that. Worry or no worry, she was entitled to the truth.'

He looked down at the potato in his hand, the skin curling under the blade.

'I didn't want to be another thing on your plate,' he said. 'You have enough.'

'You are not a thing,' she said sharply. 'You're my son. I have room.'

He swallowed. 'All right,' he said quietly. 'I'm … scared,

Mam. There you have it. For myself. For Joan. For you. For the whole bloody set-up. Happy Christmas.'

She stared at him for a moment, then stepped away from the oven and came to where he stood at the sink. She put her hand on his upper arm, fingers digging in more firmly than he'd have thought she could.

'We'll deal with it,' she said simply. 'Whatever it is. Same as everything else. One thing at a time. That's all there is. Don't be burying it inside you. You'll rot.'

He laughed weakly, tears pricking unexpectedly.

'That's an image,' he said.

'I'm full of them,' she said. 'I just don't put them in books like yourself.'

They stood like that for a second: his hands damp from the potatoes, her palm a small, fierce weight.

'Now finish them,' she said briskly, stepping back. 'We'll have half the parish in if we're not ready by the Angelus.'

He stayed for an hour, long enough to peel, to taste-test the ham, to check the back door lock twice and the immersion once.

On the drive back, the light was draining out of the sky in that early, decisive way of December. The clouds were low, tinged with a faint bruised purple. He could see already the vague promise of windows that would soon be lit.

At home, the house was warm. The smell of something sweet – Joan's last reserves of energy spent on a tray of shortbread – hung in the air.

She was on the couch, feet up, blanket tucked, watching an old film with the sound low and the subtitles on. A black-and-white man in a hat gestured dramatically at another black-and-white man in a different hat.

'How's the ham?' she asked.

'It's already in heaven,' he said. 'Mam's after testing it twenty times "to be sure".'

'She's not wrong,' Joan said. 'It's an important responsibility.'

He sat beside her, the day's efforts settling into his muscles. The radiator hummed. Outside, the wind made a low, continuous noise somewhere between a sigh and a growl.

'Will you manage the candle?' she asked, nodding toward the hall.

'I'll manage,' he said.

They waited until it was properly dusk, the street lights fully on, the sky a deep, even blue. Then he took the candle from the hall table, the box of matches from the drawer, and they went to the window together. The sill had been cleared already, wiped down, an old saucer placed as a precaution under the glass.

'Do you want to do it?' he asked.

'You do it,' she said. 'You're the one with the steady hand.'

He struck the match. The sulphur smell rose up, instant, familiar. For a second, the flame was small and wild, wanting everything. He held it to the wick. The candle caught, flared, then settled into a steady burn.

They stood in silence for a moment, watching it.

'Who's it for?' she asked, after a while. 'This year.'

They'd always joked, before, about who the candle was really meant for – long-lost relatives, emigrant neighbours, saints, strangers on the road.

He considered.

'My father. Anyone driving home in the dark. Anyone who's … between places.'

'And you,' she said quietly. 'And me.'

'And us,' he agreed.

He set the candle carefully on the saucer, making sure it

was far enough from the curtains, and stepped back. From outside, he knew, the effect would be simple: a small, steady light in a terrace of similar ones, a chain of tiny flames saying the same vague, determined thing – *here, here, here*.

They sat on the couch afterwards, the room lit only by the tree and the candle's gentle glow from the hall.

'This is surprisingly atmospheric for a pair of eejits from Leitrim,' Joan said.

'We're secretly very aesthetic,' he replied.

Her breathing had a slight hitch in it tonight, a faint effort. He could hear it now that the house was quiet – a soft catch on some inhales, as if the air were slightly thicker.

'You all right?' he asked softly.

'Just tired,' she said. 'It's been a long week of pretending to be less sick than I am.'

He glanced at the coffee table, where the hospice leaflets still sat in a neat pile, the top one folded back to a section on breathlessness.

'Do you want to ring Deirdre?' he asked.

'Not yet,' she said. 'Let her have her Christmas Eve off. She'll have enough of us in January.' She shifted a little, testing her lungs. 'If it gets worse, I'll say.'

The trust between them in that moment felt like something tangible, a rope stretched between two uncertain points.

He put an arm around her shoulders, careful, and she let her head rest against him. They watched James Stewart run down the street, shouting about Zuzu's petals, the subtitles lagging just slightly behind.

'Do you ever regret not going off?' she asked suddenly. 'Really going off to Australia or America.'

He thought of it – the half-serious conversations in smoky flats, the travel brochures left on the kitchen table, the way the words *working holiday visa* had once sounded like a spell.

'Sometimes,' he said. 'I wonder who I'd be if I'd done it. If I'd gone to some place where nobody knew me; taught history under a different sky. You?'

She considered. 'I regret things. I regret the places I didn't go to,' she said.

He felt the awareness that the roads ahead of them now were narrowing. The choices were fewer. The possibilities, once endless, had been reduced to a handful of likely paths, some of them short.

'I don't regret this,' he said, surprising himself with the certainty in his voice.

'This what?' she asked, eyes half on the screen, half on him.

'This house,' he said. 'This town. My mother talking to ghosts. The whole messy thing. I don't regret the life we actually had. Even if it wasn't the one I imagined when I was scribbling lyrics in the back of a warehouse.'

She was quiet for a moment. Then she turned her head slightly, her hair brushing his cheek.

'Good,' she said softly. 'Because I don't regret it either. Even the bad bits. Maybe especially the bad bits. They made the good bits sharper.'

He swallowed, his throat tight.

They smiled at the same time, their faces close, the candle's small flame reflected in both sets of eyes.

Later, after she'd gone up to bed – slowly, one hand on the banister, him just behind her in case her foot slipped – and after he'd checked twice that the candle was far enough from anything that could catch, he went into the small room and sat at his desk.

The notebook lay open where he'd left it days ago, the last

line of the waiting-room poem trailing off mid-sentence. He turned to a fresh page.

At the top, without thinking too much, he wrote *The Candle in the Window*.

He stared at the title for a long time, listening to the wind, the faint hum of a neighbour's television through the wall, the occasional distant pop of a firework someone had decided couldn't wait till midnight.

Then he began.

We put it there because our mothers did,
a small, stubborn flame on a wet sill,
glass collar catching drips,
match-sulphur sharp in the nose.

He paused, felt for the next line.

It's for the ones on bad roads and late shifts,
for the boy in London with cold hands,
for the woman upstairs counting tablets,
for the man in Sligo not yet seen.

He stopped, pen hovering. Too much, maybe. Too close to the bone. But the act of writing it, of putting the words *not yet seen* on the page, made the waiting feel fractionally less vague.

He crossed out *man* and wrote *file* above it, then rejected that, then left it as it was.

He wrote until the lines faltered, until his hand cramped and his back complained enough that he had to stand and stretch. The poem wasn't finished, but it existed in the world now as more than a vague shape in his head.

He closed the notebook gently, as if not to wake it.

Before he went up, he stood again at the hall window. Outside, the candle burned, steady, its small flame undisturbed by the drafts that sneaked under the door. Across the road, he could see another light in another window, and another beyond that. Little points of insistence in the dark.

He thought of his father, of the way the older man had always used his body without thinking – lifting engines, wrestling with tyres – until one day that heart, so taken for granted, had simply refused.

He thought of his own body now, asserting itself in new, unwelcome ways. Of Joan upstairs, her breathing audible even through the closed bedroom door when he listened hard enough.

He bent, checked the candle one last time, and turned off the hall light, leaving the small flame to do its work.

Upstairs, in the darkened room, Joan murmured as he got into bed.

'Did you blow it out?' she asked, not fully awake.

'Not yet,' he whispered. 'Not yet.'

He lay on his back, staring into the darkness. Beneath them, barely audible, the world turned, bringing January closer with each revolution.

But for that night, in that house, there was a candle in the window and a warm body beside him and a tree in the corner and a mother with ham in the oven and potatoes peeled, and that, he thought, would have to be enough.

For this one.

Chapter Eleven

The Gentle Hours of Christmas Day

Christmas morning arrived without ceremony.

There was no stampede on the stairs, no whispered conspiracies outside the bedroom door, no rustle of wrapping paper in the dawn. Instead there was the slow, familiar creak of the house coming awake – the heating clicking, the pipes shuddering faintly, the wind worrying the gutter.

When Ciarán opened his eyes, the light was already there: a pale, washed-out grey seeping around the curtains. Beside him, Joan lay on her back, her mouth slightly open, the thin line between her brows smoothed out in sleep. Her head was turned toward the window; the first light caught the fine hairs at her temple, making them almost silver.

For a few seconds he let himself lie very still and simply look at her. It struck him how many of their Christmas mornings together he had not done that. He had been too busy thinking about Mass, oven times and whether he'd remembered to charge the camera.

Now the time for those panics seemed to have passed, leaving a different kind of urgency in its wake – one that was quieter, denser and harder to outrun.

He eased himself out of bed. The stiffness in his back was worse in the mornings, a band of dull ache that made him move gingerly until the muscles loosened. He padded to the window and drew the curtain back two inches.

The estate lay under a cold, colourless sky. A thin sheen of frost silvered the car roofs and the tarmac. In the little green at the centre of the cul-de-sac, someone's plastic snowman leaned at an angle, its scarf stiff with last night's freeze. Here and there, lights glowed behind curtains – trees, flickering televisions, the steady square of kitchen windows where kettles would be boiling.

The candle in their own window had long since been blown out. Only a faint smudge of wax on the saucer marked where it had been.

Behind him, Joan stirred. 'Is it Christmas?' she murmured, voice rough.

'It is,' he said. 'By all available evidence.'

'We survived the night, so.' She yawned. 'Miracles never cease.'

He closed the curtain and came back to the bed, perching on its edge. 'Would you like your present now,' he said, 'or will we be modern and leave it till lunchtime?'

'Tea first,' she said. 'I can't handle joy on an empty stomach.'

In the kitchen, he put the kettle on and rooted in the cupboard for the good mugs – the ones with the chipped but beloved rims. On the counter, the plate of shortbread sat under a tea towel, the butter blooming slightly at the edges. He lifted the towel and took one, biting into it. It tasted like his childhood and like now: dense, crumbly, with that particular sweetness that came from real butter and care.

The radio was already on low, left there from the night before. A presenter with an overly cheerful voice was announcing mass times and traffic updates in the same tone.

Ciarán turned it down further until it was just a murmur, a background hum of other people's lives.

When he brought the tea in, Joan had shuffled up against the headboard, pillows propped behind her, her dressing gown wrapped tight around her shoulders. Her face was pale but her eyes were awake in that bright way they often were in the mornings before the tiredness descended properly.

'Merry Christmas,' he said, handing her the mug.

'And yourself,' she said. 'Did Santa bring you anything?'

'He brought me the gift of heightened medical awareness,' he replied. 'It's what all the boys are getting this year.'

She snorted softly. 'Lucky you.'

They drank their tea in relative silence, the comfortable kind that had grown between them over years of doing the small, ordinary things side by side.

After a while, she nodded toward his locker. 'Bottom drawer,' she said. 'The left-hand side.'

He opened it. On top of his socks and an old book of poems was a small package wrapped in the kind of paper only she would have chosen – brown with a hand-drawn pattern of stars in pen. The corners were neatly folded, the tape precise.

He sat back on the bed and unwrapped it carefully, saving the paper out of habit even as he knew there was no real practical reason to do so.

Inside was a small, hardback notebook. The cover was plain, a deep, unadorned blue. When he opened it, he saw that the pages were unlined, thick, slightly textured.

On the first page, in her careful, slightly tilted hand, she had written:

For the poems you haven't written yet.
Love, J.

He swallowed.

'You're supposed to say something clever now,' she said lightly, but he could see from the way her fingers gripped the mug that she wasn't as casual as her tone suggested.

'Give me a minute,' he said. 'The cleverness takes time.'

He ran a thumb along the edge of the paper. It felt both new and familiar, like any blank space he'd ever tried to fill.

'I thought,' she went on, 'you could keep this one for … this bit. Not the past. Not your father and the lake and the field. Not the old stories. The now. The waiting room. The candle. The ham. The whole … business.'

He looked up at her.

'I don't know if there's a market for that,' he said, attempting levity.

'I don't care,' she said. 'Not everything is a market. Some things are just … record. So you don't have to carry it all in your head. So I don't vanish into some general blur of "my wife was sick that time".'

He flinched, the words landing with their intended force.

'You won't,' he said. 'You couldn't.'

'Maybe not for you,' she said. 'But for other people. For whoever comes after. For yourself, when your memory starts to do that thing where it sands down the edges. Write us down. Not because I'm special. But because we're … ordinary. And there's a kind of holiness in that too.'

He shook his head, half in protest, half in wonder. 'You're bossy,' he said.

'I have limited time to get my way,' she said. 'I'm making the most of it.'

He closed the notebook gently. 'Thank you,' he said. The words felt small, but they were all he had.

'Your turn,' she said, nodding toward his side of the wardrobe.

He went to the bottom, where he'd hidden her present under a folded jumper. The paper he'd used was old-fashioned shop wrapping, the kind you got from the hardware when they still sold toys at Christmas: thin, with a faint imprint of holly. His corners were less precise than hers, the tape a little wonky.

She opened it more quickly, the paper tearing with a small, satisfying sound.

Inside was a scarf. He'd agonised over it for an embarrassing amount of time in town last week, standing in the tiny wool shop while the owner hovered gently. In the end he'd chosen something simple: a deep green, the colour of the hills on a good day, soft to the touch, light but warm.

'Oh,' she said quietly, running her fingers along it. 'It's lovely.'

'Alpaca,' he said. 'Apparently. It convinced me by softness alone.'

She lifted it, shook it out, and wrapped it loosely around her neck. The colour made her eyes look greener, her skin less sallow.

'Now I can pretend I'm one of those elegant women who stride around continental cities in tasteful scarves,' she said.

'You always were,' he said. 'This just makes it obvious.'

She smiled, and for a moment the years fell away. He saw her as she had been when they first met: twenty-one, hair longer, face rounder, full of opinions and nervous laughter.

'Do you remember our first Christmas here?' she asked.

He did. They'd moved into the house that October, surrounded by boxes, the wallpaper still smelling faintly of other people. That first Christmas, they'd had a tree that shed pine needles like a dog with mange, a turkey that had taken twice as long to cook as the packet promised.

'I remember you crying over the gravy,' he said.

'That's because your mother was watching,' she said. 'And

everything I did was wrong. The potatoes were too soft. The turkey was too dry. The sprouts were too sprouty.'

'She's mellowed,' he said.

'She's older,' Joan replied. 'It's not the same thing.'

They looked at each other, and the shared memory sat between them, tender and sharp at once.

By late morning, the house had taken on that particular festive air even they couldn't entirely resist. The tree lights were on; the oven was humming. On the table, the posh cloth – kept for weddings, communions, and Christmas – lay smoothed and waiting. The plates Joan insisted on using, chipped but sentimental, were stacked at one end.

They worked in tandem, though the choreography had changed. Where once she would have been darting between sink and oven and fridge, now she sat at the table, a chopping board in front of her, peeling carrots slowly while he moved back and forth, checking timings, stirring sauces, lifting pots.

'Don't overdo the sprouts,' she said, as he hovered over the pan. 'They should still be vaguely vegetable, not punishment.'

'Yes, chef,' he said.

Her breath was a little shorter today. He could see it in the way she paused between tasks, the small effort it took to get up and walk to the fridge. The colour in her cheeks was bright, but it had a slightly feverish quality.

'You sure you're up to Mama Devlin?' he asked, as he basted the turkey breast.

'She's hardly the Spanish Inquisition,' Joan said. 'And she's coming to us for once. That's practically a sign of the end times. I'm not missing it.'

He'd been surprised when his mother had agreed to come up, even just for a few hours. Her reluctance to leave the house since his father's funeral had been almost physical, as if some tether held her to the furniture. In the end, the compromise had been that he would go down, pick her up, and bring her back after the main part of the day, before the evening cold settled in.

He checked his watch now.

'I'd better go,' he said. 'Or she'll think we've emigrated.'

Joan nodded, wiping her hands on the tea towel. 'Text me when you're on the way back,' she said. 'I'll hide all the evidence of my loose morals.'

He put on his coat, scarf, gloves. As he opened the door, she called after him.

'And Ciarán?'

He turned.

'Drive slowly,' she said. 'You're precious cargo now, remember.'

'You and your campaign,' he said. 'I'll be back in a bit.'

His mother was waiting in the hall when he got there, coat on, handbag clutched, hat slightly askew.

'You're late,' she said, though he was right on time.

'You said twelve,' he replied. 'It's twelve.'

'It's twelve by your watch,' she said. 'Which is never quite right.'

He helped her into the car, noticing how carefully she lowered herself into the seat, how she held her handbag on her lap like a shield.

As they drove, she kept up a steady commentary on the houses they passed.

'They have lights on the gutters. Waste of money. That one has the good crib. Real straw. Paula down there's son came home from Australia. I saw his car yesterday. He's parked across my view. I suppose I'll let him.'

He half listened, half let the rhythm of her voice carry him.

‘And how’s Joan this morning?’ she asked eventually.

‘Determined,’ he said. ‘Tired. Bossing me around. So, alive.’

His mother sniffed approvingly. ‘She was always good at bossing,’ she said. ‘In a nice way. Not like some.’

He pulled into their drive and went around to help her out. Inside, the house was warm and smelled of roasting meat and something sweet. The combination made his stomach growl.

Joan was in the kitchen, leaning on the counter for support, her new green scarf around her neck. When his mother walked in, she straightened, face brightening.

‘Happy Christmas, Mrs Devlin,’ she said. ‘Or do I get to call you Mary yet? It’s only been twenty-five years.’

His mother rolled her eyes. ‘You can call me what you like as long as the gravy is hot,’ she said, then stepped forward and kissed Joan’s cheek.

He watched the two women together and felt, as he often did, both gratitude and a kind of vertigo at the way his life had arranged itself around these particular people.

‘Sit down,’ Joan said. ‘We’ll have the dinner on the table in no time. Ciarán’s been very industrious. I’ve just been supervising and looking decorative.’

His mother settled herself at the table, removing her hat and carefully smoothing her hair. ‘You’re thin,’ she said bluntly to Joan. ‘But you have the colour in your face. That’s something.’

‘Blush is a great invention,’ Joan said. ‘Also the heating.’

They ate.

The ritual was familiar even if the cast had shrunk slightly. Turkey, ham, roast potatoes crisped almost to destruction, carrots and parsnips, sprouts that Joan had spared from boiling into submission. The plates looked indecently full.

His mother said grace, her voice steady over the words.

There was an extra pause before the final amen, a gap where, Ciarán suspected, his father's name now lived.

Conversation at first stayed in the safe channels: the food ('The ham is very good.' 'It's the same ham you bought, Mam.' 'Yes, but it's cooked right.'), the weather ('Might snow.' 'It won't.'), the neighbours ('Kathleen's back went again. She shouldn't be lifting that grandchild. He's like a sack of coal.').

At one point, his mother gestured with her fork toward the tree.

'I like the angel,' she said. 'The girl down the road made one from a toilet roll. Not the same. Yours has a bit of class.'

After the main course, when his mother insisted on bringing her own plate to the sink despite his protests, there was trifle and shortbread and tea strong enough to stand a spoon in.

Later, they moved to the sitting room, his mother on the armchair, Joan on the couch with a cushion at the small of her back, the tree lights casting a soft glow.

His mother began to fade around four o'clock. The lines around her mouth deepened; her responses grew shorter. The effort of being out, of performing the part of herself that people expected, had taken its toll.

'I'd better bring you back,' Ciarán said, when she declined another slice of cake – a sure sign she'd reached her limit.

'I suppose,' she said. 'Sure if I stay any longer, I'll turn into a piece of the furniture.'

At the door, she patted Joan's arm. 'You did well,' she said. 'Considering.'

'High praise,' Joan replied. 'We'll talk in the week. You can tell me how I should have improved on it.'

His mother's eyes, for once, softened without a trace of criticism. 'You're all I could ask for,' she said quietly. 'You both are.'

The words made Ciarán's chest ache.

He drove her back as the sky darkened again, the thin light disappearing almost apologetically. As they turned in to her lane, he saw other candles already lit in windows, small dots of fire.

'You'll light yours?' he asked, as he helped her out.

'Of course,' she said. 'Same as always. Leave the matches out for me. I'll not be burning the place down at this stage.'

He walked her to the door. Inside, the house smelled of ham and polish and a faint, lingering trace of his father's pipe tobacco that he suspected was more memory than reality.

'Ring me,' she said, as he stepped back. 'If … anything.'

'I will,' he said. 'You too.'

She nodded, then added, almost as an afterthought, 'And write your poems. Your father was very proud of them. He'd want you to keep at it.'

The mention of his father in that context, on that day, caught him off-guard.

'I will,' he said. 'I am.'

He drove back in the deepening dusk. The road between their houses, so familiar, had taken on a new texture for him in the last few months – a stretch of tarmac laden with worry and obligation and the faint, dark humour that kept him from pulling over and screaming some days.

Tonight, the hedges on either side were edged with frost. The occasional house glowed, small tableaux visible for a second and then gone: a figure bending over a table, a tree in a corner, a child jumping on a couch.

When he pulled into their own drive, he could see the flicker of the candle in the window already lit. A small relief went through him at the sight. He hadn't realised he'd been holding that particular tension until it eased.

Inside, the house was quieter. The radio was off; the

television dark. The only light came from the tree and the candle, their glows overlapping in the hall.

Joan was on the couch, her eyes closed, the blanket pulled up to her chin. For a second, panic jumped in him – an instinctive leap toward the worst.

Then she opened one eye. 'You're back,' she said.

'I am,' he said, letting out a breath. 'How's the star performer?'

'Rating: four out of ten,' she said. 'Would not book for a full run. I had to lie down. The world started spinning a bit.'

He sat on the edge of the couch, careful. 'Breath?'

'Short,' she said. 'But manageable. I did the exercises Deirdre showed me. In through the nose, out like you're blowing out a candle without moving it. Very zen.'

He watched her chest rise and fall, the movement more shallow than he liked.

'Do we need to ring her?' he asked.

'Not yet,' she said. 'If I start sounding like your Uncle Tom's tractor, we'll consider it.'

He wanted to argue, to insist, but exhaustion hung off her like a second skin. He didn't have it in him to pick a fight she would only lose.

'All right,' he said. 'But if it's worse later, we ring. Non-negotiable.'

She closed her eyes again. 'Bossy,' she murmured.

'Occupational hazard,' he replied.

He sat there for a while, listening to her breathing, watching the candle move slightly in its glass as the draught from under the door caught it. The flame leaned, straightened, leaned again, but did not go out.

Christmas evening had settled into its routine, careful, quiet, and that old familiar cloud floated temporarily over him.

It wasn't grief exactly. The fact that they had no children. Not any more. Grief had sharp edges at the start, a sense of injury. This was something smoother, worn down by repetition. Over time, he and Joan had learned how to live around the absence, the way you learn the dark patches on a familiar road. They had stopped talking about it, not because it didn't matter, but because it had come to belong to them in a private, wordless way. Other lives had gone on: nieces and neighbours' children, classmates he taught now grown with families of their own. They had watched all of it without bitterness. Most days, he thought, they had done well.

But Christmas was different. Christmas insisted on its own arithmetic. Empty chairs became louder. Silence acquired a shape. He noticed it in the small things – the absence of wrapping paper on the floor, the lack of interruption, the way the morning passed without urgency. He could never decide whether it was the thought of what had never been, or the knowledge of what now never would be, that pressed hardest.

He thought of the years when hope had still felt reasonable, when every December carried a quiet expectation he pretended not to have. He remembered how gently that hope had withdrawn, without drama, leaving behind a space that eventually learned to stay still. Most of the time, he had grown used to it. He and Joan had built a life that worked, careful and companionable, shaped by what they could manage rather than what they had lost.

Still, on Christmas Day, the absence returned with its old clarity. It sat between him and the window, between the hours of the day, between him and the man he might once have been. He did not dwell on it for long – he had learned better than that – but he acknowledged it, the way you acknowledge a familiar ache.

Eventually he stood, stretched his back carefully, and went to the small room to fetch the notebook she'd given him.

Back on the couch, with her still dozing beside him, he opened it to the first page. He wrote the date in the corner. Under it, he let the day unspool in brief, uneven lines: the scarf, the ham, his mother's hand, the candle, Joan's breath catching on the bass notes.

There was no artistry to it, not yet. It was more list than poem. But as the words accumulated, he felt some of the weight shift from his chest to the page.

At one point, Joan stirred and opened her eyes.

'Are you writing?' she asked, voice thick with sleep.

'Trying,' he said.

'Good,' she whispered. 'Make us bigger than we are.'

He smiled. 'You're big enough,' he said.

'Don't contradict your dying wife,' she mumbled, and drifted off again.

He wrote a little more. Then he set the notebook aside and simply sat, the quiet of the house wrapping around him.

Outside, the world went on with its own noisy festivities – fireworks somewhere distant, a shout in the street, laughter from a house a few doors down. Inside, their own celebration was smaller, more fragile, stitched together from shortbread crumbs and new notebooks and the familiar click of an inhaler.

Later, when he blew out the candle before they went up to bed, the sudden absence of its light made the hall seem briefly, shockingly dark. He stood there in the thread of smoke, feeling for the banister, his other hand reaching automatically for Joan's.

Her fingers found his.

'This one wasn't so bad,' she said quietly, as they climbed.

'This Christmas?' he asked.

'This day,' she said. 'The day itself. For what it was.'

He thought of all the days before, all the ones to come, known and unknown.

'It was enough,' he said.

In the bedroom, as he lay awake longer than she did, he thought of the line she'd written in the front of the notebook: *For the poems you haven't written yet.*

He let the phrase settle in him like a small, steady flame.

There were tests ahead. Appointments. The long, white corridors of Sligo. There were decisions he didn't yet know how to make. There were days that would be brighter than this one and darker too.

Chapter Twelve

The Days Between

The days between Christmas and the New Year had always felt odd to Ciarán, like a corridor between rooms where you weren't entirely sure if you were meant to be standing or sitting.

This year, the feeling was stronger. Time seemed to move strangely – slow within the hours, quick across the days. He would look up from the kettle and realise an afternoon had gone; then, at three in the morning, every minute would drag like a bad class.

On St Stephen's Day, the town ground to a kind of halt. The supermarket stayed closed till two; the main street was quiet except for the odd car with fogged-up windows and the sound of a football thumping off the gable wall at the back of Dolan's.

He went for a walk that afternoon, leaving Joan dozing under her blanket on the couch with a book face down on her chest and the tree lights on. It was the first time in days he'd gone out purely for the sake of movement rather than errands.

The air had that raw, metallic taste of a winter day that never quite brightened. The sky was white and low; the fields beyond the estate were a patchwork of damp greens and longer grass left to seed, flattened now by rain and wind.

He walked down toward the river, hands shoved deep into his pockets, scarf tight around his neck. The path by the water was muddy in places, the gravel slick. A few other people were out – dog walkers mostly, shoulders hunched, faces set against the cold. They nodded the way country people did: a quick dip of the chin that acknowledged your existence without inviting conversation.

At the bend where the path narrowed and the trees leaned over, he stopped. The river moved with more conviction than the sky; the brown water carried bits of branches and leaves, the occasional bubble of foam.

He thought of his father then, as he often did when near moving water. The older man had always preferred rivers to lakes – *You can see where they're going,* he'd say, as if that were an argument in their favour.

Now Ciarán watched the current sliding past and thought: *You can see them moving, but you don't see where they end up.* They turned corners, joined other flows, disappeared under bridges.

He tried an old trick he'd used once with a class when trying to explain the idea of change over time. He chose a single leaf, caught in an eddy, and followed it with his eyes as it spiralled, then broke free and raced down the centre of the river. He managed to keep it for longer than he'd expected. It slid past a rock, past a floating bottle, past a pair of ducks who looked mildly offended at its speed.

Then something – a ripple, a shadow, a trick of light – made him blink, and when he refocused, the leaf was gone. It might have sunk. It might have been torn into pieces. It might have simply slipped out of his sightline, continuing another few yards before catching on something else.

He stood there another minute, letting the cold gnaw at his ears, then turned back up the path.

When he came in the back door, the warmth of the kitchen hit him in a wave. Joan was propped up on the couch, a cushion behind her, the green scarf loosely looped around her neck even indoors. The television was on low, some old film in black and white – but her eyes weren't on it. She had his new blue notebook in her hands, open on her lap.

'Caught you,' he said, shrugging out of his coat. 'That's private.'

'Is it?' she said. 'You didn't write "Dear Diary" at the top. That's the universal signal.'

He moved closer, his heart giving a small uncomfortable lurch. 'You shouldn't be rooting,' he said, though there was no real heat in it.

She held out the notebook, tapping the open page with a finger. 'You left it on the table,' she said. 'Like a man who secretly wants to be read.'

He sat beside her, scanning the lines she'd stopped at. It was the start of 'The Candle in the Window' – the parts he'd written on Christmas Eve.

We put it there because our mothers did,
a small, stubborn flame on a wet sill …

Her finger rested on the line he'd been unsure about.

…for the woman upstairs counting tablets,
for the man in Sligo not yet seen.

'It's good,' she said quietly. 'I like the "not yet seen". We're all not yet seen by someone, aren't we? Even ourselves.'

'It's clumsy,' he said automatically. 'I'll fix it.'

'Maybe,' she said. 'But don't fix the honesty out of it.'

He looked at her. 'You don't mind?' he asked. 'That you're in it. That this … is in it.'

'You'd be lying if it wasn't,' she said. 'And you're not good at lying. Your eye twitches.'

He laughed, though the sound came out thinner than he'd like.

'Read me the rest,' she said. 'From the start. You can skip the bits you hate.'

He took the notebook from her and cleared his throat, feeling more self-conscious in front of his wife in their own sitting room than he ever did in front of a class of thirty teenagers.

He read, stumbling once or twice, tempted to apologise for every line but resisting. He read the images he'd tried to catch: the match smell, the glass, his mother's porch, the boy in London with cold hands, the line about the ham in the oven that he already regretted.

When he finished, Joan's face was unreadable for a second, then softened.

'You're getting somewhere,' she said. 'With this … version of yourself. The one that doesn't flinch from what's actually happening.'

'Is that a compliment?' he asked.

'It's a warning,' she said. 'To keep going.'

He closed the notebook, feeling both exposed and oddly steadier. 'Yes, boss,' he said.

'Don't make me haunt you,' she replied.

Deirdre from the hospice came again two days later, in the limbo time when the bins were still overflowing in the estate and the recycling-centre car park looked like a scene from a documentary on modern consumption.

She arrived mid-morning, her navy fleece zipped up, her

clipboard under her arm, a small, wheeled bag trailing behind her like airline luggage. Her cheeks were pink from the cold; her breath still clouded as she stepped in.

'Happy in-between,' she said, shrugging off her coat. 'We've survived the onslaught. How are ye holding up?'

'We're in that strange phase where we're still eating leftovers and yet somehow there's nothing in the house,' Joan said. 'Metaphorically and literally.'

'We can put that in a leaflet,' Deirdre replied. 'Come here till I look at you.'

She set her bag down and pulled a small pulse oximeter from her pocket. Joan offered her index finger without protest, the small device clamping on like a tiny plastic crab.

They watched the numbers appear: heart rate, oxygen saturation.

'Ninety-two,' Deirdre said, frowning slightly but not alarmed. 'A bit lower than last time, but not panic stations. How's the breath feeling?'

'Like I'm walking uphill all the time,' Joan said. 'Even when I'm sitting. Short. Tight. It comes in little parcels instead of a full delivery.'

'Cough?'

'Dry,' Joan said. 'Occasionally productive if we're being fancy. No blood.'

Deirdre made a note. 'Any chest pain?'

'Only when my husband attempts to dance in the kitchen,' Joan said.

Deirdre smiled. 'We'll come back to that presently.'

They went through the usual checklist: pain, nausea, appetite, bowels. Some answers were reassuring, some less so. Deirdre listened to Joan's chest with her stethoscope, the cold disc making Joan flinch as she breathed in and out on command.

'How's the mood?' Deirdre asked, after the physical inventory had been taken.

'Depends on the day,' Joan said. 'Today's all right. Christmas Day was grand. St Stephen's I cried because the Quality Street tin was empty. It's a rich emotional landscape.'

Deirdre nodded. 'Totally legitimate grief response,' she said. 'We have a whole module on post-chocolate sadness.'

She turned to Ciarán.

'And yourself?' she asked. 'On a scale of one to ten, where's your head today?'

He hesitated. The temptation to say *Fine* was strong. He could feel Joan's gaze on him.

'Six,' he said, after a moment. 'Some hours four. Some hours eight. Three and a half when it's dark and the house is too quiet.'

She nodded. 'All right,' she said. 'So. The next few weeks. Let's talk about what's coming down the line. That way, when things happen, they're expected visitors, not intruders.'

Joan raised an eyebrow. 'Is there a difference?' she asked.

'There can be,' Deirdre said. 'Intruders throw you. Expected visitors still knock you back, but at least you've put the good cups out.'

She opened her clipboard to a fresh page.

'We're seeing some changes in your breathing,' she said. 'Nothing we haven't seen before, nothing we can't help with. The next sensible step would be to get you a portable oxygen concentrator. Something you can use when you're more breathless. Not all the time. Just to give you a lift when you need it.'

'Will I be trundling down the street with a tank like someone out of a film?' Joan asked.

'Not unless you're into that look,' Deirdre said. 'The new

ones are small enough. You can keep it by the chair. The neighbours will only think you've bought a fancy heater.'

Joan considered. 'If it means I can still get to the end of the garden without sounding like I've run a marathon, I'll take it,' she said.

'Good,' Deirdre said. 'I'll put the referral in today. It might take a week or two with the bank holidays and all that. In the meantime – keep using your inhaler. And when it's very bad, sit forward, arms on your knees, breaths in through the nose, out through a purse. Like we showed you. Calm and slow.'

She turned another page.

'We also need to talk about medication,' she said. 'We've been managing with paracetamol and the odd codeine. There will come a point where that's not enough. We can start a low-dose morphine now, very small. Not because you're at the end, but because it helps with both pain and breath. We don't wait till things are unbearable. We get ahead of them where we can. How do you feel about that?'

The word *morphine* made something twist in Ciarán's stomach. In his mind, it belonged to last days, to whispered instructions, to syringes in dimly lit rooms.

Joan seemed to hear his thought.

'Isn't that a bit … early?' she asked. 'I thought morphine was … you know.' She drew a finger across her throat.

'That's a Hollywood myth,' Deirdre said calmly. 'Morphine used well can give you more time feeling like yourself, not less. It's all about dose and monitoring. We're not talking about you floating off into the ether. We're talking half a millilitre here and there, to take the edge off. To let you walk to the kitchen without needing a half-hour recovery.'

Joan looked at him. 'You all right?' she asked.

He forced a nod. 'If it helps you breathe,' he said. 'If it

helps you be you for longer. I can get my head around the name. Eventually.'

She smiled at him. 'Look at us,' she said. 'Talking about drugs like sophisticated people.'

Deirdre reached into her bag and pulled out a small bottle and a syringe. She placed them on the table like part of a demonstration.

'I'll leave this with you,' she said. 'Clear instructions. We start with a tiny dose. If you don't need it, you don't take it. If you do, you try. You ring if you're worried. You don't sit in the dark panicking about every millilitre.'

She glanced between them, weighing how much more she could layer onto the day.

'There's one other thing,' she said. 'I won't force it, but it's good to start thinking. Advance care planning. What you want, what you don't. Where you'd prefer to be if things get rough. Hospital? Here? What kind of interventions you're up for. What you're not. It's not a contract with the devil. It's a set of preferences. It means that if there's a moment where decisions have to be made quickly, you've already said your piece.'

Joan was quiet, her fingers tracing the rim of her mug.

'I know what I don't want,' she said, after a moment. 'I don't want to be dragged into A&E at three in the morning, parked on a trolley under a fluorescent light, listening to drunk lads vomiting, waiting for a doctor to tell me what we all know.'

Deirdre nodded. 'We can put that in writing,' she said. 'We can put that on your file. "Avoid A&E if at all possible." It's a very popular line.'

'And I want to be here if I can,' Joan went on. 'In this house. In this stupid sitting room. Not because it's perfect. But because it's ours.'

'It's a good reason,' Deirdre said simply.

'What about me?' Ciarán heard himself ask. 'Where do I get to be in all this?'

Both women looked at him.

'You're wherever you need to be,' Deirdre said. 'Here, if that's safe for you. At your mother's some nights if she needs minding and you need a break. In the hospital beside her bed if it comes to that. None of this works if the carer collapses. That's the bit people forget.'

He thought of the Sligo letter, of his mother's warning, of his own back and bladder.

He thought of the river and the leaf he'd lost track of. Of the candle. Of Joan's gift to him, *For the poems you haven't written yet*.

'I'll try my best,' he said, though he wasn't sure how.

'That's all anyone can do,' Deirdre said. She stood, gathering her things. 'I'll be back next week. Sooner if you ring. Remember – no prizes for stoicism. Pain over four out of ten? You call. Breath less than a full sentence? You call.'

She smiled at both of them then, a smile that reached her eyes.

'You're doing well,' she said. 'I know it doesn't feel like it. But you are.'

After she left, the house felt both safer and more precarious, as if new scaffolding had been erected around a structure that was still slowly sinking.

On the table, the small bottle of morphine sat beside the salt cellar, innocuous-looking, the clear liquid catching the light.

Joan eyed it.

'It's very un-dramatic,' she said. 'I was expecting a bigger bottle. Or a skull and crossbones.'

'This is Ireland,' he said. 'All the drama goes into the funerals.'

She glanced at him, eyes glinting. 'Don't forget to write that down,' she said. 'It's a keeper.'

He sat beside her, their shoulders touching.

He thought of the blank pages waiting upstairs, of the way the pen felt heavier some days than others.

'I will,' he said. 'Tonight.'

'Good,' she said.

On New Year's Eve, the town pretended at celebration.

There were posters in shop windows for events in Dolan's and The Railway Bar – live music, DJ, free finger food. The supermarkets displayed cheap prosecco in pyramids.

Ciarán and Joan stayed home.

They had done the pubs and the countdowns when they were younger, had kissed in crowds and on pavements, had staggered home in the small hours, the cold biting and the sky indifferent.

Now the idea of being jostled in a packed bar, of shouting small talk over bad remixes, felt like something that belonged to another species.

The hospice had organised a nurse to be on call through the night. Deirdre had insisted on it, her tone brooking no argument. 'If you need us, ring,' she'd said. 'None of this "Sure we'll not bother them, it's the holidays." We are not the Guards. We want to be bothered.'

By nine, the sky outside was already filling with small fireworks. The odd whoosh-pop would puncture the quiet, followed by a cheer or a dog barking.

Inside, they watched the early film on RTÉ – a harmless comedy they'd both seen before. Joan's breathing was patchier that evening, the inhaler never far from her hand.

She had taken a small dose of the morphine for the first time that afternoon, more out of curiosity than desperation.

'It makes things … softer,' she said, when he asked. 'Not fuzzy. Just … less sharp. Like the edges of the day have been sanded.'

He watched her carefully for any sign of mental clouding, of a change in her, but the only difference he could see was that the line between her brows had eased. Her humour, if anything, was quicker.

At half ten, he stood at the window, looking at the occasional flare of colour above the rooftops. The noise seemed both too much and too little.

'Do you want to stay up?' he asked. 'For the big countdown. The twelve bongs. The whole rigmarole.'

She considered, the light from the lamp making shadows across her face.

'Part of me thinks I should,' she said. 'For symbolism. See the old year out, welcome the new, give it the fingers. That kind of thing.' She paused. 'The other part of me is wrecked and doesn't want to pretend I care more about numbers changing on a calendar than I do about how I feel.'

'Pick the second one,' he said. 'We can do symbolism at lunchtime tomorrow.'

She smiled. 'You make every party special,' she said.

They went up to bed around eleven – rebellious in their own way. As they climbed the stairs, a louder flurry of fireworks went off somewhere near town, the sound carrying on the cold air.

In the bedroom, she sat on the edge of the bed for a longer time than usual, catching her breath.

'You sure you don't want me to ring Deirdre?' he asked, watching the rise and fall of her chest.

'Not yet,' she said. 'It's just the stairs. My lungs have become dramatic teenagers. They hate any effort.'

He sat beside her, hand on her back, feeling the fine bones under the dressing gown.

'What are you hoping for?' she asked suddenly.

'Right now?' he said. 'For you to fall asleep without coughing. For my bladder to let me sleep till five. For the neighbours to run out of fireworks before two.'

She nudged him with her shoulder. 'In the big sense,' she said. 'For next year. Assuming we get any of it.'

He thought of Sligo. Of PSA numbers. Of scans and needles and words like *staging* and *involvement*.

'I'm hoping the urologist says the word "benign" in a sentence that also contains my name,' he said. 'I'm hoping your oxygen machine sounds less like a tractor than the last one we saw in the ward. I'm hoping my mother doesn't fall. I'm hoping …' He trailed off, the list suddenly too long.

'And beyond the medical,' she prompted. 'What do you want? If we strip all the appointments and numbers away.'

He stared at the pattern on the duvet – the faint, repeated motif of leaves.

'I want a summer day at the lake with you,' he said quietly. 'Just one more. Sitting on the rock, our feet in the water, a flask of tea and a ham sandwich, you giving out about the midges. That's it. That's my entire wish list.'

She took his hand, squeezed.

'I'll do my best,' she said. 'I can't promise. But I'll aim.'

'And you?' he asked.

She considered.

'I want to read one more book that's good enough to make me forget, for an hour, that I'm dying. I want to lie in this bed on a night when neither of us is thinking about doctors. Even for ten minutes.'

He nodded, throat tight.

'We've turned into very simple people,' she said.

'We were never that complicated,' he replied.

Sometime past midnight, he woke to the sound of their neighbour's distant cheering – delayed, bleary, threaded with someone attempting to sing *Auld Lang Syne* in a key not available to humans.

'Happy New Year,' he whispered into the darkness, to no one and everyone.

Downstairs, the calendar in the kitchen would still say December. The number over his life had clicked over, whether he acknowledged it or not.

The days between, he thought, were over. The year proper would begin in the morning – with the same kettle, the same aches, the same faces, the same notebook on the table.

He closed his eyes, holding that small, stubborn thought: that even in the middle of sickness and fear, there would still be days. Ordinary ones, mostly. Maybe that, in the end, was the point.

Chapter Thirteen

January Light

The new year announced itself not with fanfare but with the sight of his breath in the hallway.

On the first Monday back, Ciarán stood in the kitchen at eight o'clock, watching steam rise from the kettle and from his own mouth, the two vapours crossing each other in the cold air. The heating had gone off in the night; the house carried that particular chill that seemed to come not just from the weather but from the absence of bodies moving through it.

He stared at the calendar on the wall. The image for January showed a road through bare trees, the sky a hard, clear blue. Someone with a camera and a good eye had managed to make winter look bright instead of bleak.

He found the Biro that lived on the sill and drew a ring around a date near the bottom of the page. The 26th.

The circle looked smaller than he'd expected, unimpressive. The ink had a slight fade in the middle where the Biro had stuttered.

Behind him, he heard the soft shuffle of slippers on the lino. Joan came in slowly, one hand on the doorframe, the other already reaching for the back of the chair at the table. She wore his old college sweatshirt over her pyjama bottoms, the green scarf looped loosely around her neck like a talisman.

'You'll dent the floor if you stare at that any longer,' she said, nodding toward the calendar.

'O'Malley says it's good to prepare,' he replied. 'Mentally.'

'O'Malley also said he'd have "a word" with the consultant about your appointment,' she said. 'And yet here we are, still in the raffle. Put the kettle back on; that's preparation I can get behind.'

He made the tea the way she liked it – plenty of milk, no fuss – and set her mug on the table. As she lowered herself into the chair, he noticed the way she paused halfway, catching her breath.

'How's the going?' he asked, trying to keep his voice neutral.

'Like walking through porridge,' she said. 'Thick. Slow. But still moving. You?'

'Like waiting for an exam,' he said. 'Except this time I'm not sure I studied the right book.'

She smiled over the rim of her mug. There were shadows under her eyes that hadn't been there a few months ago, and a faint, persistent tightness around her mouth.

'You're back to school today,' she said, glancing at the clock. 'The youth of Ireland await your rants about the Civil War.'

'Cosgrave today,' he said. 'We're moving on to the Cumann na nGaedheal years. Law and order, hydroelectric schemes and the joys of proportional representation.'

'Try not to terrify them completely,' she said. 'Save some trauma for the mocks.'

He hesitated, then said, 'Are you sure you're all right with me going in? I can ring Lally. Tell him I'll start next week.'

She waved a hand. 'You've been under my feet for two weeks,' she said. 'Go and inflict yourself on someone else. I'll be grand. Maeve's calling in later. Deirdre said she'd drop by at some stage this week. I have a full social calendar.'

'You're not just saying that?' he asked.

'I'm saying it with conviction,' she replied. 'Which is nearly the same thing.'

He looked at her another moment, committing this scene – her at the table with the steam from the mug curling in front of her, the January light leaking in under the blind – to whatever part of his mind was doing the recording these days. Then he stood, took his coat from the back of the chair and shrugged it on.

'Ring me,' he said, 'if you need anything. Even just to complain about daytime television.'

'I'll ring Joe Duffy,' she said. 'He has a larger audience.'

He bent to kiss her, the familiar mix of tea and moisturiser and the faint metallic tang of the tablets on her breath.

'Mind yourself,' she said into his collar.

'You too,' he replied.

The school looked smaller in January.

It always did, he thought, as he turned in to the car park – the bright illusions of Christmas stripped away, the corridors reduced to their plain concrete and lino. The grass on the front pitch was a flat, muddy green; a lone crow strutted across it as if it owned the place.

He parked in his usual spot. The air outside was cold enough to make his teeth ache when he breathed in too sharply. He could see his breath again as he crossed the yard, the puff of vapour joining those of students huddled in clusters, shoulders hunched, phones in hand.

A few nodded at him in that semi-respectful way teenagers did when their minds were elsewhere.

'Sir,' one muttered.

'Morning,' he said. 'You survived Christmas, then.'

'Barely,' the lad replied, disappearing through the door.

In the staff room, there was a flurry of coats, bags and half-unpacked tins of biscuits that had been brought in as tributes to the gods of post-holiday goodwill. The kettle was already boiling; someone had put on a radio station that played soft rock from before most of them had been born.

'Look who the cat dragged back,' called Barry from the table, where he was frowning at a stack of Christmas exam papers as if they'd personally offended him.

Ciarán hung his coat on the back of his usual chair and dropped his bag somewhat more carefully beside it.

'The cat has no respect,' he said. 'He'd drag anyone anywhere.'

Barry stood to pour himself tea, then added a second mug and nodded toward Ciarán. 'You're on reduced hours now, is it?' he asked, lowering his voice slightly as other conversations eddied around them.

'That's the rumour,' Ciarán said. 'Two sixth-year groups, no juniors, no Transition Years.'

'Lally was going on about "supporting staff in times of difficulty" at the planning meeting,' Barry said. 'He even used the word "holistic". I nearly had to leave the room.'

'He means well,' Ciarán said. 'He can't help the language. It's the courses. They infect you.'

Barry handed him the mug. 'How's Joan?' he asked. 'And yourself?'

'We're … getting on with it,' Ciarán said. 'She's more tired. Breath's shorter. But she's still giving me orders, so the backbone is intact. I'm waiting on Sligo to tell me if my insides are decorative or not.'

Barry grimaced sympathetically. 'If you want someone

to yell about last year's All-Ireland with your crowd while you're off getting prodded, I'm your man,' he said.

'I'll keep that in mind,' Ciarán replied. 'Nothing says "compassionate leave" like a rant about referees.'

The bell went. The staff room emptied with the usual stampede, teachers grabbing copies and travel mugs, adjusting scarves, composing their faces into the expression that lay somewhere between authority and exhaustion.

He walked down the familiar corridor, the walls lined with faded posters of past achievements – debating teams with too-big blazers, GAA squads with mud on their shins, a grainy photograph of a visit from some minor celebrity no one really remembered now.

His first class was 6A History, one of the two groups he'd kept.

They were already half seated when he came in, voices bouncing off the high ceiling. The air smelled faintly of deodorant and energy drinks.

'Happy New Year, sir,' called Anna from the front row, her plait over one shoulder, pen poised.

'If by "happy" you mean "full of mock exams",' he said, 'then yes. Happy.'

There was a groan.

He wrote the date on the board, the numbers slightly skewed. The year '2024' looked wrong, like a misprint. Beneath it he wrote, in neat capitals: *The Cumann na nGaedheal Governments, 1922–32*.

'Right,' he said. 'We've traumatised ourselves sufficiently with the Treaty and the Civil War. Now we get to see what they actually did with it. Spoiler: it's not all that exciting. But the examiners love it, so you're stuck.'

There was a murmur of laughter. The mood eased.

He launched into the lesson, glad for the familiar rhythm.

He drew a rough timeline on the board, talked about new currency and Gardaí, about Shannon hydroelectric schemes and the Boundary Commission. He watched them take it in, some more interested than others, their pens moving, their foreheads creased in varying degrees of concentration.

Every so often, a wave of tiredness rolled over him, a physical sensation that made the room tilt slightly. He gripped the edge of the desk until it passed, breathed through it and went on.

When the bell rang, they packed up with relief.

'Past exam question for Friday,' he called after them. 'On public order and stability. No lists. Sentences. Doyle – no doodles in the margin this time. De Valera with devil horns will not get you marks.'

He stayed for a moment in the empty room after they'd gone, the echo of their voices still hanging in the air. The board looked suddenly bare again, the words *Public Safety Act* underlined twice.

That evening, with school's drone behind him and the mid-afternoon visit to his mother safely navigated, he came home to find the oxygen concentrator in the corner of the sitting room.

It looked, he thought, oddly unremarkable. A beige box on small wheels, a few buttons, a length of clear tubing coiled neatly like a sleeping snake. It hummed quietly, the sound like a distant fridge.

Joan was in her armchair, the narrow plastic prongs of the nasal cannula resting under her nose, the tubing looped loosely over her ears.

'How do I look?' she asked, raising an eyebrow as he stood in the doorway.

'Like you've gone up a gear in science fiction,' he said. 'Very *Blade Runner*. Very chic.'

She snorted. 'It's not exactly a glamorous accessory,' she said. 'But it makes a difference. Look— '

She took a breath, more deliberate than usual, then another.

'I can get to the end of a sentence without stopping for a committee meeting,' she said. 'It's … strange. I didn't realise how hard I was working until I wasn't working as hard.'

He crossed the room and sat on the edge of the couch, listening.

He watched the tubing rise and fall with her breathing.

'Does it hurt?' he asked. 'The … thing on your nose.'

'It's a bit annoying,' she admitted. 'Gets in the way of my glamorous lifestyle. But it's better than gasping like a landed fish. I can tolerate a bit of plastic.'

He reached for the blue notebook, which lay on the coffee table where he'd left it the night before.

'I did some more,' he said, opening it.

'Read,' she said. 'A woman likes to know she's being immortalised correctly.'

He cleared his throat, scanning for a place to begin. On the most recent page, he'd written:

January light on the radiator,
thin and precise,
picking out the dust like constellations.

He went on, the lines about the school corridor, about his mother arranging biscuits on a plate, about the ring around the 26th on the calendar.

When he finished, he was conscious of how prosaic it sounded. Not grand, no sweeping metaphors. Just bits of day.

Joan's eyes were bright.

'You're getting very domestic,' she said. 'Next you'll be writing about the washing machine.'

'I did,' he said, pointing to a line he'd crossed out. 'It squeaks. It was irresistible.'

'Keep it,' she said. 'The world needs more squeaky washing machines. The grand tragedies take care of themselves.'

He thought about that for a moment.

'Deirdre says we should start thinking about advance care planning,' he said. 'Where you want to be. What you want. What you don't. Do you hate me if I say I don't want to write that down?'

She considered.

'I don't hate you,' she said. 'I hate that it needs to be written. But I also … like the idea that there'll be a piece of paper somewhere saying "don't drag this woman into A&E at three in the morning". It feels like sending a message to our future selves. And to some poor junior doctor who'll be on his nineteenth hour and will need guidance.'

He smiled faintly.

'You're worried about the doctor,' he said.

'I'm worried about everyone,' she replied. 'It's part of my charm.'

They sat in silence for a while, the hum of the machine filling the gaps.

After a bit, she said, 'I like the "waiting for an exam" bit in your poem.'

'It wasn't really a poem,' he said. 'More a whinge with line breaks.'

'Poems are mostly that,' she said. 'Whinges with rhythm. You've always been good at them.'

He closed the notebook gently.

'You know,' she went on, 'if this goes on much longer, you might end up with a whole book out of it. *The Light at*

Evening, by our very own Mr Devlin. Subtitled: "Grumbling and Breathing Exercises".'

'The market will be clamouring,' he said. 'They'll have to form a queue.'

He didn't say what he was thinking: that the idea of a book felt both comforting and impossible. That to think of these pages as something that might one day be bound and read by others was to imagine a future in which both of them were still present enough – for him to edit, for her to roll her eyes at the proofs.

For now, it was enough that the notebook existed. That January had its own lines, its own record.

He looked at her, the thin tubing, the machine, the scarf, the steady rise and fall of her chest.

'We're living in parentheses,' he said quietly. 'Between things.'

She nodded.

'It's not the worst place,' she said. 'We have biscuits. And oxygen.'

He laughed.

Later that night, after they'd watched ten minutes of a crime drama neither of them had the attention span for, after he'd helped her upstairs, carrying the oxygen tubing like a bizarre bridal train, he lay in the dark listening to the rain ticking against the window.

The circle around the 26th glowed faintly in his mind's eye.

He thought of the men he'd seen in the waiting room in Sligo the last time he'd been there with someone else – his father, maybe, or a neighbour. Men in their fifties and sixties, jackets on laps, faces carefully blank, a quiet camaraderie in how they avoided each other's eyes.

He imagined himself among them now. A file with his name on it in a plastic tray. A consultant with a bad tie looking at a scan. The words they might use: *enlarged*, *suspicious*, *benign*, *biopsy*, *monitoring*. He tried them on silently, one by one, like suits he might have to wear.

Beside him, Joan's breathing was a little easier with the oxygen running into the cannula. The machine in the corner made a soft, regular sound.

'Are you awake?' she whispered, after a while.

'I am,' he said.

'Don't write the ending yet,' she said into the darkness. 'Of the book. Or of us. Leave room.'

'I will,' he said.

Chapter Fourteen

Sligo

The week running up to Sligo stretched and snapped like an old elastic band.

Every day had its own small structure – school, visits, pills, Deirdre's clipboard, the hum of the concentrator – but underneath it all there was a steady, insistent ticking. The circle around the 26th on the calendar took on the quality of an approaching exam date; everything else was revision, filler, distraction.

On the Tuesday before, he woke at four with his bladder burning and his thoughts already in the hospital. He lay there for a minute, willing the feeling away, as if he could out-stare an organ. The effort made his back ache. Joan's breaths came gently beside him, the tubing of the cannula catching the faint glow from the street lamp outside. He gave in and swung his legs over the side of the bed. The house was cold; the floorboards grumbled. In the bathroom, the light was brutal. The tiles threw it back at him, doubling the harshness.

He stood over the bowl and waited. A thin, unsatisfactory stream. The familiar discomfort, the sense of something unfinished. He watched, because he couldn't not. No red, no dramatic clouding. Just the palest yellow. He let out a breath then flushed and turned the light off, preferring the dark.

Back in bed, the cold sheets made him gasp. Joan shifted.

'You all right?' she murmured.

'Just the usual,' he said. 'My insides staging a protest.'

She turned, the tubes tugging slightly, and placed a hand on his chest.

'Go back to sleep,' she said. 'You'll need it. The young minds of Ireland await your wisdom..'

He put a hand over hers.

'I'm grand,' he said.

'You're not,' she replied, too tired to sugarcoat it. 'But you might be.'

He lay there, looking at the ceiling he couldn't see, feeling the small pressure of her palm over his heart, and tried to find the bit of him that believed her.

The morning of the appointment dawned grey and damp, as if the sky had decided to sit this one out.

He woke before the alarm. The numbers on the clock read 6:09, then 6:10 in that small, indifferent change. He lay there for a second, expecting to feel something profound and finding only the usual: a dull ache in his lower back, a vague queasiness, the stiffness of a man who had not been twenty for some time.

Beside him, Joan was already awake. Her eyes met his in the half-light.

'Today's the day,' she said, unnecessarily.

'Apparently,' he replied.

'Let's not be late,' she said. 'It would be very rude to keep your consultant waiting when he's about to root around your nether regions.'

'Such poetry first thing,' he said.

He'd thought about going alone. It would have been easily justified – Joan's breath, the early start, the unpredictability of hospital corridors. But when he'd floated the idea, she'd fixed him with a look.

'I'm not letting you go up there on your own,' she'd said. 'You'd come back having been told you have six weeks to live and you'd say "Ah, that's fine" and go back to school.'

So they'd worked out a plan. Maeve would drive. Joan in the front seat, oxygen in the footwell, him in the back like a child. His mother, despite protests that 'you'll be gone half the day', had agreed to let the public health nurse call in on her instead.

It felt oddly exposing, being the one arranged around.

In the kitchen, he made tea, then porridge he didn't want but knew he'd regret skipping. Joan managed half a slice of toast and a banana, chewing slowly, pausing between bites to breathe.

Maeve arrived at eight, hair damp from the morning, car keys in hand. They bundled up. Joan's scarf, his jacket, Maeve's sensible coat.

At the door, the air hit them – wet, sharp, full of the smell of winter muck. The front garden looked neglected: grass slicked down by rain, the flowerbeds a memory. He thought, absurdly, that he should have hoed it properly in September.

'Do you want to lock up?' he asked Joan.

She shook her head. 'You do it,' she said. 'My locking days are on sabbatical.'

He turned the key, feeling the small clunk of the mechanism. The ordinary sound of leaving.

In the car, the heater blew lukewarm air that smelled faintly of old crisps. Maeve adjusted the seat, set the radio low and pulled out of the drive with the careful assertiveness she had in all things.

'Seat belt,' she said automatically, glancing at them.

'Yes, Mam,' Ciarán said.

As they passed the end of the road, he saw his mother's house in the distance, the top of the hedge just visible. Somewhere inside, she'd be moving slowly through her morning: kettle, radio, rosary beads never far from hand.

He smiled, feeling the familiar tug.

The road to Sligo was one he knew well in parts and barely in others. Out of town, through the small villages with their closed shops and scattered bungalows, past fields that, today, looked waterlogged and sulky. The sky settled into a low, uniform grey that made distance hard to judge.

As they drove, the conversation came in fits and starts. Snatches about nothing – the price of diesel, the new shop in town that might be a hairdresser or a bookies. Radio headlines about the war in Ukraine, weather warnings, the endless talk of health service overcrowding that felt like listening to a report about a house that was already on fire while sitting in one of the rooms.

After a while, the talk dwindled. The tyres hummed. The windscreen wipers kept a slow, hypnotic rhythm.

In the front, Joan sat with her hands folded over the strap of her bag, the cannula snug under her nose, the tubing disappearing into the footwell where the small, portable concentrator hummed quietly.

'You all right?' he murmured, leaning forward.

She tilted her head toward him. 'Fine for a woman being smuggled across county lines like contraband,' she said.

'At least they won't confiscate you at the border,' he said. 'You're of cultural value.'

'Questionable,' she replied.

He watched the side of her face – the pale curve of her cheek, the way her jaw clenched slightly when the car hit a bump.

'How are you?' she asked, after a few minutes.

‘I don’t know,’ he said honestly. ‘Somewhere between “It’s probably nothing” and “This is the day everything changes.”’

‘Well,’ she said, ‘both can’t be true at the same time.’

He smiled, appreciating the way she braided humour through his fear.

They reached the outskirts of Sligo sooner than he expected. The town rose up slowly – the river, the bridges, the cluster of shops, the church spire stabbing at the low sky.

The hospital came into view as a set of low, spread-out buildings, a mix of old brick and newer glass. It always reminded him of something that had been added to piecemeal, never quite finished.

Maeve navigated the car park with the concentration of someone playing a difficult game. After three failed attempts to claim a space from other circling drivers, she found one at the far end, near a hedge.

‘Right,’ she said, turning off the engine. ‘We’re here. You can both start panicking officially now.’

They laughed, more out of recognition than amusement.

Inside, the hospital smelled as all hospitals did: a blend of antiseptic, boiled vegetables and fatigue. The entrance hall was busy – people in coats and wheelchairs, a child crying somewhere, the beep of machines and the low murmur of conversations in several accents.

The urology clinic was down a corridor that had seen better days. The sign above the door was slightly askew. Inside, the waiting room was almost full. Men mostly, as he’d expected. Some alone, some with wives or daughters. A few with walking sticks or wheelchairs. Newspapers in laps, phones in hands, eyes sliding off one another.

He felt, with a jolt, like he’d stumbled into some quiet brotherhood of the anxious.

They checked in at the desk. The receptionist, harried but not unkind, confirmed his name, his date of birth, his address.

'Take a seat, Mr Devlin,' she said. 'They're running a bit behind.'

Of course they were. Time in hospitals, he'd learned, was a suggestion rather than a promise.

They found three chairs together near the wall. The television mounted high in one corner played a daytime show with the sound off; captions crawled across the bottom, talking about decluttering your life.

'Do I count as clutter?' Joan asked softly.

'You're a permanent fixture,' he said.

'Same thing,' she murmured.

He scanned the room. A man in a suit in his sixties, tapping his foot. Another in his forties rubbing his hands together. An older man asleep, head back, mouth open. A younger fellow, maybe late thirties, staring so intently at his phone that his knuckles were white.

He wondered what their letters had said. What their PSA numbers were. How long each of them had spent imagining their own funerals.

On the opposite wall, there were posters: one about testicular self-examination, another about urinary symptoms, one cheerfully titled *Know Your Prostate*. The drawings were anatomically vague; more cartoon than body.

Joan followed his gaze.

'Very handsome,' she whispered. 'I see the attraction now.'

'Jealous?' he replied.

'Utterly,' she said.

They waited.

The names being called from the inner door came in bursts. 'Mr O'Rourke?' 'Mr Mahon?' 'Mr Kavanagh?' Each man stood, adjusted his jacket, and disappeared. Each time the door swung shut, there was a small pressure drop, as if the room exhaled.

After forty minutes, his own name came.

'Mr Devlin?' The nurse at the door looked around. Her badge said *Sinéad*.

He stood. His knees felt suddenly loose.

'You coming?' he asked Joan.

She shook her head. 'You go,' she said. 'Too many bodies in there and I'll be gasping. I'll stay out here and read about optimal prostate shape. Maeve can supervise my commentary.'

He hesitated.

'Go on,' she said. 'I'll be here. I'm not going anywhere quickly.'

He nodded and followed the nurse through the door.

The corridor beyond was narrow, lined with closed doors and more posters. He had the fleeting, irrational thought that he could still turn around and leave – that he could step back out into the waiting room, grab Joan and Maeve and drive home, pretend the letter had never arrived.

Instead, he went where he was directed. A small examination room, a desk, a computer, a trolley with instruments laid out neatly. The smell of disinfectant was sharper here.

'Take a seat there,' the nurse said gently. 'The doctor won't be long. We'll probably be doing a little scan today as well, so I'll explain that in a minute.'

He sat on the chair by the desk, his hands resting on his knees, his feet not quite sure where to be.

He'd barely had time to look around properly when the door opened again and a man in a white coat came in, glasses sliding slightly down his nose.

'Mr Devlin?' he said, holding out his hand. 'I'm Dr Kearney. Dr O'Malley sent you up to us.'

His accent was Dublinish with hints of somewhere else. He

looked to be in his fifties, with the brisk manner of someone whose life was segmented into fifteen-minute units.

'How are you keeping?' Kearney asked, that opening question that meant everything and nothing.

'Grand,' Ciarán heard himself say, automatically. Then, because of Joan, because of Deirdre, because of Maeve, he added, 'A bit worried.'

Kearney nodded once, as if that were the right answer.

'Well, let's see if we can give you less to worry about,' he said.

He tapped at the computer, pulling up Ciarán's notes.

'O'Malley says your PSA jumped,' he said.

It was strange seeing the numbers there, on the screen, clinical and neat, when in his head they were messy and loud.

'I'm fifty-eight,' Ciarán said, before he could stop himself. 'My father died at eighty-four, but of the heart. Not this. Not that we knew anyway.'

Kearney nodded again. 'PSA is a useful marker,' he said. 'But it's not a cancer test. Lots of things can cause it to rise. Benign enlargement. Infection. Even a cycle on a bumpy road. What we need to do is get a better look.'

He explained, in simple, precise terms, what that would involve.

'We'll do a physical exam today,' he said. 'And an ultrasound from here.' He tapped the lower abdomen on a diagram. 'Depending on what that shows, we may schedule an MRI. A biopsy if necessary. We don't rush to the big guns unless we need to. The important thing to know is that even if we were to find something concerning, most prostate cancers are slow-growing. We are not talking about a train you're already under. We're talking about a train in the distance that we may or may not see, and if we do, there are ways to deal with it.'

The words eased something in him, but only slightly. Trains in the distance, he thought. He'd still heard the word *cancer*.

'I've a wife with lung cancer at home,' he blurted, surprising himself. 'She's ... on treatment. Palliative. Oxygen. Hospice. I'm ... already on one platform.'

Kearney's face changed, the professional anxiety replaced by something softer.

'Right,' he said quietly. 'That's a lot.'

'It is,' Ciarán said.

'It also means,' Kearney went on, 'that I'm going to be particularly careful with our decisions. We don't want to over-treat you for something that's not life-threatening in the context of your life as it is. But we also don't ignore things that need attention. We find the middle ground.'

He looked at Ciarán directly.

'Bottom line,' he said. 'You did the right thing getting checked. We'll take it one step at a time. Today is step one.'

The physical exam was as undignified as he'd expected, but over quickly. He lay on his side, knees drawn up, staring at a crack in the paint on the wall while gloved hands pressed and probed. He focused on the sound of the clock ticking, on the distant muffled voice of the television in the waiting room.

'Enlarged,' Kearney said, afterwards, notes in hand. 'Doesn't feel rock hard. That's reassuring. We'll do the ultrasound now. Nurse Sinéad will get you ready.'

The ultrasound gel was cold. The scanner pressed into his lower belly felt like a blunt question.

'Just breathe normally,' Sinéad said. 'Think of nice things. Holidays.'

He thought of Lough Allen instead, of the grey sky and the rock where they always sat. Of Joan with her feet in the water, complaining about the midges. It helped more than generic sunshine.

When it was done, Kearney wiped his hands, looked at the screen, then back at Ciarán.

'Mr Devlin,' he said, sitting down. 'From what I can see today, you have a significantly enlarged prostate. That can explain a lot of your symptoms and the PSA. I'm not seeing any obvious signs of something nasty infiltrating the surrounding areas. That doesn't give us a one hundred per cent guarantee, but it's a good sign.'

Ciarán felt the room tilt slightly.

'So …?' he asked.

'So,' Kearney said, 'I'd like to arrange an MRI to give us a more detailed look, just to be thorough. We'll prioritise you given the PSA rise. If the MRI is clear, we will likely manage this with medication and monitoring. If it throws up anything suspicious, then we talk about a biopsy. But based on today, I'm … cautiously optimistic that we're dealing with a benign enlargement.'

The word *benign* landed like a small, unexpected gift.

He realised, with a jolt, that he'd been bracing himself for *malignant*, for *aggressive*, for *spread*.

'You won't have to wait as long this time,' Kearney added, perhaps reading his face. 'Two weeks, maybe less, for the MRI. I'll have my secretary ring you with the slot. Do you have any questions?'

He had hundreds, but they were tangled.

'What happens if I ignore it?' he asked, the one that surfaced.

'Your urinary symptoms will worsen,' Kearney said. 'Risk of retention, infection. Maybe catheter. It'll make your life miserable. I don't recommend ignoring it.'

'I've enough misery,' Ciarán said weakly.

'Exactly,' Kearney said. 'So we'll start you on medication today to relax the muscle around the prostate and shrink it a bit. See how you get on. Any problems – pain, blood, inability to pass urine – you ring immediately. Don't be stoic. Stoicism is overrated in urology.'

He found himself almost smiling.

'All right,' he said.

As he left the room, clutching a new prescription and a sheet of instructions, he felt oddly light and heavy at the same time. The big axe he'd been imagining had not fallen. Instead, he'd been handed a complex, annoying toolkit and told to get used to carrying it.

In the corridor, he stopped for a moment, leaned briefly against the cool wall. He let the word run through his head again.

Benign. Possibly.

Probably.

Benign-enlarged. Like a half-compliment.

He took a breath, straightened, and went back into the waiting room.

Joan's eyes went straight to his face.

'Well?' she asked.

He sat beside her, suddenly aware of all the other ears in the room and yet sure no one was really listening.

'They think it's enlarged,' he said. 'Not … the worst thing. They're "cautiously optimistic" that it's benign. I have to get an MRI. More checks. Tablets. Monitoring. But … no one mentioned "terminal" or "spread" or "kiss your secrets goodbye". Not today.'

Joan exhaled, a sound that was half-sigh, half-laugh.

'That's good,' she said. 'That's … very good. That's buying time. That's "You're still allowed to worry more about me." I can work with that.'

Maeve, on his other side, put a hand on his arm. He hadn't noticed how tightly he'd been holding his shoulders until they lowered under her touch.

'We'll take that,' she said. 'With bells on.'

He felt tears prick his eyes, unexpectedly. The relief wasn't pure; it was threaded with guilt. He got the 'probably all right' while Joan carried the 'definitely not'.

'I'm sorry,' he said to her, the words out before he could catch them.

'For what?' she asked, genuinely puzzled.

'For … not being … worse,' he said, hating how stupid it sounded.

She rolled her eyes.

'Don't start,' she said. 'If you apologise for not having cancer, I'll hit you with the oxygen machine. This is good news, Ciarán. In a hospital. For us. We're not idiots; we'll take it.'

He let himself smile then, a painful, shaky thing.

'All right,' he said. 'We'll take it.'

On the way out, the rain had eased. The sky was still low, but there were lighter patches between the clouds.

'Will we go straight home?' Maeve asked, as they turned out of the car park.

'Stop at the lake,' Joan said, before he could answer. 'If we're passing. I need to check that it's still there. For future reference.'

'It's January,' he objected. 'You'll freeze.'

'I'm not planning on skinny-dipping,' she said. 'Just looking. From the car if necessary. Consider it a reconnaissance mission.'

Maeve glanced in the rear-view mirror, judged the energy in both their faces, then nodded.

'All right,' she said. 'Five minutes. No more. I've no

intention of explaining to Deirdre why I let you both get pneumonia.'

The road up toward the lake was familiar in its bends and rises. The hedges were slick with rain, the ditches full. The fields beyond rose toward low hills, the colours muted – brown, green, a yellowish tinge where rushes had taken over.

When they crested the last small hill and the lake spread out below them, Ciarán felt something in his chest ease in a way that no consultant could manage.

Lough Allen lay flat and grey under the winter sky. The far shore was a smudge; the island a darker lump. The water had that heavy, metallic look it got when the wind was low.

Maeve pulled into the small lay-by where they always parked, the gravel crunching.

'Five minutes,' she said again, but her voice was softer.

They sat for a moment inside the car, the windows beginning to fog.

'Will we risk getting out?' Joan asked.

He looked at her, at the slight flush in her cheeks, the way her breathing had picked up slightly with the small climb in the car.

'You tell me,' he said.

She paused, assessing herself.

'I can manage the few steps to the wall,' she decided. 'If you bring the portable oxygen. And if someone promises to carry me back if I stage a dramatic collapse.'

'We'll roll you,' Maeve said. 'To save our backs.'

Getting out was a small operation. He lifted the concentrator carefully, making sure the tubing didn't snag. Maeve went ahead, checking for ice on the tarmac, holding the car door open.

The cold when it hit them was sharp enough to make his

eyes water. The air off the lake had a bite, a purity that the hospital air had lacked entirely.

They made their slow way to the low wall at the edge of the lay-by. Joan took each step as if it were a minor negotiation, her hand light on his arm, the cannula in place, the tube looped down to the small machine that hummed reassurance at her feet.

When they reached the wall, she leaned on it, catching her breath. He watched her chest rise and fall, counted to ten in his head, then saw her shoulders loosen slightly.

'Now,' she said, looking out.

The lake stretched, indifferent to appointments and PSA scores, to oxygen concentrations and morphine doses. A bird skimmed low over the surface. Somewhere on the far side, a dog barked faintly, carried by the air.

'It's still here,' she said. 'Good. I'd have been very annoyed if it had packed up and gone.'

He stood beside her, his hands in his pockets, the cold seeping through his coat. For a moment, they were simply two people looking at water.

'It looks like every January since we were kids,' he said.

'It looks like every January before us and after us,' she replied. 'That's the point. That's the comfort and the insult.'

He glanced at her.

'What are you thinking?' he asked.

She considered.

'I'm thinking,' she said slowly, 'that you just got a reprieve of sorts. Not a pardon. A stay. There's work to be done. Tablets to be taken. Scans to be endured. But you're not on the cliff edge I thought you might be. And that means …'

She trailed off, staring at the water.

'That means?' he prompted.

'That means we have more time where both of us are here,'

she said. 'Even if it's messy. Even if I'm attached to machines and you're attached to a bathroom. Even if we're never again the people who ran into the lake in April on a dare. We are here. Together. For more than we feared.'

He nodded, his throat tight.

'I'm also thinking,' she added, 'that we need to plan a proper day here when it's less freezing. With a flask and ham sandwiches and you can finally write your big lake poem instead of all these little ones.'

'I've written plenty of lake poems,' he said.

'Exactly,' she said. 'This one will have more equipment in it. A new phase.'

He smiled.

'We can do that,' he said. 'When you're up to it. When the grass is less like soup.'

She took another breath, deeper this time, the oxygen doing its quiet work.

'Do you feel lighter?' she asked suddenly.

He thought about it.

'I feel … different,' he said. 'Like I've been carrying two sacks up a hill – yours and mine – and someone has told me that mine is mostly full of towels, not rocks. It's still a sack. It still has weight. But I'm not going to be crushed under it today.'

'That's a very Devlin analogy,' she said. 'But I'll accept it.'

'And you?' he asked. 'How do you feel?'

She looked at the lake, at the strip of reed that marked the water's edge, at the empty sky.

'I feel,' she said, 'like I'm still carrying rocks. But I have more hands around me now. Yours. Maeve's. Deirdre's.'

The wind picked up, sending a small shiver through them.

'That's your five minutes,' Maeve called from behind,

stamping her feet. 'Back in the car before I get hypothermia and start blaming your prostate.'

They turned, slowly. Joan's legs were already complaining, but the oxygen had given her just enough.

On the way back to the car, she stopped once, hand on the bonnet, eyes closed.

'All right?' he asked.

'Just … resetting,' she said. 'It's like the hill to the GPO in town. Looks like nothing till you're halfway up it.'

He waited, patient, the concentrator humming between them.

When they were all back inside, doors shut, the car filled quickly with the smell of cold air and their three different anti-perspirants.

As Maeve started the engine, Joan turned to him.

'You know the title,' she said.

'Of what?' he asked.

'Your book,' she said. 'The one with all this in it. The poems. The waiting. The lake. The candle. The prostate. All of it.'

He half laughed. 'I haven't decided there is a book,' he said.

'There is,' she said, with the certainty of someone who had already decided. 'And you already know what it's called.'

He looked out at the lake receding as they pulled away, at the pale evening light dragging itself along the surface of the water.

The Light at Evening, he thought, Joan's phrase dropping into him with a quiet inevitability.

'Yes,' he said aloud, almost to himself. 'I do.'

The road wound away from the lake, back toward the town, the hospital behind them, the calendar ahead. Between the two, there was this: three people in a car, one of them a bit more hopeful than he had been that morning, one breathing easier with the help of a machine, one concentrating on the road and on not saying everything she wanted to say at once.

It wasn't a miracle. It wasn't a cure. It was something more ordinary and, somehow, more precious.

It was time.

Chapter Fifteen

Margins

The MRI appointment came quicker than expected, the way some bad-weather fronts did – one moment only a rumour on the forecast, the next already at the edge of the field.

The hospital rang on a Wednesday afternoon when he was in the staff room, pretending to care about a discussion on the new digital roll system.

'Mr Devlin?' the voice said, when he stepped out into the corridor with his phone pressed to his ear. 'This is Radiology in Sligo. We've a cancellation for Monday morning, eight-fifteen. Would you be able to attend?'

He said yes before his mind had time to erect any obstacles. The sooner the better. Less time for the imagination to turn shadows into tumours.

When he told Joan that evening, she nodded, unsurprised.

'Good,' she said. 'While you're at it, ask them can they scan my patience. It's thinning.'

'Multi-buy deal,' he said. 'Buy one organ, get the second half price.'

She smiled, but he could see the flicker of worry under it. The word *scan* did that to people now.

The MRI building was in a separate pre-fab near the main

hospital, as if the machine were a temperamental relative that needed its own space.

It was still dark when they arrived that Monday. The car-park lights cast a yellowish glow on the wet tarmac. Their breath hung in the air in small clouds as they walked in; Maeve had insisted on driving again.

'I can wait here,' Joan said, when she saw the sign warning of 'strong magnetic fields' in capital letters. 'I have enough metal in me between fillings and resentment.'

'You're not supposed to have oxygen near it,' Maeve added. 'You'd probably blow the place up.'

'Tempting,' Joan said. 'But fine. I'll sit in the boring waiting room and read the leaflets about cholesterol.'

The MRI waiting area felt like an anteroom to a spaceship. Bright, too clean, a bit too warm. Posters warned about pacemakers, aneurysm clips, metal shavings in the eye. The receptionist behind the desk wore a lanyard full of keys and a look of tired patience.

He filled out the form they gave him – tick boxes about metal, operations, implants. He thought, not for the first time, how much of a person could be reduced to boxes and lines and a signature at the bottom. Afterwards, he went into a changing booth, got undressed, put on a gown and waited for a knock on the door from the radiographer's assistant.

The radiographer, a young man with a Donegal lilt and a ponytail, explained the drill.

'We'll put you in feet-first,' he said. 'You'll be in up to about your chest. It's noisy. Like someone building a house around your head. You'll have ear defenders on, but you'll still hear the bangs. It's normal. Don't move. Breathe like you usually do. If you feel panicky, squeeze the little alarm thing and we'll pull you out. No shame in it. But try to stick it out if you can. The clearer the pictures, the less we have to repeat.'

The machine itself looked like a prop from a film he wouldn't have gone to see – white, impersonal; a giant ring with a narrow bed feeding into it.

'Lie down there,' the radiographer said. 'Head on the pillow. Hands by your sides.'

He did as he was told. The mattress was firm. The ceiling above him had one of those fake-sky panels fitted into it – a sort of blue with clouds that never moved.

'We'll be in the next room,' the radiographer said. 'We can see you and hear you. Do not, under any circumstances, try to sit up. You'll knock yourself out, for one thing. We'll tell you when we're done.'

The table began to move. Slowly at first, then with more determination. The tunnel closed around his lower body; the edges of his vision filled with white plastic.

He felt his throat tighten as the ceiling came closer.

Don't start, he told himself. *It's only a tube. You're not underground. You're not buried. You can breathe.*

The radiographer's voice came through, tinny in the headphones.

'Okay, Mr Devlin. First scan. This one's about three minutes. You'll hear some loud banging. That's just the magnets doing their thing. Don't move.'

The noise, when it started, was worse than he'd imagined. Metallic clacks and thuds, like someone dropping scaffolding around him. At first his body flinched instinctively; then, as the pattern settled, it became almost rhythmic. Terrifying, then tedious.

He fixed his eyes on the fake-sky panel, even though he could only catch a glimpse of it near his feet. He counted his breaths. On the thirty-sixth, he lost count and started again.

His mind, unhelpfully, ran backwards and forwards along his life as if flicking through a book. His father at the kitchen table, cigarette smoke curling. Joan on the bridge that first time they'd walked together, her hair wild in the wind. His mother's hands on the rosary. The students' faces when he drew the map of Europe on the board from memory and got one border slightly wrong.

He thought of Joan lying in similar machines, of the first scan that had shown the tumour in her lung. The relief that it had been stageable then; the way that relief had changed shape over time as the treatments failed to shrink it the way they were meant to.

'You're doing great,' the radiographer's voice said, cutting across his thoughts. 'Two more short ones and then a longer one. Nearly there.'

He wanted to laugh. Nearly where? At the end of the tube? At the start of a different kind of waiting?

He thought of Joan out in the waiting room, flicking through an outdated magazine, oxygen tubing draped like jewellery. He pictured the expression on her face when she was concentrating on not thinking too far ahead, the slight narrowing of her eyes, the way she tapped her toe.

He let that image anchor him.

When the table slid back out, it felt like emerging from a burrow.

'There you are,' the radiographer said, cheerfully. 'You did well. No emergency button. You'll be very popular with the consultant. Results will go back to Dr Kearney. He'll be in touch. Might take a week or two. The usual.'

Another corridor. Another waiting room. Another *might*.

He dressed slowly, his fingers fumbly on his belt.

In the main waiting area, Joan and Maeve looked up almost in unison when he came out.

'How was it?' Joan asked.

'Loud,' he said. 'Like being inside a washing machine with a hangover.'

'Any revelations?' Maeve said.

'Not that they told me,' he replied. 'They made polite noises about image quality and told me to wait. One of them complimented my stillness. It's the first praise I've had for staying still since secondary school.'

Joan reached out, touched his arm.

'Come on,' she said. 'Let's escape before they find something else to scan.'

The letter with the results arrived ten days later.

The envelope lay on the hall floor when he came back from school, half tucked under the radiator. The hospital crest on the corner made his stomach clench.

He stood there for a moment, his bag still on his shoulder, the house quiet except for the faint hum of the concentrator in the sitting room. He could hear Joan coughing, a thin, dry sound.

He picked the envelope up. It felt innocuous. Light. He turned it over, as if expecting it to reveal its contents by weight.

'Is that it?' Joan called, voice hoarse. 'You've gone very quiet. Have you been turned to stone?'

He walked into the sitting room, the envelope held as if it might bolt.

She was in the armchair by the window, blanket over her legs, the nasal cannula in place. The light was coming in low now, that particular late-afternoon yellow that made everything look briefly more substantial.

'Results,' he said. 'MRI.'

'Well it's either going to tell you you're dying or not,' she said. 'So open it before the kettle boils twice.'

He sat on the couch and tore the top of the envelope more roughly than he intended. The paper inside crackled.

Dear Mr Devlin, it began. *Following your MRI prostate scan, the images show marked benign prostatic enlargement with no suspicious focal lesions identified …*

He read it twice to make sure he wasn't missing some hidden caveat.

No suspicious lesions. Enlarged. Benign features. Recommend medical management. Repeat PSA in six months. Review in clinic.

His body reacted before his mind caught up. He let out a long breath, the sound almost a laugh.

'Well?' Joan demanded.

He looked up, the paper trembling slightly between his fingers.

'They say it's benign,' he said, the word tasting unfamiliar and wonderful in his mouth. 'Big as a tennis ball, apparently, but no obvious cancer. Tablets and monitoring. No knife. No chemo. Not now, anyway.'

Her eyes closed briefly, her head falling back against the armchair.

'Thank God,' she said. 'Or medical science. Or both. I don't care who takes the credit.'

He blinked, feeling suddenly wobbly.

'I was … more scared than I thought,' he said.

'I know,' she replied.

He moved to her, dropped awkwardly to his knees beside the chair, the paper still clutched in his hand. She reached for his head, like his mother used to, her fingers tangling gently in his hair.

'So,' she said, a smile tugging at the corner of her mouth. 'Your bits are irritating but not lethal. That's very on-brand for you.'

He laughed, a watery sound.

'Seems so,' he said.

She tightened her hand.

'Listen to me,' she said. 'And take this in, because I'm only going to say it once and you know my breath is expensive now. You are allowed to be relieved. Fully. Without guilt. Without the "but I'm fine and you're not" nonsense. We both walked up to a door marked *Cancer*. Mine opened. Yours, for now, hasn't. That's not your fault. That's not justice or injustice. That's just … biology. Bad luck and good luck tangled. Don't make it into a moral failing.'

He rested his forehead lightly against her knee. The blanket smelled of washing powder and the faint medicinal tang of the cream she rubbed on her legs for circulation.

'I was half planning your widowhood,' he said, the confession muffled.

'Don't,' she said. 'You're terrible at interior design.'

He smiled against the fabric.

'Seriously,' she added. 'I need you. In one piece. Or as close to one piece as a man of your vintage can be. I need you with your annoying bladder and your bad jokes. So forgive yourself for the reprieve and take the bloody tablets.'

He lifted his head and looked at her.

'I don't know what to do with the … space,' he said. 'The bit of me that was already halfway into the worst-case scenario.'

'Fill it,' she said. 'With poems. With walks. With the washing. With ringing your mother. With sitting in hospital chairs beside me. With looking at the lake. With being very boringly alive. That's what we do when we step back from the edge. We don't stand there regretting that we nearly fell.'

Her words, as ever, dropped into him with more precision than any doctor's.

He nodded.

'All right,' he said. 'I'll … practise being boring.'

She raised an eyebrow.

'You've had years of rehearsal,' she said.

He rang his mother that evening, sitting at the kitchen table with the letter in front of him as if it were a script.

'Hi, I got my results back today from the MRI scan' he said.

'Well?' she said, without preamble. 'What did they say to you?'

He could hear the television in the background – some quiz show. The faint clatter of cups.

'They say it's enlarged,' he said. 'Benign. I have to take tablets and be watched. But they didn't say the word we were afraid of. Not in the bad way, anyway.'

There was a sharp exhale.

'I lit a candle,' she said. 'In case. I'll light another now to say thanks. That's two you owe.'

'I'll pay in ham,' he said.

'And your wife?' she asked. 'How is she taking it?'

'Better than me,' he said. 'Relieved. Bossy. She's already telling me how to live my extra non-cancer days.'

'She's right,' his mother said. 'Don't waste them. And don't be thinking you're invincible either. You'll still mind yourself. You still have the age you have. I'm not losing you to stubbornness after surviving the MRI.'

He smiled.

'Yes, Mam,' he said.

'You'll call in tomorrow,' she added. 'Bring the letter. I like to see these things. I don't trust you to summarise properly.'

'I will,' he said.

When he hung up, the letter on the table seemed smaller now, its power diminished.

He took out the blue notebook, opened it to a fresh page, and wrote at the top: *MRI Results*.

The words that followed came easier than he'd expected.

The man in the white coat says benign,
says enlarged and awkward and in the way,
but not the thing we feared,
not the dark flower in the bone.

He wrote about the tube, the banging, the fake sky, the weight of the envelope, Joan's hand in his hair, his mother's candles, the thin thread of reprieve.

Halfway down the page he stopped, stared at what he'd written, then crossed out *reprieve* and wrote *margin* above it.

It felt more accurate. Not acquittal. Not sentence. Space at the edge of something.

In the weeks that followed, life didn't improve so much as rearrange itself again around the new information.

The tablets Kearney prescribed made him light-headed for a few days, then settled into the background. His trips to the bathroom became less urgent, less painful. The dull ache eased. He still woke at odd hours, but now the panic that accompanied those wakings had lost some of its bite.

His mind, having been deprived of one catastrophe, diverted its energy back to the other.

Joan's breath shortened further as February slid into March. The oxygen concentrator hummed for more hours of the day; the portable machine became as much a part of their keeping-safe kit as coats and keys.

Deirdre increased her visits, always framing each new

intervention not as an admission of defeat but as a way to extend the radius of Joan's world.

'This isn't about keeping you alive at all costs,' she said once, kneeling to adjust the tubing. 'It's about keeping you living as much as we can. There's a difference. You tell me what matters to you – getting to the garden, going to the shop, sitting at the lake – and we try to facilitate that. You're the boss. We're the assistants.'

Joan looked at her oxygen cylinder like a slightly sulky pet.

'Today,' she said, 'it matters that I can get to the kitchen without feeling like I've just run a marathon. Tomorrow, we'll see.'

They experimented with the morphine, small doses calibrated like spices. Too much and she felt muzzy, detached. Too little and every breath was a negotiation. They hovered around the edge of comfort, adjusting by millilitres.

One Friday afternoon, when the house was already full of the smell of roasting chicken and the muffled shouts of children in the estate coming out of school, Deirdre arrived with a thin folder.

'This is the advance care planning stuff,' she said, placing it on the table. 'We don't have to fill it in today. Or tomorrow. But I'd like you to have it. Look at it. Think. Scribble on it. It's not a contract; it's a conversation starter.'

Joan opened it; flicked through the pages.

'"Do you want to receive CPR?"' she read aloud. 'Tough first question.'

Deirdre smiled ruefully.

'They don't ease you in,' she said. 'But we can talk through it. A lot of the telly CPR is fantasy. On real bodies, at certain ages, with certain lungs, it's not always kind.'

They talked about it that evening, when Deirdre had gone

and the house was in that early-night lull, the lamp on, the television flickering quietly with something neither of them were fully watching.

'What do you think?' Ciarán asked, the folder open between them on the coffee table.

'I think if my heart stops when my lungs are already this bad, I don't want some stranger breaking my ribs to drag me back for more of the same,' she said, with no drama. 'I think if there's a good chance of meaningful recovery, that's one thing. But we're not in that story now, are we? We're in the long goodbye, not the surprise twist.'

He swallowed, the phrase catching.

'The long goodbye,' he repeated.

'It doesn't mean it has to be miserable,' she said. 'It just means we get to decide how long we spend at the door, putting our coats on. I'd rather not have someone shove me back into the hall if I've already stepped outside.'

He nodded, even as parts of him resisted the practical clarity of it.

'And hospital?' he asked. 'If you get an infection?'

'Short stays, if they help,' she said. 'No long stints on trolleys. No ICU with machines breathing for me. Not unless there's a realistic chance they can switch them off and I walk out. I don't want you sitting under fluorescent lights for weeks, living on vending-machine coffee, while I look like a prop in a sci-fi film.'

He thought of the hospital corridors, the smell, the waiting rooms.

'I'll write it,' he said hoarsely.

'You'll write it,' she agreed. 'And sign it. And then we'll go back to arguing about what to watch.'

When he filled in the sections later, pen hovering over boxes, the act felt both traitorous and loving. To write *Do not attempt resuscitation* beside the name he had written a thousand times on birthday cards and cheques and envelopes was to admit openly what had so far only been acknowledged in sidelong glances.

He placed the completed form in the folder, and put the folder on the shelf by the phone where Deirdre had suggested. It looked ordinary there, among the cookbooks and old takeaway menus.

'Do you hate me?' he asked that night, as they lay in bed, the dark familiar.

'For what?' she murmured.

'For agreeing,' he said. 'For signing things that … let you go.'

She turned her head on the pillow, made a small sound that might have been a laugh.

'I'd hate you more if you didn't,' she said. 'If you insisted on heroic measures so you could say you'd tried everything while I lay there suffering for your conscience. This way, when the time comes, we've already had the fight. We leave only the necessary grief for later.'

He let her logic settle, heavy and necessary.

In the morning, the folder was just another object in the house, like the concentrator, like the blue notebook, like his PSA result letter now shoved into a drawer.

The margins of their life had shifted again; the core remained strangely intact.

One Saturday in late March when a pale, watery sun made a half-hearted attempt at being cheerful, Joan surprised him.

'Get your coat,' she said, as he was washing up after lunch. 'And the portable oxygen. And the blue notebook.'

He turned from the sink, suds on his hands.

'Why?' he asked. 'Are we going on the run?'

'We're going to the park,' she said. 'The one with the duck pond. I want to see something that isn't our street or the hospital or the lake from inside a car. And I want you to bring that notebook and write something that isn't about waiting rooms.'

'You'll be wrecked,' he said automatically.

'I'm wrecked anyway,' she replied. 'Might as well be wrecked with ducks.'

It took them half an hour to get ready. Layers, inhaler, morphine dose timed, oxygen battery checked.

At the park, the air was colder than it had looked from the kitchen window, but there was a brightness in it. Children shrieked from the playground; dogs chased each other along the paths, their owners trailing behind.

They made their slow progress along the path that looped the pond. Joan held his arm; the concentrator trundled obligingly. Her breath was audible but not ragged, the oxygen doing its work.

The pond itself was a grey oval, reflecting the sky. A contingent of ducks bobbed on the surface, the drakes' heads a glossy green that always looked painted on. Someone had left slices of bread on the bank; the birds clustered and pecked with ruthless efficiency.

'They're fierce little yokes,' Joan said, watching them. 'No manners.'

'I like them,' he said. 'They know what they're about.'

They found a bench. It was slightly damp, but a folded scarf and his coat over the metal made it bearable.

'Sit,' she commanded. 'Write something. Not about death. Or hospitals. Or bodily fluids. See if you can remember how.'

He hesitated, then laughed. 'You're very demanding,' he said.

‘I have limited time to mould you into the writer you were supposed to be,’ she said. ‘Get on with it.’

He took out the blue notebook and the Biro he’d slipped into his pocket. The blank page stared back.

For a few minutes, nothing came. His mind kept reaching for the old themes – waiting, tests, machines, numbers. He let those thoughts move past and instead focused on what was directly in front of him.

The pond. The ducks. A child in a red hat throwing bits of something, her hands sticky. A man on a bench across the way, hunched in a big coat, eyes closed as if pinned to the moment by the weak sun. The faint smell of mud and water and fried onions from a food van somewhere at the edge of the park.

He began.

Spring pond, ducks carving grey water,
their bodies small, efficient machines of want.
Behind them, a girl in a red hat conducts,
her hands tossing crusts like blessings.

Beside him, Joan leaned her head back against the bench, eyes half-closed.

‘Read,’ she said, without opening them.

He did. His voice sounded tentative at first, then steadier.

‘It’s a start,’ she said, when he finished the fourth line. ‘You should put in the man over there. He looks like a metaphor waiting to happen.’

‘You’re incorrigible,’ he said.

‘That’s why you married me,’ she replied.

He added further lines, obediently:

On the far bench, a man in a borrowed coat

falls asleep in the weak sun,
his mouth open to whatever comes.

When he read it, she smiled properly.

'There,' she said. 'See? You can still do it. The world is not made entirely of test results. Ducks persist.'

He closed the notebook gently.

'I'm glad we came,' he said.

'Me too,' she said. 'I can't walk far any more, but I can sit. Sitting is underrated.'

They stayed another ten minutes, maybe fifteen. The air bit at their fingers; the light flattened further. When Joan's colour started to fade, he stood.

'Ready to go?' he asked.

'Reluctantly,' she said. 'But yes. I don't want Deirdre to have to scrape me off a park bench and give me a lecture on pacing.'

On the way back to the car, Joan's breath hitched a bit more, the effort of the afternoon catching up.

'Thank you,' she said quietly.

'For what?' he asked.

'For bringing me,' she said. 'For not wrapping me completely in cotton wool. For letting me be tired because of something other than our house.'

He squeezed her hand. 'Thank you,' he said. 'For telling me to write about ducks.'

She laughed, then coughed, then laughed again.

At home, when she'd rested and eaten and the oxygen had restored some colour to her face, he went into the small room and copied the pond poem, lengthened now, onto a fresh page. He added a title at the top: *Margins*.

The word seemed to fit. Not only for the ducks on the edge of the pond, but for the whole season they were in – living in the white space around bold black text that spoke of diagnoses and prognoses and plans.

He knew, with a clarity that didn't make it easier, that there would be more letters, more forms, more decisions. His prostate might stay behaved or not. Joan's lungs would not suddenly regrow. The folder on the shelf would not disappear.

But there would also be benches and ducks and babies learning to walk and students rolling their eyes and mothers wanting the details and sisters turning up with apple tart. There would be poems about washing machines and ponds and hospital chairs. There would be lake days and park days and days where getting from the bed to the kitchen was the full achievement.

That night, he felt something he hadn't felt in a long time. Not hope exactly. That suggested a future he didn't dare to sketch too clearly. More like … permission.

Permission to inhabit the days they had, without always standing in them as if in a rehearsal for the end. Permission to be relieved about his own reprieve without apology. Permission to write about ducks.

In the darkness, he reached for her hand.

'Awake?' he whispered.

'Mmm,' she said. 'Half. Which half do you want?'

He smiled.

'Thank you,' he said.

'Again?' she said. 'You'll wear it out.'

'For telling me not to write the ending,' he said. 'I nearly did.'

She squeezed his fingers.

'Leave room,' she murmured. 'That's where the light gets in.'

He lay there and thought: this is what margins are for. Not emptiness, but space for notes. For corrections. For additions no one saw coming.

Chapter Sixteen

The Letter

It arrived in a plain white envelope, the address written in tidy, unfamiliar script. There was no sender marked, only a postmark from Birmingham. Ciarán found it sitting on the hallway floor that morning, half buried under junk mail and takeaway menus. He picked it up with mild curiosity, expecting a misplaced bill or some clerical error, and slid it into the inside pocket of his coat before heading out the door.

He didn't open it until much later, after returning from his mother's, where the evening had been spent watching her slowly plate a dinner for two, only to set one back in the fridge.

He sat at the kitchen table and slit it open. The paper inside was thin, blue-lined, folded twice with care. He unfolded it slowly, almost reverently, and began to read.

Dear Mr Devlin,

I hope this letter finds you well. You don't know me, but I knew your father many years ago. We worked together on a tunnelling crew in the West Midlands in the 1960s. My name is Frank Hanratty. I came across your father's death notice in The Irish Post *a few months back, and it stirred up more than I expected. Memories, mostly. But also a photograph I found among my old papers that I thought might be of interest to you.*

Your father was a quiet man, not the type to boast, but I remember him well. He saved my arm once – we were pouring concrete into a formwork when the mix burst loose. I would've been crushed if he hadn't pulled me back. We were both young and far from home, trying to make something better for the people we left behind. He talked about you – even then, though you were only a baby. Always with pride.

I don't mean to intrude. I just thought you might want to know that, over here, someone remembered him. He mattered.

Yours sincerely,
Frank Hanratty

Ciarán read it twice. Then a third time, the words becoming quieter each time, until they settled into something like silence. He noticed his hands trembling, just slightly, as he set the page down.

He hadn't expected to cry. But something about the matter-of-fact kindness, the detail about the tunnelling crew, the memory of his father's strength – it reached deeper than he was ready for. There was, tucked neatly behind the letter, a photograph. Black and white. Six or seven men in work coats and flat caps, standing by the mouth of what looked like a shaft. Mud on their boots. A small crane in the background.

There he was.

His father. Sean Devlin.

Not yet the man who ran a machinery business, or paced the length of a workshop with an invoice in hand. Not yet the man who sat in the same armchair each evening, quiet, watching the news with arms crossed. Here he was a young man, laughing. His arm slung around another lad's shoulder. His face thinner, but recognisably the same. And that smile – almost wild with youth.

Ciarán stared at the photo for a long time.

Later, he showed the letter to Joan. She sat propped up on the sofa, a hot-water bottle under her blanket and a tea cooling on the side table.

'He saved someone's life,' she said, quietly.

He nodded. 'I didn't know that.'

'Of course you didn't. He wouldn't have told you.' She took the photo from him, studied it carefully. 'He looks different.'

'Younger.'

'Freer.'

Ciarán nodded again. There was a strange ache at the edge of his throat. 'I always thought he resented leaving Ireland. Like it had broken something in him.'

Joan looked at him. 'Maybe it had. But he didn't let it show.' They sat in silence for a while. Then she said, 'You should write back.'

'To Frank?'

'Yes. Let him know it meant something. That it mattered.'

That night, Ciarán couldn't sleep. The letter rested on the bedside table, the photograph tucked inside it again. He kept turning it over in his mind – this version of his father that had existed long before him, a man with laughter on his face and calluses on his hands, living in damp boarding houses, wiring home a few shillings every week.

He'd never once heard that story about the concrete pour. Never heard the name Frank Hanratty. How many stories had vanished with his father?

The next morning, he went to his father's workshop again.

Not to fix or clear; just to sit. Dust shimmered in the beam of light falling through a cracked pane. He found himself scanning the old drawers again, more carefully this time. Letters, receipts, warranty slips. A stub of a blue pencil. A licence from 1973. Everything brittle at the edges.

He sat on an old stool and thought about how much of a person's life disappears, how much remains only in memory – and, when memory falters, in silence.

In the afternoon, he wrote back:

Dear Mr Hanratty,

Thank you for your letter. It reached me at a time when I needed to hear it. My father didn't speak much about his time in England. I always assumed it was a difficult chapter he preferred not to revisit. But reading your words, and seeing the photograph – it's like finding a small window into a room I never knew existed.

Thank you for remembering him. For reminding me that he lived more than one life, and that it mattered.

Warm regards,

Ciarán Devlin

That evening, he visited his mother. She was in her armchair, knitting a scarf that had grown impossibly long. She looked up as he entered.

'You look tired,' she said.

'I am, a bit.'

He took out the photo and placed it in her lap.

She stared at it for a long time. Her fingers trembled slightly as they traced the image.

'I remember that coat,' she murmured. 'He sent me a letter saying he'd bought it in Wolverhampton. Cost him half a week's wages.' She smiled, soft and distant. 'He always looked good in navy.'

Ciarán sat beside her and didn't say anything.

After a while, she said, 'He was lonely, I think, when he was over there. He was proud, but he hated the damp. Said the walls wept at night.'

'Why didn't he ever talk about it?'

She shrugged, her knitting abandoned on her lap. 'Men didn't. Not then. They just carried things.'

On the way home, he pulled into the lay-by near the lake. The same spot where he used to sit as a teenager with a notebook, scribbling lyrics, dreaming about getting out.

The water was still. A single heron stalked the shore in the gathering dark.

He thought of his father standing in Birmingham muck, smiling for the camera, proud and weary and alive.

He thought of himself now, stretched between generations, between silences and stories.

And he thought of Joan, waiting at home, warm under her blanket, watching the clock for his return.

He stayed until the dark folded itself completely over the lake. Then he turned the key and drove home.

Back at home, Joan had brought out the old record player. A stack of vinyl sat beside it like a forgotten shrine.

'You remember how to work that thing?' he asked.

She gave him a look. 'I'm not ninety.'

She chose Nina Simone – '*I Loves You, Porgy*' – and set the needle down gently. The room filled with that voice, warm and aching.

They didn't talk much. They didn't need to. The music threaded through the silence like a stitch.

'I always loved this one,' she said.

'You used to play it in the flat in Ranelagh,' he said. 'When I'd be trying to write poems and you'd be making pasta.'

She smiled. 'And you'd sulk because I was humming.'

He smiled too. 'I was a brooding artist.'

'No,' she said. 'You were a gobshite.'

He laughed. Loudly. The sound startled a bird outside.

Joan stood slowly and offered him her hand.

'Come on,' she said.

'What?'

'Dance with me.'

'Are you serious?'

'Yes.'

They moved to the centre of the conservatory. The record skipped slightly as it looped into the next track. Nina kept singing.

They danced. Slowly. Carefully. Her hand in his. His arm around her waist. Her head resting on his shoulder.

He felt the sting behind his eyes, sharp and sudden. The breath caught in his throat. But he kept smiling.

Joan couldn't see his face, and he was glad.

Later, after the music ended and she was resting again on the sofa, he went to the kitchen.

Then he opened the notebook and wrote:

Today, the world stopped breaking.
Just for a little while.

He underlined the last line, shut the book, and put it back on the shelf. Then he made tea, brought it in, and kissed her forehead. She smiled up at him and said, 'Still a gobshite.' He laughed. And loved her.

Chapter Seventeen

A Different Weather

By April, the rain had learned new tricks.

It came in sideways now, bullying the bare branches and rattling the windows. Some mornings the sky sat so low over the town that the roofs looked as if they were holding it up by themselves. Other days there was a brighter, thinner light, a suggestion that somewhere, beyond all this grey, spring was thinking about the place.

On one such morning, Ciarán sat on the edge of the plastic chair in O'Malley's surgery, looking at a poster about cholesterol and a clock that insisted it was ten past ten when his body was convinced it was at least noon.

O'Malley, behind his ancient computer, peered at the screen, his glasses low on his nose.

'Well now,' he said, dragging the words out as if they weighed something. 'Here we are.'

'We are,' Ciarán agreed, trying not to watch his own file being opened.

'You've been on the tablets nearly six weeks,' O'Malley went on. 'Any bother? Dizziness, fainting, loss of your legendary vigour?'

'I get light-headed if I stand up too fast,' Ciarán said. 'And

I'm up less in the night. My visits to the bathroom are less dramatic. As medical adventures go, it could be worse.'

O'Malley grunted approvingly. 'Good,' he said. 'We'll keep you on them so. Give me your arm there and we'll take the blood pressure while we're at it. Make a day of it.'

The cuff tightened around his upper arm with the familiar, unpleasant squeeze. He watched the digital numbers climb, then fall.

'Not bad,' O'Malley said. 'A bit on the lower side than before, but that's the tablets.'

He clicked a few more times. 'PSA's down as well,' he added, almost casually. 'Not dramatically, but a notch.'

It was such a small number in the grand scheme of things, but it felt like moving a rock uphill with one shoulder.

'That's good?' Ciarán asked, needing it said aloud.

'That's good,' O'Malley confirmed. 'It's going in the right direction. We don't chase it down to zero at your age with that prostate. We just don't want it sprinting. A gentle amble is acceptable.'

He turned from the screen and looked at him properly.

'And yourself?' he asked. 'Aside from the plumbing.'

'I'm … functioning,' Ciarán said. 'I teach. I pee. Joan still tells me what to do. My mother still complains about the weather. The world turns.'

O'Malley tilted his head. 'Sleeping?'

'Some nights,' he said. 'Others I lie awake thinking about tubes and letters and lungs and what kind of eejit waits till fifty-eight to discover he has a prostate.'

'Ah, we've all sorts,' O'Malley said. 'There was a man in last week who thought his liver was on the left. You're ahead of the field.'

He folded his hands, steepling his fingers.

'You know,' he said, 'they asked me at the case conference

if you'd like to talk to someone. Counsellor in the hospice. Or one of the men in the support group. Prostate lads who've been through the mill. They say it helps. Sharing.'

Ciarán pictured himself in a room full of strangers, all of them taking turns to describe their bodily functions and fears while a well-meaning facilitator nodded in circles. The idea made his skin crawl and yet, somewhere under that, there was a tug of recognition.

'I don't know,' he said. 'I … talk to Joan. And your man in Sligo. And you.'

O'Malley smiled briefly.

'I'm not here to force you,' he said. 'I'm here to remind you the option exists. You don't have to be the strong one in every room, you know.'

'I don't feel particularly strong,' Ciarán said. 'I feel like someone who's been told to carry two buckets while wearing a pair of shoes he's not sure fit.'

'That's more self-awareness than half the parish,' O'Malley said. 'We'll call it a win.'

He leaned back, the chair creaking in that way it had for twenty years.

'Look,' he said. 'In simple terms: your prostate is behaving itself under medication. Your bladder will hopefully stop shouting at you quite so often. You will still have to get up once a night; that's the privilege of age. We'll check your bloods again in six months. Unless you have new symptoms, you're not on my urgent list any more.'

The phrase *not on my urgent list* landed with mixed feelings. Relief, certainly. But also a strange emptiness, as if he'd been pushed a few rows back from the front of some invisible queue he'd been braced to stand at the head of.

'That's good,' he said, because it was.

'It is,' O'Malley said. 'It means you can put more of

your worry into Joan, if you insist on worrying. But I'd still recommend you save some for yourself. Eat a vegetable now and then. Walk. Try to have one thought a day that isn't about illness. That kind of thing.'

'I'll write it down,' Ciarán said.

'Do,' O'Malley replied. 'But don't write it in a poem. Poems make everything too important.'

At school, the weather in the corridors had changed as well.

The Easter exams and holidays had come and gone, leaving a trail of red pens and resigned sighs. The sixth years moved through the days with that peculiar mix of bravado and panic that always appeared around this time of year.

In 6A History, he handed back their essays on the Economic War.

'Overall, not bad,' he said, standing at the top of the room. 'A few of you have grasped that cows and tariffs can be dramatic. Some of you still think "de Valera fixed everything by being tall". We'll work on nuance.'

There was a low chuckle.

He moved down the rows, leaving papers on desks. A few students glanced at their marks, groaned or breathed out. Doyle at the back flipped his over, unread, as if postponing the inevitable.

Ciarán smiled to himself. He recognised the tactic; he'd used it often as a student.

When he reached the front again, one of the quieter girls – Aisling, hair tucked behind her ears, copy always immaculate – raised a hand.

'Sir?' she said. 'Can I ask something not about cows?'

'That's a relief,' he said. 'Go on.'

She hesitated. 'You know the poem we did last Autumn,

when you were teaching us English,' she said, 'the Heaney one about his father and the ploughing?'

'"Follower",' he supplied.

'Yeah,' she said. 'You said sometimes people write poems about … like … ordinary things. Their houses. Their parents. And they're actually about big things underneath.'

'That sounds like something I might say,' he said.

She fiddled with her pen. 'There's this thing,' she went on, 'where … like … my dad is sick. Not … like … as bad as some. But he has this thing with his heart. And he keeps making jokes about it. And we all keep making jokes about it. And I was trying to write about it for English and it came out weird. Like it was either too jokey or too serious. I don't know how you … balance it.'

The room had gone unusually quiet. Even Doyle had stopped doodling.

He glanced around at them, aware of their eyes, their self-consciousness, their curiosity.

'First of all,' he said, 'I'm sorry your dad is sick. That's a lot, even if he's making jokes about it.'

She shrugged, looking down. 'He says it's not a big deal,' she muttered.

'People say a lot of things,' he said. 'Sometimes to protect themselves. Sometimes to protect the people around them. Sometimes because they don't know how to say "I'm scared" without the whole world collapsing.' He paused. 'Sometimes teachers do that too.'

A few heads tilted.

'To your question,' he went on. 'If you're writing about something like that, you don't have to pick one tone at the expense of the other. Jokes can sit beside fear. Ordinary details can sit beside big truths. Maybe you write about your dad buttering toast with his tablets lined up beside the knife. Or about the way he holds his chest when he laughs, like he's checking it's still there. You don't have to say "my dad might die" for the reader to understand there's something serious happening. You just show us how he butters his toast.'

Aisling's pen hovered over her copy. 'So … like … showing instead of telling,' she said.

'Exactly,' he replied. 'The old cliché has some use. You show us what the kitchen looks like. The sounds. The smells. The way you feel when you hear the doctor's name on the phone. Let the humour in. Let the fear in. They can share the page. They share your house every day anyway, by the sounds of it.'

He felt, as he spoke, that he was not just answering her.

'So yeah,' he added. 'You can write whatever helps. Just … be kind to yourself when you read it back. Don't mark it like a Leaving Cert paper. It's not for that.'

Aisling nodded slowly, her eyes brighter than they had been.

'Thanks,' she said.

'You're welcome,' he replied.

He turned back to the board and wrote in neat capitals: *ORDINARY DETAIL = BIG FEELING*.

'Right,' he said. 'Back to cows and coal.'

The bad spell came on a Thursday morning, quick as a weather change.

He was in the utility room, wrestling laundry into the dryer, when he heard a sound from upstairs that sent a cold spear through him. A gasping, strangled cough, followed by a thud.

He dropped the clothes, the damp bundle hitting the floor with a soft slap, and took the stairs two at a time – his back complaining, his heart thudding.

The bathroom door was half open. Inside, Joan sat on the

closed toilet lid in her dressing gown, one hand gripping the sink, her face chalk-white. The towel she'd been using hung from the rail, damp. The portable oxygen machine hummed at her feet, tubing in place, but her chest heaved shallowly, her mouth open in a silent attempt to catch air.

'Joan,' he said, his voice too loud in the small room.

She turned her head a fraction, eyes wide.

'Got … ahead … of myself,' she managed between breaths. 'Shower. Stupid.'

He was already on autopilot. Move. Do. Fix.

He turned the concentrator up a notch, moved it closer, untangled the tubing with shaking hands.

'In through your nose,' he said, trying to keep his own voice calm. 'Out like you're blowing out a candle gently. Like Deirdre said. Small breaths. Don't chase the big one.'

She tried. The first few attempts were ragged, panicky. He crouched in front of her, one hand hovering near her knee, not quite touching, as if any contact might break the fragile line of breath.

Her chest still hitching, she managed two, three shallow pulls through her nose, letting them out slowly through pursed lips. Little by little, the wildness in her eyes receded. The muscles in her neck loosened a fraction.

'Better?' he asked, after what felt like an hour but was probably two minutes.

She nodded, the movement tiny.

'Stupid,' she whispered, when she could trust her voice. 'Thought I could manage a proper hair wash. Moron.'

'You're not stupid,' he said. 'You're bored. There's a difference.'

He stayed there, crouched on the tiles, until her breathing had settled into its new, normal-for-now rhythm. Only then did he feel the delayed shakiness in his own limbs.

'I'm ringing Deirdre,' he said. 'She'll kill me if I don't report this.'

'She'll give out,' Joan said weakly. 'She loves giving out.'

'Good,' he said. 'We need someone with energy for that.'

He helped her back to the bedroom and dried her hair gently with the towel, the domesticity of it almost absurd after the panic. Then he put the phone on loudspeaker on the locker while it rang.

Deirdre's voice, when she answered, was brisk, but softened quickly as he described what had happened.

'And now?' she asked. 'Breathing?'

'Slower now,' Joan said, leaning toward the phone. 'Like a woman sitting on a chair, not climbing a mountain.'

'Any chest pain?' Deirdre asked. 'Sharp? Tight?'

'More like someone sat on a corner of me,' Joan said. 'But it's easing.'

'And colour?' Deirdre continued. 'Any blueness?'

'She's pale,' Ciarán said. 'But that's normal. No Smurf effect.'

'All right,' Deirdre said. 'Good job with the breathing. That's exactly what you're meant to do. You've had what we'd call an exertional episode. You pushed past the limit your lungs can tolerate right now. It happens. It's scary, but we can manage it.'

'Should we come in?' he asked. 'Hospital?'

'Not if we can avoid it,' she said. 'Not for this. Here's what we'll do. I'm on my way out to see someone near you anyway. I'll call in within the hour. In the meantime, keep the oxygen on. Keep her sitting up. No heroics. If, and I mean if, her breath shortens again to the point where she can't get a sentence out, and the oxygen and breathing exercises don't touch it, then you ring me again and you ring 999. But from what you're describing, we can handle this at home.'

The phrase *at home* felt like mercy.

True to her word, Deirdre arrived forty minutes later, cheeks pink from the weather, clipboard under her arm.

She checked Joan's oxygen saturation, listened to her chest, watched her walk the few steps from the bed to the door and back.

'You scared yourself,' she said, when Joan had settled again. 'But you did exactly the right thing. You stopped. You sat. You used the oxygen properly. You let the panic peak and pass.'

'I panicked,' Joan said dryly. 'That was the main skill.'

'Panic is normal,' Deirdre replied. 'What matters is what you do in it. You've both earned gold stars for this one.'

She turned to Ciarán.

'And you,' she said, 'you didn't fling her into the car and drive like a mad yoke to A&E. That's progress. You rang. You stayed. You breathed with her. That's the job.'

He felt his shoulders loosen a little at the affirmation.

'It's hard,' he admitted. 'Every time something shifts, my brain goes straight to "This is it".'

'I know,' she said. 'It's a horrible way to live – always braced. Let me say this clearly: there will be more episodes like this. Some worse, some better. They are not each "the end". They are bumps. Important ones. We respond. We adjust. We don't rehearse the funeral every time.'

Joan gave a small, wry smile. 'You've been talking to my husband,' she said.

'I talk to everyone,' Deirdre said. 'It's a curse.'

She sat on the edge of the bed, looking at them both.

'Look,' she went on. 'We're on a hill that slopes, yes. We're not pretending otherwise. But we're not on a cliff face. We have room for pacing. Today's lesson is that showering is a two-person job now. You'll need help. Or you do it in stages. Hair one day, body another. Glamorous? No. Effective? Yes.'

Joan sighed. 'I hate it,' she said. 'The needing-help part.'

'I know,' Deirdre said. 'But think of it this way: the less energy you spend on washing your hair, the more you have for the ducks. We prioritise.'

After she left, the house felt at once safer and more precarious again, as it always did after medical visits. The bathroom, still smelling faintly of shampoo and steam, seemed like a small hazard course.

'Back to sponge baths in the bedroom like the old Westerns,' Joan said. 'You can hum the theme tune.'

'I'll get you a cowboy hat,' he said.

'You'd like that,' she replied.

He laughed, but later, when he was alone in the kitchen making tea, he had to lean his hands on the counter for a moment to steady himself. The image of her gasping on the tiles kept replaying. His own helplessness in that first second felt like a physical bruise.

He picked up the blue notebook from the table where it had been left open the night before. Without consciously deciding to, he wrote:

You are sitting on the closed lid of the toilet,
towel half on, half off,
your breath like someone else's radio
breaking up in the next room.

The pen trembled a little on the strokes, but the act of putting it there, outside his body, calmed something in him. By the time the kettle boiled, the lines had settled on the page. The worst of the panic had leaked into the ink.

A week later, the crisis had receded into the category of Things They'd Managed.

The weather shifted in small ways. A day of unexpected sun. In the corner of the garden, the lilies began their tentative emergence, green shoots pushing up through the grass.

On Friday, Maeve rang.

'There's a thing on in the library,' she said. 'Poetry evening. Open mic. Some local crowd. And one fella they got from Galway who's published. I'm going. You should come.'

'I'm not sure I'm up to being publicly depressed,' he said.

'Don't be dramatic,' she said. 'You can sit at the back and heckle. Or – mad thought – you could bring that blue notebook and read something. You know, like a person who actually writes.'

The idea made his stomach flip.

'Jesus, Maeve,' he said. 'I'm not twenty. I can't be getting up in front of strangers with my midlife angst.'

'Who better?' she said. 'We're in an epidemic of midlife angst. You'd be among your own.'

He hesitated. He thought of Aisling in his class, of her question. Of telling her to let humour and fear share the page. Of telling her not to mark herself like an exam.

'I'll think about it,' he said.

Joan, when he mentioned it that evening, was more direct.

'You're going,' she said. 'And you're reading. Otherwise I'll ring the library and tell them you're a fraud.'

'You can't come,' he said. 'It'll be crowded. The air will be bad.'

'I know,' she said. 'That's why you're going. You're my envoy. I want to hear you've stood up in a badly lit room and inflicted your lines on innocent people.'

'You're very supportive,' he said.

‘I am,’ she replied. ‘I just don’t want to miss the chance to annoy you into doing something good.’

In the end, he went.

The library’s meeting room was half full when he and Maeve slipped in. The chairs were arranged in loose rows facing a makeshift lectern. A table at the back held tea, instant coffee and a plate of biscuits already showing gaps.

The crowd was a mix – students in hoodies, older women with colourful scarves, a retired man from the town he recognised vaguely from GAA matches, a couple in their thirties holding hands.

The Galway poet, a slight man with hair that seemed to belong in another decade, read first. His work was careful, intricate, full of seas and stones and fathers who rarely spoke. Ciarán listened, appreciating the craft even as a part of him floated elsewhere, thinking of Joan on the couch at home, of the oxygen machine’s unwavering hum.

When the organiser opened the floor for anyone who wanted to share, there was the usual awkward silence while people negotiated internally with their own dares.

A young woman went first, reading a short poem about leaving home for the city and the smell of her mother’s kitchen. A man in a fleece read something overlong about politics, his anger drowning his imagery. There was a haiku about the river that was more enthusiastic than precise.

Maeve nudged him.

‘Now or never,’ she whispered.

His heart thudded. His palms were suddenly damp.

He thought of Joan’s voice in his ear: *Don’t write the ending yet. Leave room.* He thought of the candle, the lake, the bathroom tiles.

He stood up before he could talk himself out of it.

At the front, the lectern felt taller than necessary. The room blurred at the edges. He cleared his throat.

'Erm …' he began. 'I'm Ciarán. I teach History and English. I also … apparently … write poems. This one is called "The Candle in the Window".'

He opened the notebook, the familiar pages steadier than his hands.

As he read, his voice shook at first, then found a rhythm. The poem spoke of matches, of glass, of his mother's porch, of the woman in the upstairs bedroom counting tablets, of the boy in London with his phone screen for light. It ended with a line he hadn't planned until it was on the page:

We light it for the ones who are not lost yet, only delayed by weather.

When he finished, there was a small silence. Then a modest round of applause, the polite, earnest kind people gave in these rooms. He felt his face flush.

Back in his seat, Maeve squeezed his knee.

'Proud of you,' she murmured.

Afterwards, over too-sweet tea in polystyrene cups, a woman with short grey hair approached him.

'Excuse me,' she said. 'I liked your poem. The candle one. My husband is in the hospice. We have a candle in the kitchen window every night now. I hadn't really thought about it until you said that. The … "delayed by weather" bit. That's … yeah. That's it.'

He swallowed.

'Thank you,' he said. 'For telling me.'

On the walk home later, the air sharp, his breath puffing, he felt strangely lighter. Exposed, certainly – his private lines had been out in the open – but also connected, as if the poem were a small bridge between his house and someone else's.

When he came in the door, Joan was half asleep on the couch, the television flickering low.

'Well?' she said, without opening her eyes. 'Did they boo?'

'Only once,' he said. 'And that was at the man with the politics manifesto.'

She smiled.

'How did it feel?' she asked.

'Like jumping into the lake,' he said. 'Cold. Shocking. And then, once you're in, you realise you can move.'

She opened her eyes then, looked at him.

'Good,' she said. 'You need to move. Even if I'm stuck on this couch half the time, I don't want your brain ossifying.'

He sat beside her, the weight of the evening settling gently into his bones rather than crushing them.

'Maybe there's a book in it,' he said, half joking.

'There is,' she said. 'You know there is. You've already named it.'

He looked at her, at the way the lamplight caught the lines on her face, at the cannula looping under her nose like a small, persistent question mark.

That night, after she'd gone up to bed – carefully, step by step, his hand hovering near her elbow – he stayed at the kitchen table with the blue notebook open for longer than usual.

He wrote at the top of a fresh page:

The Light at Evening.

And then, slowly, feeling his way, he began:

Not the blaze that makes headlines,
not the first fierce shock of morning,
but the thin, patient radiance

that finds its way under doors
and through old curtains,
laying itself quietly along the sill.

He paused for a few minutes to read over the words, listening to their rhythm.

Then he wrote on.

It colours the washing on the radiator,
turns the steam from the kettle into ghosts,
settles on your hand as you reach
for the tablets, the pen, the match.

He thought of all the evenings they'd lived through in this house, the ordinary ones and the ones that had lodged in the bone – the night after his father's funeral, the evening of Joan's diagnosis, the Christmas just gone with his mother at the table.

We learn to live here, in this sideways brightness,
where nothing is promised past the next breath
and yet we still put the kettle on,
still hang the towel on the back of the door,
still argue about the best way to cut bread.

He stopped there, the words sitting heavy and right.

Chapter Eighteen

The Lake Day

The first truly fine day came disguised as an ordinary Saturday.

There had been hints, of course – a softening in the air, the daffodils in the front garden making a half-hearted attempt at cheer, a brightness that lingered ten minutes longer in the evenings. But this was different. When Ciarán opened the back door at eight that morning to shake out the crumbs from the breadboard, he stepped into a world that smelled faintly of cut grass and warmed tarmac instead of wet soil and oil.

The sky was a pale, washed blue. Thin clouds drifted without much conviction. The air had that particular softness that made you acutely aware of your own skin.

He stood there a moment, breadboard in hand, listening. Somewhere in the estate, a lawnmower coughed into life. A blackbird was giving out from a television aerial. The day felt less like a punishment and more like an invitation.

From the kitchen, Joan called, 'Are you eloping?'

'Tempting,' he said, coming back in. 'It's decent out. Proper spring. The world has remembered how to be outside.'

She was at the table, dressing gown on, hair scraped back, oxygen tubing in place. Light from the back door caught the small silver strands at her temple.

'Is it?' she asked, eyes flicking to the patch of sky she could see through the gap in the blind.

'It is,' he said. 'We could hang clothes on the line instead of turning the house into a steam room.'

She hesitated, then said, 'Could we …?'

He knew what she meant before she finished.

'The lake?' he asked.

She nodded. 'Not today, necessarily,' she said quickly, as if afraid of jinxing it. 'Soon. Before it gets too hot. I know that sounds ridiculous in Ireland, but you know what I mean. While I still have enough in me to get from the car to the rock without collapsing into some heroic tableau.'

He put the breadboard down, sat opposite her.

'We could do it,' he said. 'With planning. The portable oxygen. The wheelchair from the hospice if we need it. A flask. Ham sandwiches. The whole kit.'

She smiled, a small, cautious thing.

'I've been thinking about it,' she admitted. 'Every time we drive past in the car, my lungs sulk. They remember walking down to the shore with no second thought, no mental maths about energy. I'd like to remind them what it feels like. Even if it's just sitting in the car with the window down.'

He looked at her, weighing her colour, the way her shoulders rose when she breathed.

'We'll ask Deirdre,' he said. 'See what she thinks. Make a plan that doesn't involve you being heroic. I'm done with heroics in bathrooms.'

She wrinkled her nose. 'Me too,' she said. 'Though I did enjoy the drama of you barging in like a man in a soap opera.'

He laughed. 'My acting career peaked in that moment.'

Deirdre's response, when he brought it up at her next visit, was characteristically direct.

'Yes,' she said, before he'd finished the sentence. 'Go. As long as we don't do it like amateurs.'

They sat around the table – their unofficial war council. Joan with her mug of tea, Ciarán with a pen poised over a page, Deirdre with her clipboard, Maeve who'd dropped in ostensibly to return a book but clearly had no intention of leaving while plans were being made.

'What counts as amateur?' Joan asked, amused.

'Throwing yourself into it on a day when your breath is bad,' Deirdre said, ticking points off on her fingers. 'Forgetting the portable oxygen. Deciding to climb a hill "while we're there". Wearing shoes you haven't worn in three years. Refusing the wheelchair out of pride. That kind of thing.'

'I see you,' Joan said. 'And I feel deeply attacked.'

'Good,' Deirdre replied. 'Spite can be a motivator.'

They agreed on a day the following week when the forecast promised dry weather and mild temperatures. Deirdre would organise a lightweight folding wheelchair from the hospice. Maeve would drive.

In the days leading up to it, the trip took on an almost ceremonial quality. Ciarán found the old flask in the press, washed it so thoroughly that the lingering taste of last decade's soup finally faded. He bought sliced ham and a decent loaf of bread. Joan insisted on supervising the sandwich assembly.

'Thick, not mean,' she said, watching him spread butter. 'We're not on a health kick.'

He cut the sandwiches into triangles, the way he always had for lake days, and wrapped them in greaseproof paper. An apple or two found their way into the bag, more out of habit than desire.

The blue notebook went in as well, slipped between the tea towel and the flask.

'Write something nice,' Joan said. 'If you write about my breathing, I'll flick crumbs at you.'

On the morning itself, the weather held.

The sky was not the perfect blue of postcards, but it was high and unthreatening. The air had that fresh, just-washed feeling that made his lungs feel greedier.

They took their time getting ready. Joan showered in stages, with him in the bathroom and the door open, oxygen cannula firmly in place. The panic of that earlier episode hovered, but stayed politely in the background.

'See?' she said, when she was dressed and sitting on the bed afterwards. 'No drama. Very disappointing.'

'I prefer boring,' he said. 'We should have a loyalty card for boring days.'

Maeve arrived with the car at eleven, having done a supermarket run for extra snacks 'in case the ham sandwiches aren't enough', as if famine were a likely consequence of a two-hour outing.

She and Ciarán manoeuvred the wheelchair into the boot, arguing over angles and the best way to fold it. The portable concentrator, fully charged, sat by the front door like a small obedient dog.

'Have you told your mother that we are going out for the day?' Joan asked, as he checked the house for the third time.

'Yes. She said to tell you not to fall in. And she made that face she makes when she wants to say more and doesn't,' he said.

'I like that face,' Joan said. 'It means she's thinking, not just worrying.'

When they finally set off, Joan in the front seat, him in the back with the bag, the house looked smaller in the rear-view mirror. The estate slipped past in familiar scenes: children on scooters, a man washing his car with conscientious swipes, a woman hanging a line of clothes that snapped gently in the breeze.

The road to Lough Allen had not changed. It rarely did. The ditches were a little more overgrown; a cottage that had been empty for years now had fresh paint and a new car outside. Sheep stood in fields with that combination of blankness and mild suspicion they always had.

As they drove, Joan's hand rested lightly on the dash, her fingers drumming occasionally to some inaudible rhythm.

'You all right?' Ciarán asked, leaning forward.

'So far,' she said. 'It's strange. My chest feels both tight and … hopeful. Like it's not quite sure which way to go.'

He knew what she meant. The car carried not just their bodies but a cargo of past and future. They'd driven this road as young teachers with weekends ahead of them, as a couple escaping for an hour from arguments or long silences. To drive it now, with oxygen tubing and a wheelchair in the boot, was to overlay all those journeys on this one.

When they crested the last hill and the lake appeared, he felt the familiar shift inside – the sense of something in him opening, even now.

Lough Allen lay broad and grey-blue under the high sky. The far shore was clear, the hills beyond softened by distance rather than fog. There was a slight ripple on the surface where the wind moved, but no white horses. It looked, he thought, less like an image and more like a fact.

They pulled into the small lay-by. The rough gravel crunched under the tyres. The familiar low wall marked the drop to the shore.

'Right,' Maeve said, switching off the engine. 'Operation Lake. Slow and no heroics. Remember the rules.'

The first decision was whether to use the wheelchair or

attempt the few steps down to the rock unaided. The path from the lay-by was short but uneven, a mix of compacted earth and stones, sloping slightly.

Joan eyed it, measuring.

'I want to try it on my own two legs,' she said quietly. 'If it goes wrong, you can roll me back in the chair and I'll listen to you say "I told you so" for the rest of my natural life.'

Deirdre's voice was still in his head. No heroics. No pride. He weighed that against the look on Joan's face – the mixture of determination and fear.

'We'll do both,' he said. 'You walk. I bring the chair beside you. If anything feels off, you sit. No arguments. Agreed?'

She nodded. 'Agreed,' she said.

He unfolded the chair, its metal joints clicking into place with a sound that made him feel older than ever. The portable concentrator hummed when he switched it on; the tubing looped over Joan's ears and under her nose like a thin, clear bridle.

They set off.

The first few steps were tentative, but her legs remembered their job. She placed her feet carefully, feeling for the solidity beneath the mud. His hand hovered near her elbow, not quite touching. Maeve rolled the empty chair behind them, a slow metal shadow.

The air off the water hit them – a coolness that carried the smell of lake and reed and distant turf smoke. A few gulls wheeled. Somewhere a dog barked, invisible.

By the time they reached the rock that had become *their* place over the years – a flat, slightly lichenous slab near the edge – Joan's breath was faster. Not quite panicked, but working.

She sat down heavily, one hand on the rock, the other on her chest.

'All right?' he asked, crouching.

'Give me … a minute,' she said between breaths. 'My lungs are … filing a complaint.'

They waited. The concentrator hummed. She took small, steady pulls of air, letting each one out slowly. Her shoulders, which had been up around her ears, began to lower.

'Okay,' she said at last. 'This is … okay.'

They arranged themselves on the rock, Joan at the flattest part, a folded coat under her for comfort. He sat beside her, feet braced against a smaller stone, the bag between them. Maeve parked the wheelchair a little way back and leaned on the wall, giving them space.

For a few minutes, they simply sat, the three of them, looking.

'You know,' Joan said eventually, 'I always forget how big it is until I see it again.'

'It's like that with certain people,' he said. 'You get used to them in the kitchen and then you see them in a different light and remember.'

'Are you calling me a body of water?' she asked.

He smiled. 'Among other things,' he said.

The lake stretched away, indifferent to their metaphors. The light shifted on it in slow, subtle ways – small ripples catching the sun, darker patches where clouds passed. The island sat squat and patient. The hills on the far side were a softened green with tufts of gorse.

He felt his own breath deepen, as if his chest took its cue from the water.

'Tell me,' she said quietly, 'what it looks like.'

He glanced at her. Her eyes were open, but he knew what she meant: she wanted words, not because she couldn't see, but because she wanted to hear it filtered through him, the way she always had.

'It's … wide,' he began, aware of his own inadequacy. 'Flatter than you'd think a lake would be. The colour's … between slate and steel. There's a line of reeds there' – he pointed – 'like brittle hair. The hills beyond are … half asleep. And there's a boat.'

A small rowing boat, barely more than a dot, moved sluggishly near the far shore.

'Idiot,' Joan murmured fondly. 'Out there with no coat. That's very Irish.'

He could feel her hand, resting palm-down on the rock between them, close enough to touch. He placed his own hand on top of it, the contact both familiar and newly precious.

'We used to swim from here,' she said, after a while. 'Can you believe we were ever that mad?'

'We weren't mad,' he said. 'We were different. Our joints hadn't filed their objections yet.'

'I remember the shock,' she said. 'The way the cold hit your skin and then your bones and you thought you'd never be warm again – and then, ten minutes later, you were laughing.'

He could see it – the younger versions of themselves, splashing, half daring each other. Those days seemed at once impossibly distant and only just past.

'Do you wish we'd done more?' he asked suddenly. 'When we could. More trips. More swims. More … living.'

She considered, eyes still on the lake.

'Yes and no,' she said. 'It's easy to look back and see the days we stayed home and think we wasted them. But those days were life too, you know. The ones where we did the big shop and watched some bad film and fell asleep halfway through. I don't want to erase those because they don't look impressive in hindsight.'

He nodded slowly.

'I wonder sometimes,' he said, 'if I should have taken you

more places. Abroad. Paris. Rome. Somewhere with heat and a guidebook.'

'We went to Achill,' she said. 'That was abroad enough. Besides, I had everything I needed here. Books. You. A lake. Small towns. Weather to complain about. I wasn't under-served.'

He smiled, but a part of him still ached. The idea of the un-lived holidays had become, in his mind, a shorthand for all the things he feared he'd failed at.

She seemed to sense it.

'Don't rewrite our marriage now,' she said gently. 'We did all right. We fought. We sulked. We laughed. We bored each other. We surprised each other. That's what a life is. Not a brochure.'

He breathed in the lake air, letting her words settle like silt.

'I brought the notebook,' he said, after a while. 'In case the ducks have any insight.'

'Good,' she said. 'Write something that isn't morbid or I'll push you in.'

He took it out, the blue cover a little worn at the edges now. The pen felt light in his hand.

For a while, nothing came. He watched the lake, the movement of the small waves on the stones at the edge, the way the reeds shivered slightly even when the surface looked still. He listened to Joan's breathing beside him – still laboured, but steadier than it had been in the bathroom that day.

The first line, when it arrived, was simple:

We brought your lungs to the water to remind them.

He wrote it down, the words making more sense on the page than they had in his head.

They sit, stubborn, in your chest,
huffing, counting, filing complaints,
while the lake barely notices,
moving in its old, unhurried way.

He paused, listening to the small scrape of his pen on the paper.

Beside him, Joan tilted her head.

'Read,' she said.

He did, cheeks colouring slightly as he heard his own voice speaking her lungs into the open.

She smiled.

'I like the idea that they have union rules,' she said. 'Lungs on strike at Lough Allen.'

He added another stanza.

We used to run straight in,
skins shocked blue, mouths open on swear words,
now we walk five careful steps,
wheelchair waiting behind us like a folded apology.

When he read that, both of them went quiet for a moment, the truth of it landing in a way that wasn't entirely comfortable but wasn't cruel either.

'It's not an apology,' she said finally. 'It's … an accommodation.'

He nodded, and under the line he wrote, in smaller letters: *accommodation, not apology*.

Maeve wandered over then, hands in pockets.

'How's the poetry?' she asked.

'Wet,' he said. 'And unionised.'

'Good,' she said. 'I like my metaphors with benefits.'

They ate the ham sandwiches on the rock, greaseproof

paper crinkling, crumbs falling on their laps. The tea from the flask had that particular metallic taste that only ever seemed to exist in flasks, but it was hot, and it did the job.

For a few minutes, as they chewed and swallowed and watched the light move, the whole thing felt almost like the old lake days, just … smaller. Slower. Framed more tightly.

When the wind picked up a little, Joan pulled her coat closer around her.

'Time?' she asked.

He checked his watch. They'd been there just over half an hour.

'We should head back soon,' he said. 'Before your lungs write to the union rep.'

She rolled her eyes. 'They've already drafted something,' she said. 'But yes. Let's not push our luck.'

The walk back to the car was shorter, as it always felt after an outing, as if distance measured differently depending on direction. She managed it without needing the chair, though he could see the effort in the way she placed each foot. At the car, she sank into the seat with a small, involuntary sigh of relief.

On the way home, they were quieter. The day had taken its share of her energy; he could see the slight grey tinge around her mouth, the way her hands trembled faintly when she lifted the water bottle.

But there was also a brightness in her eyes that hadn't been there for a while.

'That was worth it,' she said, as they turned back in to the estate.

'Even the bit where I talked about your lungs like trade unionists?' he asked.

'Especially that bit,' she said.

That evening, after Maeve had gone and the dishes were done, after he'd helped Joan up the stairs and settled the oxygen, he went back down alone to the kitchen with the notebook.

The day had already started to reassemble itself in his mind – the drive, the path, the rock, the lake, the small boat, the way the light caught the upturned edges of the waves.

He copied the draft from the rock into a cleaner version, adding, at the top, almost without thinking: *Lake Day*.

Halfway down, he stopped, pen hovering.

He thought of all the people he'd seen in waiting rooms, all the stories in Deirdre's quiet references, all the candles in kitchen windows. He thought of his mother, lighting one now, no doubt, for sheer habit if nothing else.

He wrote:

Some days we live in the scan,
the numbers, the what-ifs,
but today we lived in the weather,
in the way your breath kept time
with the small waves on stone.

He sat back, reading it over. It wasn't perfect. It wasn't anything grand. But it felt like a fair record of the day.

He closed the notebook, placed it gently beside the kettle.

Upstairs, Joan called down.

'Are you writing an epic?' she asked. 'Or making tea?'

'Both,' he said. 'One takes longer.'

'Bring the tea first,' she replied. 'The epic can wait.'

As he climbed the stairs with the cups, he realised that something in him had shifted.

The lake day had not changed the prognosis. It hadn't strengthened her lungs or shrunk tumours or erased fears. It had cost her energy she would feel the lack of tomorrow. He would see it in the slope of her shoulders, in the extra millilitres of morphine, in the way she might sleep through a television programme she normally commented on.

But it had also given them something: a shared memory that wasn't clinic or corridor or crisis. Another day to put on the shelf beside all the others, ordinary and not so ordinary.

In the bedroom, she was propped up on pillows, the lamp casting a gentle pool of light. The cannula sat under her nose; the concentrator hummed in the corner like a tired, faithful thing.

'How are you?' he asked, handing her the mug.

'Wrecked,' she said. 'Contentedly wrecked. I'll be paying for that outing in breath for a few days. But it was worth it. I got sun on my face. Real sun. Not filtered through double-glazing and worry.'

He sat on his side of the bed, the cup warming his hands.

'Thank you,' she said, after a moment.

'For what?' he asked.

'For carrying the bag,' she said. 'For walking at my pace. For not making a speech about it while we were there. For writing about it instead.'

He smiled.

'I could still make a speech,' he said.

'Don't ruin it,' she replied.

They drank their tea, cups clinking softly as they put them down.

Outside, the day had given way to that long, drawn-out spring dusk – a lingering grey-blue that kept the shape of things visible for longer than winter would have allowed.

He pulled back the curtain a little, glanced out. Across the road, in someone else's window, a lamp was on, casting a warm, rectangular glow onto the darkening street. The sky above the roofs was a deepening blue, the first star visible, faint.

‘We should get a candle for the window again,’ he said. ‘Just because. For whatever’s delayed tonight.’

‘For us,’ she said. ‘We’re always delayed.’

He lit one – a small stub they’d never got round to using at Christmas – and placed it on the sill. The flame wobbled, then steadied, reflected faintly in the glass.

He knew there would be worse days ahead. Darker evenings. Hospital corridors and forms and decisions. But there would also be more of this: cups of tea after small adventures, jokes about lungs, poems that tried and failed and tried again to catch the shape of what they were living.

The lake was still there. The rock was still there. The path, the wall, the reeds. They might not see it again in this exact way, or they might. Either way, the fact of its existence felt like a kind of reassurance.

Chapter Nineteen

The Light at Evening

The school year ended not with a flourish but with a loosening. A gradual untying of small knots. Essays handed up. Desks cleared. The corridors emptying day by day until even the echo seemed surprised to hear itself. On the final morning, Ciarán locked his classroom and stood for a moment with the key in his hand, unsure what to do next. The summer stretched ahead of him, unfamiliar in its openness.

The light had begun to linger again, easing itself into rooms rather than falling suddenly. Not dramatically, not with any announcement – just a steady lengthening of days that caught him out if he wasn't paying attention. The house filled with light earlier each morning, the kitchen bright by half four, the hill beyond the back garden already warm. Some mornings Ciarán woke to birdsong he had forgotten how to hear.

The house felt different without the pressure of term time. No essays stacked at the corner of the table, no alarm slicing the dark at half six, no low-grade dread pacing him through the week. The holidays came like a held breath finally let go. He still rose early – his body had not forgotten decades of habit – but the hours stretched more kindly now, unclaimed.

Joan noticed it before he did.

'You're not rushing,' she said one morning, watching him

move about the kitchen with a mug in his hand, the radio murmuring quietly. 'You're hovering.'

'I'm thinking,' he said.

She smiled. 'That's what I mean.'

The days arranged themselves more gently. Joan slept later now, the worst of the treatments behind her, though tiredness still claimed her without warning. Ciarán found himself sitting at the table with his notebook open, not quite writing, but not not writing either – reading back, crossing out, changing a word here, a line break there. The poems had been accumulating for years, scattered through notebooks, envelopes, margins. Now they had begun, quietly, to cohere.

He printed them one afternoon while Joan rested upstairs. The printer whirred and paused, whirred again, each page sliding out warm and faintly curled. He stacked them carefully, tapped them into order, and sat looking at the small, surprising weight of them. A life, of sorts. Or at least a record of attention.

The manuscript lay on the desk in the spare room, the one that had once held boxes and coats and was now, by quiet agreement, his. It had taken him years to arrive at it – not the writing itself, which had come in scraps and clusters over time, but the decision to gather it together and call it something finished. Poems written in hospital cafés, in the car outside his mother's house, in the margins of notebooks he'd carried like talismans. He had pared them back, cut lines he loved, resisted the urge to explain. What remained felt … honest. Still, he had no great faith in its future.

He had lived long enough to know how these things usually went. Poems were admired politely and set aside. Emails went unanswered. Rejection slips arrived with careful kindness, praising tone or sensitivity while declining to take things further. He told himself – truthfully – that he had not written it for publication. It was enough, he thought, that it existed at all.

When Joan came down later, wrapped in her cardigan despite the heat, she saw the pages on the table.

'What's that?' she asked.

He hesitated. 'Nothing finished.'

She smiled. 'That's not what I asked.'

'My poems,' he said. 'All of them. Or most.'

She came closer and ran her hand along the top page, as if smoothing a sheet on a bed. 'They look finished to me.'

'They're not,' he said quickly. 'They're … close. Probably.'

She pulled out a chair and sat. 'Have you a title?'

He hadn't meant to tell her yet, but it was already there, sitting in him, clear and unarguable. '*The Light at Evening*.'

She nodded, as if that were exactly what she'd expected. 'That's right.'

He laughed softly. 'Is it?'

'It is,' she said. 'You've been writing it all along.'

'Thank you, Joan, the title was your suggestion.'

For days afterward, the stack stayed on the table. He moved it from one end to the other, from table to desk and back again, as if testing where it might best belong. Sometimes he'd lift the first page and read the opening poem, then stop, suddenly embarrassed, as though he'd been overheard. He told himself the usual things: that poetry books were hard to place, that publishers had enough, that his voice was too quiet, too late. He was nearly sixty. What was the point now?

Joan watched him circle the matter. 'You have to send it,' she said one afternoon, sitting opposite him at the table. The summer light caught the thinness at her wrists, the faint blue of veins beneath skin made translucent by treatment and time.

'To whom?' he said, though he already knew.

'To people who publish books,' she said. 'That's generally how it works.'

He smiled despite himself. 'I don't think it's what anyone's looking for.'

'Since when have you written to suit demand?' she said.

He had no answer to that.

'You must send it.'

'I could,' he said. 'And it would come back.'

'So what?'

'So, it would come back,'

She leaned against the table. 'Ciarán. Everything comes back. Bills. Blood results. Bad news. This is the nicest thing that could. Just send it, then it's not only yours any more.'

He said nothing.

Joan was not inclined to let him retreat so easily.

They talked about it over several days, not in long conversations, but in fragments – over tea, while folding laundry, as they sat with the windows open in the evening listening to the faint sounds of neighbours' lives drifting in. She never pushed hard, never raised her voice or framed it as a test. She simply assumed it would be done and waited for him to catch up to that assumption.

Eventually, worn down by her calm certainty rather than convinced by argument, he sat at the desk and opened his laptop. He sat there a long time after she went back upstairs. Outside, a tractor passed on the road, the sound steady and unhurried. He typed, deleted, typed again. Attached the manuscript. Removed it. Attached it again. He thought of his father's yard, the ledgers filled with careful figures. Of things made solid by being written down.

The email was brief. Almost apologetic.

Dear Editor,

Please find attached a poetry manuscript titled The Light at Evening. *I hope it might be of interest.*

He read it several times, wondering if he should say more, then less, then nothing at all. In the end he sent it as it was – to one publisher, then another, then two more he had researched quietly, without optimism.

When he pressed send on the last one, nothing dramatic happened. No release, no panic. Just the ordinary hush of a room holding its breath.

'Well?' Joan asked from the doorway.

'It's gone,' he said. 'Out of my hands.'

'Good,' she said. 'That's where it belongs now.'

He expected to feel exposed, foolish, the way he had in his thirties when he'd sent poems out with too much of himself wrapped up in their fate. Instead, what he felt was a kind of tired peace. He had done the thing. Whatever came next would come.

The rest of June unfolded in its usual Irish way – brightness tempered by cloud, heat interrupted by rain. One evening near the end of the month, they drove north, the road unwinding easily into wider skies, fields opening and closing, the land thinning toward the coast. The sea appeared and vanished at the edges of vision like a thought you don't chase too hard. Mullaghmore rose ahead of them, the headland dark against a sky already beginning to soften. Joan dozed with her head tilted toward the window, her scarf loose around her neck, the car filled with the low, steady sound of tyres on tarmac.

When they arrived, the beach was busy in the loose, unselfconscious way of summer evenings. Families with towels still damp from swimming, teenagers orbiting one another in bright, nervous clusters, older couples walking slowly along the edge of the water, shoes in hand. The smell of salt and sunscreen hung in the air, mixed with frying oil from the chip van parked near the car park. The Atlantic lay calm, improbably blue, the surface catching fire as the sun tipped lower.

Ciarán went to the van and returned with paper-wrapped parcels. They ate fish and chips in the car, salt on their fingers, vinegar sharp in the air. Seagulls cried overhead, bold and hopeful.

'Do you ever watch people and wonder where they're going next?' Joan said, nodding toward a young couple arguing quietly by the dunes, their hands still linked despite it.

'All the time,' he said. 'Most of the time they don't know either.'

The sun slid lower, the sky beginning its slow transformation as it opened into colour – orange deepening to red, then bruised purple, then a soft, luminous gold that seemed to hold the clouds, catching fire at their edges.

The sunset surprised them both. Joan leaned her head against his shoulder. He felt her weight there, light and familiar. Neither of them spoke; falling quiet without quite realising it, drawn into the same shared attention. The people on the beach became silhouettes, then shadows, then simply movement. The sun touched the edge of the water and lingered, as if reluctant to go.

For a moment – not a dramatic one, not even a particularly articulate one – he felt an easing. Not a solution, not an answer.

'This is enough,' Joan said quietly.

He nodded. He knew what she meant. Not enough to fix anything. Enough to be held.

That whatever the autumn brought, whatever news came back in emails polite or otherwise, this evening would remain.

The light at evening, he thought, was never about endings. It was about what stayed visible longest.

They stayed until the light thinned and the sea turned dark, until the cars around them began to leave and the air cooled. When they eventually drove home, the road unspooled ahead of them, pale and uncertain, the long day finally, gently, letting go.

Ciarán thought of the manuscript sitting somewhere now beyond his reach, travelling its own slow way. He thought of the light over Mullaghmore, the way it had not hurried. Whatever came back, he thought – yes or no – this had been written. This had been lived.

Chapter Twenty

Mabon

By late September the light had changed again.

It came in lower now, slanting through the kitchen window in the evenings, catching the dust in gold streaks along the radiator. The leaves on the small tree in the front garden had begun to yellow at the edges, as if someone had dipped them in weak tea. School was back in its full, exhausting rhythm; first years roamed the corridors in packs like bewildered birds.

On a Tuesday afternoon, Ciarán stood by the photocopier, watching it spit out yet another stack of history handouts, when his phone buzzed in his pocket.

A new email. Subject line: *Re: Poetry Manuscript – The Light at Evening.*

His stomach did the now-familiar small flip. He glanced around the staff room, as if someone might tell him to wait, then tapped it open.

Dear Ciarán,

Thank you for sending us your manuscript. We read the poems in one sitting. There is a quiet power in the way you write about illness, ordinary days and love. We would be interested in publishing The Light at Evening, *contingent on some light editing and funding approval …*

He read it twice, slowly, each sentence settling like a stone placed gently under water.

He felt oddly detached from his own hands, his own chest. The photocopier whirred on, oblivious, coughing out paper.

'Everything all right?' Barry asked from the corner, where he was mutilating a stapler.

He looked up, dazed.

'I think … I think I'm going to be a poet,' he said.

Barry snorted. 'Only now?' he said. 'I thought you'd been that for years. What happened? Did they catch you?'

'They want to publish … the book,' he said, still hearing the uncertain note in his own voice. 'The one I sent in. *The Light at Evening*.'

Barry's face softened.

'Christ,' he said. 'That's brilliant. You're going to be insufferable.'

'Probably,' Ciarán said.

He felt a laugh bubbling up, half hysterical.

'Congratulations,' Barry added. 'Seriously. You deserve it. We'll all pretend to understand the metaphors at the launch.'

He nodded, the words still swirling in his head.

In the car on the way home, the town looked slightly different, as if someone had adjusted the focus. The houses, the shops, the traffic at the roundabout – it was all the same, and yet there was a new thin thread running alongside it now, labelled *book*.

It felt almost indecently lucky, in the middle of everything else.

At home, the smell of soup greeted him in the hall. The oxygen concentrator hummed its low, faithful note. The September light stretched a long bar across the sitting-room floor.

Joan was in her armchair by the window, blanket over

her legs, a book on her lap. The nasal cannula sat in place; her cheeks were a little more hollow than in spring, but her eyes still had that hard, bright intelligence that made him feel caught out when he tried to fudge anything.

'You're late,' she said lightly. 'Were you seduced by the lure of double-sided printing again?'

'I've been offered immortality,' he said.

She frowned. 'By who? The religion teacher?'

He held up his phone.

'A publisher,' he said. 'The small crowd in Galway I sent the manuscript to. They want to do it. My manuscript. *The Light at Evening*. At the end of the year, if the Arts Council doesn't decide to spend all the money on interpretive dance instead.'

Her face changed in stages – confusion, comprehension, delight. Her hand went instinctively to her chest, as if to steady something there.

'They're publishing it?' she asked. 'Properly? With … covers and pages and all that?'

'Apparently,' he said. 'They used words like "quiet power" and "book". They want to talk about edits. It's … real.'

For a moment, they simply looked at each other, the words hanging between them.

Then she smiled, a wide, unguarded grin he hadn't seen in months.

'I told you,' she said. 'I told you there was a book. You doubting Thomas. Come here and kiss your literary wife.'

He laughed and crossed the room, careful of the tubes. Her hug was different now – less strength in the arms, more bone beneath the jumper – but the warmth was the same. Her breath puffed lightly against his neck.

'This is good,' she said into his shoulder. 'This is … very good. The words, the poems aren't just floating around in your head. It's on paper. It'll be on shelves. Other people will … see it. Carry it. Maybe some other gobshite sitting in a waiting room will read a poem about a bloody washing machine and feel less alone.'

He felt his throat tighten.

'I wish …' he began, then stopped.

'What?' she asked, pulling back enough to look at him.

'I wish …' he tried again, choosing the words carefully. 'I wish we weren't … in the middle of the material. That the book was about something else. Fields. Birds. Traffic lights.'

She tilted her head.

'The material would have found you anyway,' she said. 'If it wasn't this, it'd be something. Age. Loss. Some lad in your class who broke your heart by spelling "Parnell" with one "l". You'd have written. That's what you do.'

He smiled, despite himself.

'And now,' she went on, 'we get to have a launch. In the library, probably. Under awful fluorescent lights. With bad biscuits. It'll be magnificent. I will be there, even if Deirdre has to smuggle me in in an oxygen tent.'

'You might not feel up to it by then,' he said, before he could stop himself.

She narrowed her eyes.

'Are you trying to get disinvited from your own launch?' she asked. 'Listen to yourself. "You might not feel up to being present at the thing that is literally about our lives." Don't write me out yet. I'll decide how up to it I am when the time comes.'

He held up a hand in surrender.

'Fair enough,' he said. 'I withdraw my pessimism.'

'You can keep a little,' she said. 'It's part of your charm. But not today. Today we're allowed to be delighted.'

He sat on the edge of the couch, the phone still in his hand, the email open. The words looked different now that he'd said them out loud, more solid.

'How's the breath?' he asked, after a moment.

'Like an old bellows,' she said. 'But working. Deirdre has upped the dose again. I'm officially allowed to be dozy for longer stretches.'

She looked more tired, he realised, than she had in the summer. The trip to Mullaghmore, to the sea, had been their last proper outing; since then, their radius had shrunk again to house, garden, short drives around the town. The wheelchair lived now in the hallway, folded but ever-present. The folder with the advance care plan sat, unassuming, on the shelf by the phone.

But there was also a new steadiness in the way they moved around each other, a practiced choreography. He knew which side to stand on when brushing her hair. She knew exactly how long she could talk on the phone before her chest protested. They had learned their routes.

He showed her the email again, read it aloud, stumbling slightly over the praise.

'"Quiet power",' she repeated. 'They must have mixed you up with someone else.'

He threw a cushion at her.

The days that followed had a slightly altered charge.

He still went to school, still argued with sixth years about treaty clauses and Free State policies, still sat with his mother over tea while she detailed the ailments of people he barely remembered. He still emptied the dishwasher, still cursed when the washing machine squeaked, still stood in the chemist waiting for prescriptions.

But in the evenings now, when the light stretched thin and clear across the table, he opened the blue notebook not just as a pressure valve but as a draft folder. He spread the poems out, marking some with asterisks, striking through lines, writing small question marks in the margins.

He printed out the email and placed it inside the notebook's cover, a talisman.

'Look at you,' Maeve said one evening, peering. 'Real edits. Next thing you'll be talking about "my editor" and we'll all have to slap you.'

'I already have an editor,' he said. 'She's sitting in that chair.'

Joan gave a small bow, as far as her lungs allowed.

'I'm very expensive,' she said. 'I charge in biscuits.'

They sat together at the table – him with a pen, her with a pencil, the photocopied manuscript between them. They argued, gently, over line breaks and titles. They moved poems around, trying different sequences.

'This one should be near the start,' she said, tapping 'January Light'. 'It sets the tone. The kettle. The calendar. The crowd of doctors in the background.'

'And this?' he asked, pointing to 'Lake Day'.

'Near the end,' she said. 'But not the last one. You don't end on the lake. You end ... here.' She pointed to 'The Light at Evening'.

'Why?' he asked, genuinely curious.

'Because it's about ... the ordinary,' she said. 'About the washing and the bread and the way the light comes in. That's the real thing. The lake is dramatic. That's for postcards. The radiator is where we live.'

He looked at the poem she was pointing to – the one he'd written after that night at the kitchen table, with the line about cutting bread.

'All right,' he said quietly. 'We'll end there.'

They worked until her breath shortened, until the morphine

tablet started to soften her speech, until her pencil slipped from her fingers and she smiled apologetically.

'I'm fading,' she said. 'We'll resume tomorrow. Tell your editor to rest.'

He walked her back to the armchair, trailing the oxygen tubing like the tail of some strange kite. Then, later, he returned to the table alone and made the changes they'd agreed, hearing her voice in his head.

As the evenings drew in, the candle returned to the window.

It had started almost by accident – his mother dropping off a bag of potatoes one evening and leaving behind a small glass candle holder 'because the light looks nice in your front room, and it's good for the angels'. They'd lit it that night and, without quite deciding, had kept lighting it.

Sometimes he did it; sometimes Joan insisted on being the one to strike the match, her movements slower but precise. The flame would flare, then settle, throwing a small, warm circle of light on the glass.

'Who's it for tonight?' she'd ask.

'For whoever's delayed,' he'd say, the phrase having lodged itself in their lexicon. 'For you, for me, for my mother's knees, for the man with the bad suit in the urology clinic, for the woman in the hospice whose daughter leaves her crying in the car park.'

'For the eejits who cut us off at the roundabout,' she'd add.

'For them too,' he'd agree.

One such evening, rain streaking the glass, the candle burning steadily, they sat on the couch together, the television murmuring something forgettable. The blue notebook lay on the coffee table, a pen resting across it.

Joan's head was on his shoulder, her breath a little raspier than it had been in spring but still moving in and out with that stubborn persistence he'd come to recognise as her defining trait.

'Are you scared?' he asked quietly, the question having sat between them for weeks, maybe months.

She didn't answer immediately. He felt her fingers twitch in his.

'Yes,' she said finally. 'Sometimes. In spikes. When it's hard to breathe. When I wake up in the night and the room feels small. When I think too far ahead. But mostly … no. Or not in a way that's useful. Fear doesn't change the fact that my lungs are gobshites.'

He huffed a laugh.

'And you?' she asked. 'Are you scared?'

He thought about it.

'Yes,' he said. 'Of losing you. Of being left in the house with your mug in the press and your book on the chair. About Mam. Of my own body deciding to start another subplot. Of … all of it. It comes in waves. Some days it knocks me sideways. Some days I barely notice it.'

She nodded, as if this confirmed something she'd already suspected.

'Good,' she said.

'Good?' he echoed, startled.

'It means you're paying attention,' she said. 'I'd be worried if you said you weren't scared at all. That would either mean you're in denial or you've joined some cult.'

He smiled.

'I am also … something else,' he said slowly. 'Grateful, I suppose. That we've had … this. This extra. The lake. The ducks. The poems. The bad telly. The days where nothing happens except we manage to get from morning to night without a crisis. I didn't think we'd get as many of those as we have.'

'Me neither,' she said. 'Remember when they first told us? It felt like we were standing in the path of a train that was already on top of us. Turns out it's more like … a train we can hear, somewhere down the track. It's still coming. But we've had time to sit on the platform and drink some very bad tea.'

He pictured the corridor at Sligo, the waiting room, the lake, the park, the kitchen, the classroom.

'You know,' she added, 'most people don't get a rehearsal. They just … go. Heart attack. Crash. Whatever. We got the gift and the curse. A long, messy preface. We've used it well, I think. We've fought. We've cried. We've made plans and torn them up. You've written. I've nagged. It's not nothing.'

He swallowed.

'It's not nothing,' he echoed.

She shifted slightly, winced.

'I'm not saying I'm not raging sometimes,' she said. 'I am. At my lungs, at the unfairness, at the bloody cough that won't piss off. But I'm also … weirdly … at peace. Some of the time. More than I thought I would be. When the light comes in like that' – she nodded toward the window, where the last light of dusk was shining – 'it's hard to feel entirely robbed.'

They sat there in silence for a while, listening to the rain, watching the small flame hold its own against the gathering dark.

At some point, he reached for the notebook and opened it to the last poem, the one they'd agreed would end the book. 'The Light at Evening'.

He read it softly, almost to himself.

… We learn to live here in this sideways brightness,
where nothing is promised past the next breath
and yet we still put the kettle on,

still hang the towel on the back of the door,
still argue about the best way to cut bread.

When he finished, he felt her hand squeeze his.

'That's the one,' she said. 'They'll like that.'

He smiled, feeling a small, fierce warmth in his chest.

'Do you ever imagine,' he asked, 'that none of this had happened? The cancer, the prostate, the appointments. That we'd just … got old in the boring way. Complaining about the TV license and the price of bread.'

She was quiet for a long time.

'Yes,' she said eventually. 'Of course. I'd swap this for a mundane life in a heartbeat. But if I can't, and I can't, then … this is the version we have. And in this version, we got a book out of it. We got lake days. We got your mother lighting candles. We got Maeve, bossing everyone into coping. We got … you and me, here, now, still able to hold hands and drink tea. That's not a consolation prize. That's … life. Just … tilted.'

He felt tears prick the corners of his eyes.

'You'll put that in something,' she said. 'I know you. "Tilted life". Don't pretend you're not already thinking of lines.'

He laughed, wiped his face.

'You know me too well,' he said.

'That's the point,' she replied.

Chapter Twenty-One

Samhain

In October the days still came, but they no longer lingered. The air carried that faint, unmistakable smell of rot and smoke – leaves breaking down, turf fires being coaxed back to life.

Ciarán parked the car at the edge of the wood just before dusk.

It wasn't a place people went in Autumn. In summer there were dog walkers, children with sticks, the occasional runner with earbuds and determined purpose. Now the track lay empty, the mud dark and slick, the trees closing in on themselves as if for counsel. A sign at the gate warned of uneven ground. Someone had scrawled *Happy Halloween* across it in marker, the letters already bleeding in the damp.

He zipped his coat and set off.

The wood swallowed sound quickly. The road noise faded within a dozen steps, replaced by the soft, irregular hush of leaves underfoot and the faint creak of branches shifting against one another. The ground was thick with last year's fall – layers of brown and black and rust, damp enough to give slightly with each step. Somewhere above him, unseen birds moved, disturbed by his passing.

He had come without much thought, or at least without admitting the thought to himself. Halloween had always unsettled him, even as a child – the way it leaned into darkness without apology, the way it pretended playfully at fear while brushing up against something older and less amused. In recent years it had begun to feel less like a festival and more like a marker. Another notch in the year's slow tally.

His father's anniversary was coming.

Early December. The thought arrived without ceremony, as it had been doing more often lately, slipping into his mind while he stood at sinks or waited at traffic lights. One year. A phrase that sounded neat, manageable, but wasn't. It implied a closing of something, a rounding off. As if grief kept calendars.

The path dipped slightly and narrowed, roots breaking the surface like knuckles. He slowed, careful where he placed his feet. The light filtering through the bare branches had taken on a greenish cast, as if the wood itself were holding its breath.

He wondered how his mother would manage it.

She spoke less about his father now. Or perhaps she spoke of him more obliquely, folding him into stories about the boiler or the weather or some half-remembered errand. She still listened for him at night, though she rarely admitted it outright any more. Instead she complained of draughts, of the house settling, of foxes moving through the yard.

He had learned to hear what lay beneath those explanations.

She was ageing faster than she had before, or perhaps he was only noticing it now. The careful way she rose from chairs. The slight tremor in her hands when she poured tea. The way she watched him as if memorising. He thought of the coming winter, of darker evenings and longer nights, and felt the familiar tightening in his chest.

He walked on.

The trees grew denser deeper in, trunks dark with rain, bark slick and shining in places. Ivy climbed everywhere, patient and insistent, threading itself through branches and choking light from the lower ground. He had the sudden, childish sense of being watched – not by anything supernatural, not really, but by the accumulated presence of the place itself. Woods remembered. They always had.

He thought of his father here, thought of him moving through his own landscapes – the yard, the shed, the narrow roads he knew by heart. His father had belonged to places in a way Ciarán never quite had. There had been no hesitation in him, no second-guessing. He had stood where he stood and done what was in front of him.

Ciarán had always lived slightly to the side of himself, watching.

He stopped where the path opened briefly into a small clearing. Someone had once built a rough bench there from fallen timber, but it had collapsed back into itself, half reclaimed by moss. He didn't sit. Instead he stood and listened.

The silence was not empty. It had texture. Drips from unseen leaves. A distant thud as something fell – a branch, perhaps, or an old cone breaking loose. His own breathing sounded too loud.

A year, he thought. In a few weeks they would stand again at the grave, his mother gripping his arm, the ground colder now, harder. There would be talk of how fast time had gone. There always was. As if speed were consolation.

He wondered, not for the first time, how many such anniversaries he had left. The thought was not morbid, just factual. He felt older now in a way that had nothing to do with numbers. His body reminded him daily, quietly but persistently. A stiffness that took longer to ease. Fatigue that lingered. The unignorable sense that he was moving into a narrower corridor of time.

And Joan.

He pictured her as she had been that morning, wrapped

in a cardigan at the table, her hair thin but growing back, her smile steady but careful. Some days she was almost herself again; other days she moved as if through water. They did not speak much about the future any more; not because they were afraid of it, but because it had learned to keep its distance from certainty.

They had learned instead to mark the present. A cup of tea finished while still hot. A walk taken without hurry. An evening where neither of them was too tired to talk.

In the wood, the light shifted again, sliding toward blue. Dusk was approaching with intent now. He checked his watch, surprised by how much time had passed. The days shortened without asking permission.

As he turned back toward the car, the path felt different – less welcoming, more intent on reminding him that he was a visitor. The air cooled perceptibly, a dampness seeping into his coat. Somewhere, far off, a dog barked, the sound thin and lonely.

At the edge of the trees he stopped and looked back once.

The wood stood dark and indifferent behind him, already closing ranks. It would be here long after he was gone, after his mother's house was emptied, after the yard rusted into nothing. The thought did not trouble him. It steadied him.

He drove home as darkness gathered fully, the first of the trick-or-treaters already moving through the town in bright, unreal costumes, their laughter carrying briefly before dissolving into night. He turned the car toward the house where Joan waited, toward warmth and light and the small, hard-won continuity of shared evenings.

Chapter Twenty-Two

Solstice

The evening of the book launch came sooner than he expected.

The library's meeting room had been strung with fairy lights to disguise the harshness of the ceiling panels. A makeshift podium stood at the front, the librarian fussing with the microphone.

On the small table at the back, there was a neat stack of slim books, the covers a soft grey with the title in simple black type: *The Light at Evening – Poems by Ciarán Devlin*.

He stood staring at them for a moment, feeling oddly out of his own body.

Joan arrived in the wheelchair, pushed by Deirdre as if she were guarding the crown jewels. The oxygen tubing was in place; her face was thin, but her eyes were alight with mischief.

'Look at this,' Joan said, taking in the room. 'Our very own local celebrity.'

'You got a whole book,' he said. 'You're practically the protagonist.'

She looked at the books, her hand reaching out to touch the cover of one as if checking it were real.

'Well now,' she said softly. 'Would you look at that. That's yours, all of it.'

'Some of it is ours,' he said.

The room filled with the expected faces – colleagues, neighbours, two of the sixth years he'd bullied into coming by promising extra feedback on essays. His mother came, wrapped in her good coat, clutching a bunch of supermarket flowers as if she were attending a graduation.

When it was time, the librarian introduced him with more fuss than he felt he deserved. He stepped up to the podium, his hands shaking just enough to make the paper tremble.

He read three poems: 'January Light', 'Lake Day', and finally 'The Light at Evening'. As he read, he kept his eyes mostly on the page, but every now and then they flicked up.

He saw Maeve, watching him. He saw his mother, lips moving as if in prayer. He saw the sixth years trying to look unimpressed and failing. He saw Deirdre, leaning against the back wall, arms folded, a small approving nod every now and then.

And he saw Joan, in the second row, blanket over her legs, oxygen tubing gleaming in the fairy lights, her gaze fixed on him as if she were memorising the shape of him.

When he reached the line about the towel on the door, he saw her smile.

Afterwards, there were handshakes, compliments, polite platitudes. People told him which poem they liked best, which line had stuck. The woman from the hospice whose husband had died that summer said quietly, 'Thank you. For the waiting-room one. That was ours.'

He signed a few copies, his name looking strangely official on the title page.

At one point, he turned and saw Joan looking a little greyer, her mouth tight. Deirdre was already at her side, checking the oxygen flow, murmuring something in her ear.

He went over.

'Too much?' he asked, guilt pricking.

'It's … a lot,' she admitted. 'In a good way. My lungs are drama queens.'

'We can go,' he said. 'Now. You've done your civic duty. You've witnessed the poet in his natural habitat.'

When they finally left, the air outside was cold and clear. The sky was a deep, dark blue; a scatter of stars pricked through. The library's lit windows looked like a stage set from across the car park.

They got Joan into the car carefully, the wheelchair folded and stowed, the oxygen checked. He sat in the back with her while Maeve drove.

'Well?' he asked quietly. 'How was that?'

She turned her head to him, her face tired but radiant.

'It was good,' she said. 'You were good. The poems … worked. People heard them. That's all we can ask.'

She closed her eyes briefly.

'I'm glad I saw it,' she added. 'In person. Not on some angelic live stream.'

He took her hand. 'So am I,' he said.

At home, later, when she was in bed and the house was finally quiet again, he stood for a moment at the sitting-room window, looking out at the street. The candle was lit on the sill, its small flame reflected in the glass.

He thought of all the nights they'd lived through since Joan's diagnosis. The fear, the appointments, the scans, the bathroom tiles, the lake, the park, the ducks, the students, the poems. The folders and forms and tablets and breaths. The laughter that had sneaked in even when they'd thought there was no room for it.

He knew there would be harder nights ahead. Nights of sharp breath and sharp decisions. Nights where the light would be harder to see.

But standing there, the book in his hand, the candle burning, her breathing audible from upstairs, he felt something steadier than hope.

A kind of acceptance, perhaps. Not of loss – not yet – but of the fact that this, all of this, was life. Not a pause before it. Not an afterword. The thing itself.

He went upstairs, his book under his arm.

In bed, Joan was half asleep, the lamplight making her skin look almost translucent. The blue notebook lay on the locker, its pages full.

He slid into bed beside her, careful of the tubing. Her hand found his in the dark with the ease of long practice.

'Did we do all right?' he whispered, not entirely sure what he meant – the launch, the book, the year, their whole shared life.

She squeezed his fingers, a slow, deliberate pressure.

'We're doing,' she murmured. 'That's all there is.'

He lay awake for a little while longer, listening to the soft rasp of her breath, the distant hum of the concentrator, the quiet of the street outside.

The light at evening, he thought, wasn't a single moment, a lyric line, a perfectly framed sunset. It was this: the ordinary miracle of having come this far together, of still being here, of still putting the kettle on and cutting bread and arguing over line breaks, even as the dark gathered at the edges.

Eventually, his eyes closed. Sleep came, not as escape, but as another kind of margin.

Tomorrow, there would be pills and visits and classes and maybe a new poem about the way his mother had tried to pay for a book that already belonged to her. There would be more breaths, counted and uncounted. There would be more light, thinner now, but still finding its way under doors.

For now, there was this: their two hands, linked, warm, in the quiet of the evening.

The Light at Evening

The light at evening comes softly here,
not with fanfare or fire,
but with the hush of old hands folded,
and boots left by the back door.
It touches the field in slow forgiveness,
finds the rust on the gate,
the crack in the step,
the place where the nettles returned.
It remembers a man who said little,
whose laughter stayed behind his eyes,
and a woman who still stirs the tea
even when no one is looking.
There is silence in the kettle's boil,
and meaning in the way
she tucks the blanket at her feet,
asks nothing, but sees everything.
We were never promised more than this –
a porch at dusk,
a hand in mine,
and the long, low breath of staying.
The past is not a wound here.
It is a weight we've learned to carry –
folded like shirts in a drawer,
creased, but clean.
And as the first bat flits above the hedge,

and the stove crackles to itself,
I write this down
not for them,
not even for her –
But for the light at evening,
that came,
and stayed.

Acknowledgements

I would like to thank Ross Dickinson and Debbie Chapman for their excellent work in shaping my original manuscript into its final form. Their careful editing and thoughtful attention brought clarity and structure to what began as something far less certain. A special thank you to Ross, whose support throughout the publishing process – and early belief in the manuscript – meant a great deal.